THE DEAD AND THE WASTED

JORDAN VEZINA

Copyright © 2022 by Jordan Vezina

All rights reserved.

No part of this book may be reproduced in any form or by any electronic or mechanical means, including information storage and retrieval systems, without written permission from the author, except for the use of brief quotations in a book review.

Cover by Deranged Doctor Design

PROLOGUE

THE FULBRIGHT BUILDING
  Houston, Texas

It was perfect. Colonel Maxim Lebedev of Alpha Group Command opted not to follow the next logical thought, which was that it was too perfect. Yes, it was important to make smart tactical decisions, particularly in what could only be considered a non-permissive environment, but it was also important not to look a gift horse in the mouth for too long. That was how a fool was most likely to lose his head.

The helicopter pad on the roof of the Fulbright Building was large enough to accept the bulk of the

Mi-17 helicopter, and the landing lights were even lit. He wondered about that for a moment. Supposedly the entire Texas power grid had experienced a catastrophic failure quite some time ago, yet it appeared that every light in the Fulbright building was still on. The rest of the city was dark, but this one tower was lit up like the proverbial Christmas tree.

There was already one helo on the small auxiliary pad beside the main one, but that was not unusual. A building like this was expected to have a helicopter on stand-by, particularly during times like these.

Lebedev reached down and triggered the emergency relay that would burst transmit his coordinates to the nearest receiving station, but he knew it was to no avail. The nearest division that could have received his signal and decrypted it was the Third Motor Rifles, and at that specific moment in time, those soldiers were wandering Central Texas with black eyes seeking human flesh.

He thought about that for a moment and wondered if Warrant Officer Balakin had died in his final defense of the hill top, or if he too was now one of those black-eyed things.

Lebedev snapped himself back to reality and began the process of deploying his landing gear and maneuvering the helicopter toward the rooftop. Landing one of the big helos wasn't exactly a one-man task, but he also had no other option. He had been in tighter spots before and had even had to perform a solo landing much like this, so he knew that he was capable of doing it.

He also understood that it was important to get the intelligence they had uncovered at the Third Motor Rifles encampment to someone who could use it. But before he did that, he needed one last piece of the puzzle. Specifically, he needed to find out if this Doctor Gregory Wilson person was still residing in the Fulbright Building. If he was there, and if he was a part of what General Zhukov had thought was happening, there was no time to waste in securing him.

Colonel Lebedev allowed himself a smile as he touched down on the helipad. The landing could not have been smoother if it had been a simulation.

Despite the dire nature of the situation and the need for brevity, he still followed proper procedures in shutting down the aircraft and waited patiently for the rotors to stop spinning. It was quiet. This high up there was no sound other than the gentle blowing of the wind across the rooftop. It was peaceful—peaceful in a way he had not experienced in quite a long time.

A couple dozen feet away was what appeared to almost be a small building on top of the Fulbright, and he could see large double doors in the relative darkness. Lebedev walked back to the rear of the helicopter, reached inside, and retrieved his gear. For a moment, he thought about going in slick, but then decided against it. He kitted up completely with his plate carrier, ballistic helmet with NODs, and then stuffed loaded magazines and fragmentation grenades into any pouch or pocket that would accept them. He wasn't as big as many men in the Russian Special Operations community, standing only five foot ten, but he was built like a fire hydrant and had carried much more weight than this through much less forgiving terrain.

Finally, he checked his rifle and did a quick function check of his night vision device and the aiming laser on his weapon.

He listened again, but still heard nothing. He turned to where the second helicopter sat on the auxiliary helipad and moved toward it. The aircraft was secured, and there was nothing to indicate it was something he should be concerned about. Still, he peered in the windows but again saw nothing. For a moment he thought about putting his NODs down and performing a closer inspection, but he was also aware that time was not on his side.

The inside of the building was well-lit, but clearly by emergency lighting. It was running off of a generator and Lebedev wondered how long that could last. He moved silently down the stairwell until he reached a heavy door that looked like it would bring him into the main building. He pulled the stock of his suppressed AK-74 into his shoulder, reached out, and opened the door.

There was no hesitation in the seasoned special forces officer. He pulled the trigger of his rifle as the first black-eyed cannibal pushed towards him, teeth snapping and saliva flying. From there, he took three steps back and continued firing, not bothering to bring his eyes to his optic, as it was impossible to miss at this point-blank range.

There was no adrenaline, no panic, no jerky movements. It was all business for the Russian commando as he moved from target-to-target, taking clean headshots that dropped the cannibals in their tracks. No one had told him that shooting these things anywhere other than the head or the heart was futile, it was simply the mark of a consummate professional. Why would he aim anywhere other than the head or center mass?

He had dropped the first wave of cannibals with little effort and watched a second wave of perhaps a dozen storming toward him from the other end of a long hallway. With little fanfare, Colonel Maxim Lebedev performed what amounted to an administrative reload of his rifle, then brought it back into alignment and took smooth, controlled shots, executing what remained of the horde.

Lebedev kept his rifle at the ready and scanned the hallway. There was nothing. He walked forward and gently kicked the bodies, making sure to also hit a few in the groin. Finally, he took a knee and thumped one in the eyeball. In the unlikely event they were not completely dead, the eye thump was likely to shock them enough to move.

He looked forward to the door at the end of the hallway. There would almost certainly be more of them beyond it, but there was no other option. He knew that he may have to fight his way through a building of these things, but it had to be done.

In a strange moment of clarity, Doctor Gregory Wilson realized that he should not have gotten down on his knees when Ralph Finley told him to. After all, what was the Fluid Dynamics security chief going to do if he didn't comply? Shoot him?

He had only done it because that's what everyone did in the movies when they were about to be executed.

Executed. He thought about that for a moment. They were going to execute him. Was this really happening? He had four PhD's, dammit! They were just going to put a bullet in his head?

"Why are you doing this?" Gregory asked.

"It's not personal," Ralph replied. "It's business. I know that sounds like something a movie villain would say, but it's the truth. There's a lot at stake here."

"What did he tell you I would do?" Gregory implored. "Mister Rampart told you to do this, didn't he?"

"That's not important."

"Did he tell you about the antidote for the vaccine?" Gregory asked. "I'm betting he didn't!"

There was a brief look of curiosity on Ralph's face, but then he over-rode it.

"That's above my pay grade," Ralph replied as he flicked the selector switch on his M4 to "semi."

"I saw a flare!" Gregory blurted. "On the edge of the city before you arrived."

"What?" Ralph asked.

"A flare!" Gregory insisted. "It could be important. I know where it was, but you don't. I can take you to it."

"It's not important," Ralph said flatly and put the suppressor of his rifle to Gregory's forehead.

Gregory closed his eyes, then felt a thump beside him on the floor. His eyes snapped open and he saw Ralph lying beside him with a hole in his head. The scientist looked up and saw glass shattering and other security men firing at something across the room, but one-by-one they were also dropping to gunshot wounds.

Again, it was like something out of a movie. He watched as a man in some sort of foreign uniform crossed the large open floor with his rifle up, scanning for any further threats. The man finally lowered his rifle and turned to where Gregory was kneeling on the floor.

"Doctor Gregory Wilson, I presume?" Lebedev asked in his accented English.

"Russian?" Gregory asked.

"Stand up," Lebedev ordered. "I'm getting you out of here."

"Where are we going?" Gregory asked, switching to Russian.

This took Lebedev by surprise, but he quickly recovered and also switched to Russian.

"Would you prefer to stay here?" Lebedev asked. "I ran into several of your countrymen upstairs. I'm sure they would be happy to make your acquaintance."

Behind him, Lebedev could hear the fast, labored breathing of one of the men he had shot. He turned and saw the man's hand sliding into a pouch mounted on his chest rig. The Russian had no idea what this man was doing, but his reflexes took over. He turned, brought his rifle up, and put a round through the man's head.

Too late.

The building shook and Lebedev knew what had happened. It was the same thing he would have done, and he did indeed have an identical failsafe on his helicopter. He turned and watched the wreckage raining down the side of the building in the darkness. With his last breath, this man had detonated the helicopter that Lebedev had seen on the auxiliary helipad when he flew in. Of course it had been theirs.

"I'm guessing we're not flying out of here," Gregory said quietly.

Lebedev turned to him.

"I heard you were a genius," he said. "Apparently the rumors were true."

"What do we do?" Gregory asked.

"I heard what you said," Lebedev said. "When I was coming in. About the flare and then about the antidote to the vaccine. What was that?"

Gregory opened his mouth to answer and then stopped.

"I know things," he said. "Important things. Things that your people would want to know."

"So, tell me."

"First you have to get me out of here."

"I'm not even sure I can get myself out of here," Lebedev replied. "Tell me about the flare."

Gregory walked to the window and pointed into the distance.

"It was out there," he said. "It was a green flare. Do you think it was your people?"

Lebedev shook his head.

"No, they aren't this far out yet."

"Chinese deep recon?" Gregory probed.

"Unlikely. No, it was someone else, but whoever it was, they may be our only option." He scanned the city beneath them. "In a place like this, in circumstances such as these, whoever it is, we will have a common ground. We may be able to work together."

"Common ground?"

"To not become dinner," Lebedev replied coldly. "This flare, do you know where it came from? Can you estimate the distance?"

"I can't be sure, but I think it came from City Hall. If it did, it's only ten blocks away."

"*Only* ten blocks?" Lebedev said with a laugh. "It might as well be a hundred miles. If we're going to get there, you will have to fight."

He picked up one of the rifles the dead men had been carrying and pushed it into Gregory's hands. The scientist looked at it as if it were some sort of foreign object that had fallen from space.

"I— I don't know the first thing about how to use one of these," he stuttered.

Lebedev took it back, checked that there was a

round in the chamber and flicked the safety selector back and forth, then pointed to the trigger.

"This makes the boom," he said and shoved it back at Gregory. "Not a perfect tutorial, but it's an imperfect world."

"I don't kill people!" Gregory insisted.

"That's good," Lebedev said with a nod. "Because those things out there aren't people."

"I won't do it!"

"Do or do not as you please, but I'm going to city hall."

Lebedev walked away toward the door to the stairwell.

Gregory sensed that the Russian was serious and jogged to catch up.

"Wait, you can't leave me!"

Lebedev turned back to him. "My curiosity compels me," he said. "Where did you learn Russian?"

"YouTube."

"That explains your shitty accent."

Harris County Hospital
    Houston, Texas

. . .

Doctor Adelaide Freer dropped the casing from the flare he had just set off and watched as the green illumination lit up the night sky above him. He looked out from the roof of the Harris County hospital and saw only the same darkness covering the city that had enshrouded it the night before, when it all started happening.

He hadn't taken the Gen 2 Pandemify because he thought he was doing the right thing, perhaps even the noble thing by making sure all of his patients and the everyday people of the City State of Houston received access to it first. That was part of his oath, at least as he understood it.

Instead, it had been the reverse. Without knowing it, he had doomed everyone else to become these mindless, black-eyed things that now rampaged through Houston, killing everyone in their path, while he survived.

Had it not been for his access to the infectious disease ward with its heightened security measures, he would have been one of the many casualties that now littered the streets below.

No, that wasn't correct. It wasn't the casualties that were strewn about the streets of Houston. *It was their bones.* That was all that remained. Even those bones were not quite whole. He had observed this from his vantage point on the rooftop, that some of these black-eyed cannibals took pause and actively chewed upon the bones of the dead, while others did not. He wondered why that was.

He looked back to the sky as the green flare arched back downward and the light dimmed.

"Where are you?" he asked himself.

Nothing. Once again, there was no response. He was following emergency protocol, yet no one was following up. Deep down, even if he didn't want to admit it to himself, he knew why no one was responding.

Because there was no one left to respond.

Freer turned and walked to the access door. He reached into his pocket and retrieved the small flashlight he kept there. He had wrapped scotch tape over the lens, which served to dim the light quite a bit, at least enough that it would not be seen from far away. He was fairly certain that the stairwell was free of the black-eyed cannibals, but he couldn't be sure. Going to the roof had been a necessity, but he understood that it was not without risk.

He opened the door and quietly closed it behind him, then began navigating downward to the fifth floor. As he did this, his thoughts wandered back to just the week prior. He had really thought that things were going to get back to normal somehow. He'd thought the vaccine would be the final step they needed.

The reality was that he had grown complacent, just like everyone else had. The City State-run copies of Youtube and Facebook had been a big part of that, lulling everyone into a false sense of security. After all, if they still had social media, how bad could things really be? People were doing all of the silly things online they had done before, and the fact that all of the original pre-apocalypse videos had been copied along with the Youtube architecture made it even easier to slip into a warm bath of "normalcy." Just as long as you didn't try to venture beyond the boundaries of the city.

If he hadn't let his guard down, if he'd been living in the real world, he would have known something like this could happen. He might have been ready for it.

Doctor Freer turned and pushed open the door to the fifth floor. Then he stopped. He turned back to the darkness. He had heard something. He knew he had. What was it? Some kind of murmuring. Was it voices? Were there other people alive in the hospital? It couldn't be. After the slaughter in the Emergency Room, the black-eyed cannibals had left looking for a new food source. He had locked himself and his patients in the infectious disease ward. That was the only reason they were still alive. No one else could have survived that onslaught. Yes, there may have been something below him in the stairwell, but it was not a someone. Whatever it was, it was no longer human. All the more reason to get back to the ward.

Freer secured the door behind him and walked down the dimly lit hallway. The emergency lights were still on from when the power had failed the day before, but he knew they wouldn't last. The generators had kicked in, but at best they would sustain basic functions for only ninety-six hours.

At the end of the hallway, he found the re-enforced double doors that led into the infectious disease ward. For a moment, he stared at the bloody smears on the thick plexiglass. The things had hammered on them for nearly an hour. He remembered watching one of them, how his hands had started to come apart he was punching the window so hard.

Freer snapped out of it and swiped his card to enter. It occurred to him that when the power finally quit, the electronic locks wouldn't work anymore. He had no idea what would happen then. Would they stay locked or would all of the doors open? Either version was a problem, which meant he didn't have much time to figure out what to do next.

Reginald Moore met him at the door with a broad smile.

"Reginald," Freer said and returned the smile as best he could. "Everything okay?"

"It's fine, Doc," Reginald replied and put a hand on the physician's shoulder. "Just fine."

Freer looked to the rows of beds and saw that his oncology patients were all sitting and looking at him. Every one of them was terminal. Freer had saved them by getting them into this empty section of the ward. They had not received the Gen 2 vaccine because of their prognosis.

Their situation was unique, as many people, even those with terminal diseases had seen remissions after the admission of the Gen 1 Pandemify. Not only did it work on the virus, but it seemed to supercharge the body's immune system and speed up healing processes. For whatever reason, though, it had not worked on these patients.

"Any news?" Reginald asked. "From the roof? From the flares?"

The rest of his patients looked at him expectantly, clearly hoping for an answer he did not have. In that moment, Doctor Freer knew the truth of his situation. He knew the absolutely hopelessness of it. He could not possibly save them, because he could not even save himself.

"Yes," Doctor Freer said with a smile. "Orange flare response. They're coming to get us."

The patients all cheered, some embracing each other and Reginald reached out and gave the physician a big bear hug.

"I knew it!" Reginald declared. "I knew it, Doc! I knew you'd get us out of this."

Doctor Freer walked to where the rest of his patients were gathered in their beds. He strained to keep his smile in place.

"How is everyone feeling?" he asked. "Rested?"

"I wouldn't say 'rested'," a woman named Gracie said. "This has been—well, it's been hell, Doctor Freer. I feel like my nerves are fraying at the ends."

"Not to worry, Gracie," he said and placed a hand on her shoulder. "We'll be on the other side of it soon."

"How long do you think it will take, Doc?" Reginald asked. "For the rescue party to get here?"

"They'll be here in the morning," Doctor Freer said. "But it won't be easy. You'll all have to have your strength up to make it onto the trucks."

Reginald looked confused.

"Trucks?" he asked. "We're driving through that?"

"Armored trucks," Freer reassured him, thinking on the fly. "They'll be able to get us back out of the city."

"That makes sense," Reginald agreed. "Only way they could do it, I suppose."

Doctor Freer walked back to his office, where he had set up a series of Dixie cups. Normally they would contain the nightly medications for his patients, but already knowing what direction things were going in, he had made a modification to the nightly regimen.

He stopped and looked at the pills in the cups. Was he doing the right thing? He knew he was. They were all terminal anyway, and with the way things were going, that situation would not be improving. Not only that, but once the hospital finally lost power, they would be overrun, and that was not going to be good.

This was not only the right thing to do, it was the merciful thing.

Freer carefully lined the cups up on the rolling table and then pushed it out of his office and into the ward.

"I made some substitutions," he said. "Just something to give you a little immunity boost and help you sleep. I know getting good sleep isn't easy right now, but you'll need it for the morning."

"When the trucks come," Reginald said.

"That's right," Freer confirmed. "For when the trucks come."

CHAPTER 1

Harris Hawthorne watched the road ahead of him intently, continually scanning the forty degrees of bluish-black and white landscape as he drove the Winnebago through the night. He knew that people often drove under night vision, but he had never actually done it before.

Of course, this lack of experience didn't stop him from answering in the affirmative when Roland Reese asked him if he could drive under NODs.

"Sure."

After all, how hard could it be?

The truth was that it wasn't that hard once you were used to not having peripheral vision. In fact, it was a lot of fun.

The decision had been made to not delay their

departure from Oatmeal so that they could get to Houston as fast as possible. It was reasonable to assume that with every passing minute, they were losing the element of surprise.

They also knew (in line with Cotton's comment about pulling the fifty-caliber machine gun from the top of the Winnebago) that they would want to run as incognito as possible, which meant driving at night, under NODs, with no lights on. Under a full moon, there was enough ambient light that Harris could see clearly pretty far down the road without any additional IR light, but it was unlikely anyone would be able to see them unless they were right up on the vehicle.

"This is terrifying," Fred said from the co-pilot's seat.

They had blacked out the cabin with heavy curtains and disconnected the fuses from the dashboard lights, so that she was sitting in complete darkness, looking out into darkness, hurtling down the road.

"What do you mean?" Harris asked as he turned to her.

"Please look at the road!" Fred urged.

"Oh, sorry," Harris replied.

"You don't find this to be the least bit unnerving?"

"Well, I can see fine with these night-vision goggles."

"Fair enough," Fred replied, thinking about the situation for a moment. "Wait, why am I even up here if I can't see anything?"

"Keep me company," Harris replied.

Roland Reese stood in the fore of the Winnebago, watching Jean Wiley as she thumbed through a book in the rear of the vehicle. It had been two years since he had seen her last, but it felt like much longer. The girl was so different than she had been. Even as she was flipping through this book, her jaw was set, her eyes resolute. It was clear that her young mind was working on a problem.

"You knew her?" Sheila asked from the bench seat across from Roland.

He turned to her and managed a smile.

"Long time ago. Me and Cotton ran together in the Teams, but it wasn't just a Team. It was... a family, I guess. I was at the hospital with him when she was born."

"You and Cotton were close then?"

"Maybe as much as we ever could be. Not like the way normal folks think of friends. More like brothers that fight all the time, but when the chips were down, we were there for each other."

Sheila nodded.

Rolland smiled. "You can't hear shit, can you?" He laughed.

"Nope," Sheila replied. "Mostly reading lips."

"Think it'll come back?"

"Hard to say," she said. "But I can still hear her, so I wonder when it does come back if I'll keep hearing her."

"What's she say?" Roland asked, referencing the Cannibal Queen.

"Seems like a lot of gibberish, almost like she's speaking in tongues."

"You know, I've been meaning to tell you, what you did back there in Oatmeal was some next level shit. The way you blew the hell out of everything and took on that horde. If I'm being honest about it, not sure I'd have had the balls to do it." Roland paused. "If you weren't all disfigured with your arm missing, I might be getting a crush."

"You really know how to sweet talk a girl."

Roland turned and pulled up the top of one of the bench seats. He reached inside and retrieved a

10.5" 300 Blackout rifle with a suppressor, aim point and CQB-L aiming laser mounted. He walked back to the rear of the RV and stopped where Jean was sitting.

"Howdy," he said with a smile. "Been a minute."

Jean returned the smile.

"What are you reading?" Roland asked.

Jean held up the book. It was the 31-21 Guerrilla Warfare and Special Operations field manual.

"You always were a weird kid," Roland said and held out the rifle he was holding.

"What's that?" Jean asked.

"It's yours if you want it. 300 Blackout. It's got some mags split out between 125 and 220 grain. I figure there's some night fighting coming, so those 220 grain rounds will let you go as dead silent as you'll get on account of being subsonic."

Jean sat up and took the rifle. She dropped the magazine and locked the bolt back, checking the chamber. She looked up at Roland.

"This an LMT?" she asked, indicating it was a Lewis Machine and Tool Works rifle, one of the best made.

"I was saving it for a special occasion," Roland said with a shrug. "Didn't figure there was much sense in giving it to someone who might get smoked the next day."

Jean met his eyes. "Thank you," she said.

Roland sat down on the bench seat beside her and looked to the front of the RV, where Harris sat in the driver's seat. Fred was across from him in the co-pilot's chair.

"How's he doing?" Roland asked. "Your dad."

"Well as can be expected, I suppose," Jean replied. "End of the world and all."

Roland laughed. "Seems like he's doing okay," he said.

"It's a distraction," Jean went on. "From the real thing."

Roland understood. Neither of them needed to say anything more about it. The end of the world, at least for Cotton Wiley, was a welcome distraction from the loss of his wife.

"So, you're pretty smart, right?" Harris asked as he drove the vehicle with Fred in the co-pilot's seat.

These sorts of questions always made Doctor Frederique Van Sant uncomfortable. Yes, she knew she was smart. Objectively (even before the virus), she was probably one of the smartest people on the planet. It had been that way ever since she was two years old and her mother realized she had memorized all of the books on her bookshelf. It quickly became a sort of family game. Her father would put her on his knee and begin reading a book, and anywhere he stopped she would pick up the story. The thing about it was, she wasn't really even reading the books. When she did what became known in the Van Sant household as "the trick" she didn't even need to look at the page.

Within a short amount of time, she had memorized every children's book in the house. Even then, her parents did not fully understand what they were dealing with. Not until her father left one of his Popular Mechanics magazines open on the kitchen table. She looked at the pages for a moment and then looked up at him and began reciting them verbatim. She was three years old and had taught herself to read.

In short order, she was sent to a private school for gifted children, and it was the worst thing that ever happened to her. Even at a young age, she knew this, but the consensus was that a mind like hers could not be allowed to wither within the public school system. By the time she was ten, she was solving college level math problems and beginning her study of quantum physics.

Her recollection that this meteoric course of study was the worst thing to happen to her was because it had replaced her childhood, robbing her of those years. Despite her rigorous study schedule and early pioneering work in mathematics, her father always did what he could to give her some respite. For the two of them, this had meant spending Sunday mornings in the garage working on one of his classic cars.

As these memories ran wild through her consciousness, Fred wondered if that was why she had been so diligent about restoring the old DeSoto that was now upside down on the road in Marble Falls. Perhaps she had been trying to recapture some of the feeling of innocence she'd had as a child.

"Yeah, I'm smart," Fred replied. "But all things being equal, considering the current state of the world I'd rather be a fast shooter."

Harris laughed.

"World still needs smart people, Fred," Harris said. "That's what they call you, right? Fred?"

Fred nodded.

"Frederique always just sounded a little too... aristocratic."

"You grow up out here?" Harris asked. "In Texas, I mean?"

"No, Massachusetts."

"Thought you had a funny accent," Harris said in his Texas drawl.

"I've tried to get rid of it," Fred lamented. "But some things stick with you."

Harris drove in silence for a moment before continuing his train of thought. "You know, I ain't dumb, but there's some things... well sometimes it takes me a minute to grasp. Reason I say that is y'all were talking about an EMP?"

"Yes. An electromagnetic pulse."

"Oh, I know EMP's," Harris said with a smile. "Preppers, that's our stock in trade."

"Then what didn't you get?"

"Well from what you were saying, it sounds like this might all be part of a plan? The virus, then the vaccine, and now maybe the lights going out?"

"It's a possibility," Fred replied. "Whenever I say it out loud it sounds so crazy, but unfortunately, I don't think it's crazy at all."

"And this place we're going, the guy we're trying to find—you really think he can stop it?"

"Gregory makes me look like a high school dropout," Fred said. "But he also makes really bad decisions about the jobs he takes on. If anyone's tangled up in this, and more importantly knows how to stop it, it's him."

"Remind you of old times?" Jorge asked as he drove the Toyota truck down the highway ahead of the RV. Both him and Cotton wore night vision devices to navigate their way through the darkness.

Cotton reclined in the passenger seat, scanning the horizon while April had taken up position in the bed of the truck behind an M240B machine gun. This had been an acceptable compromise of Roland's original vision, replacing the much bigger fifty cal he had mounted to the roof of the Winnebago. This had also required bolting the tripod into the bed to stabilize it.

This arrangement had not been April's favorite idea, as it required her to be strapped in to the bed of the truck and riding in the open. The weather was warm enough that she didn't get cold, but it still wasn't the most comfortable way to travel. However, all had agreed that it was definitely a "better to have a machine gun and not need it, than need a machine gun and not have it" type of scenario.

"Little bit," Cotton replied. "Just don't know yet if it's the good old times or the bad old times."

Jorge laughed.

"Well, I always had fun. Even when it was bad, it was good."

"When did you go in? If you don't mind me asking."

"I was late to the party," Jorge replied. "I was in high school when the first Battle for Fallujah went down, when they were stringing up those contractors. 9/11 happened when I was a freshman, and I wanted to be a part of it, wanted to... I don't know. Get even I guess, but I was just too young. Then I was eighteen when Fallujah hit the news and I was just glued to it. Watched everything I could, read the reports. Finally, it came to a head and I went to the recruiter's office. Told him I wanted in."

"Still in high school?" Cotton asked with a wry smile. "I can guess how that went."

"Yeah. I was pissed, but looking back on it he did the right thing telling me to finish high school first. I only had a month left. Would've been dumb to trash that thinking I was going to get into the fight faster. Knowing now how the pipeline works... I still didn't get overseas for three more years."

"The old pipeline," Cotton echoed.

"Yeah," Jorge said with a smile. "When you're a kid, you think it'll be fast. Just have to get my rifle and I'll be on the next helo to Iraq, because they need Jorge Ramirez and his M4 to wrap this thing up."

"I thought I was going to Vietnam," Cotton offered. "Back in the nineties. We all thought we were going to the 'nam."

Jorge laughed. "I just never understood how much went into making, well, one of us."

Cotton nodded. "Lot of schools," he said. "So did you go Ranger or Green Beret?"

"Rangers," Jorge replied. "Second Battalion. Did my first rotation in Afghanistan and didn't really do much of anything. Just a lot of patrolling, lot of training, but not much action. Then in 2006, I took my first trip to Iraq."

Cotton let out a long whistle.

"Good time to be there."

"Freaking Wild West," Jorge said. "I mean, we were getting in fights near every day. It was nuts. Then after a while, I don't know. It was just normal."

"When did you go to the Unit?"

"I went to Selection in 2008 after my second trip to Iraq. Went through OTC and wrapped up just in time to go to Afghanistan in 2010."

"Not sure if you have the best luck in the world or the worst," Cotton said, indicating the high operational tempo during that period in Afghanistan.

"Wait a minute," Jorge said as he slowed the vehicle steadily enough that he knew Harris would be able to sync up with him from behind. "You see that?"

Cotton leaned forward and looked into the greenish landscape he could see from behind his RNVG's. Roland had asked him if he wanted to swap out the older style green phosphor night vision device for one of the newer "high speed" white phosphor units they had, but Cotton had declined. Years ago, he had noticed that he just felt better looking through the green phosphor device than the white ones. Later, a neurologist had explained that different areas of the brain were activated by different colors, and that his specific brain-based issues may respond better to a green tint than a blueish one. Despite the fact that everyone was advocating for more white phosphor units, Cotton had elected to stick with his OG green tubes.

"I see lights," Cotton said, then tilted his head back to look under his night vision into the naked darkness. "IR lights."

"Who in the hell is running around in the woods with IR lights on?"

"People who don't know how to use night vision," Cotton replied.

"What is it?" Roland asked as he keyed the radio in response to Cotton's call.

"Got some IR in the woods ahead, possible hostiles under NODs. We're stopping."

"Roger that," Roland replied, parting the curtains that were blacking out the cabin while Harris was driving. "You get that?"

"Got it," Harris said, steering the RV off the road behind the lead vehicle and onto a large shoulder.

They continued from the shoulder onto a dirt patch that was partially obscured by tall trees. They had left behind the open and arid landscape of Central Texas an hour prior and were coming up on the unincorporated community of Ledbetter.

Harris shut off the engine and flipped his NODs up on the ballistic helmet he wore, rubbing his eyes and letting out a yawn. He had opted not to take the lighter "bump" helmet he had been offered, as despite the heavier weight of the ballistic helmet compared to the plastic bump, he placed great value on not getting shot in the head. After he felt that his eyes had taken the moment they needed to rest, he placed the night vision device back over them.

Roland opened the door and dropped his NODs as well, then stepped out into the darkness with Harris behind him.

Jean peered out the window and watched the men gathering on the side of the road. She wanted to be out there with them, not sitting inside and waiting with the women.

"Your time will come," Sheila said from behind her.

Jean turned and looked at the woman, then down at what remained of her left arm.

"Did that hurt?" Jean asked.

"No more than anything else that's happened to me," Sheila replied.

Jean turned and looked back out the window.

"What's the play?" Cotton asked, addressing the question toward Roland.

The former SEAL Team Six Command Master Chief looked down the road through his NODs and saw the same IR lights moving through the woods ahead of them.

"Can't just drive thought that," Roland replied. "And can't just hang out here waiting for 'em to go away."

"Whoever they are," Jorge interjected, "they probably ain't friendly."

"More U.N.?" Harris asked.

"Possible," Roland confirmed. "But at this point it could be freaking anybody. And I do mean anybody."

"Patrol up?" Cotton asked. "Get eyes on and go from there?"

Roland turned to Harris. "You ready for this?" he asked.

"Yes, Sir," Harris replied.

"Stop calling me sir," Roland said. "You're freaking me out. Makes me think I'm about to die."

The four men moved silently through the woods in a modified wedge formation. Ahead of them, they could still see the intermittent use of IR lights as well as strangely loud talking. Finally, Roland called the patrol to a halt. He turned and spoke in a low voice, as whispers would carry much further than just quiet talking.

"Are you hearing what I'm hearing?" he asked.

"Yeah," Cotton replied. "They're speaking Chinese."

"What in the hell are they doing up here?" Jorge asked. "Deep recon?"

"Only thing that makes sense," Cotton replied.

"Either way we need to get eyes on," Roland continued. "Know what we're dealing with here and then find a way around it."

Jean kept her face pressed to the window of the RV and stared out into the night. She looked into the woods across the street and scrunched her eyes together.

Sheila took notice. "What is it?" she asked.

"I don't know," Jean replied as she stood up and walked to one of the bench seats. "Maybe nothing."

She lifted the lid on the bench seat and pulled out the smallest helmet she could find with a set of DTNVS night vision attached. There was no plate carrier small enough for her frame, but she was able to tighten down a chest rig enough to make it work and then retrieved the 300 Blackout magazines loaded with 220 grain subsonic rounds that Roland had mentioned.

Fred walked back from the cabin and watched the scene unfold with Sheila.

"What in the hell are you doing?" Fred asked, and when she received no reply, she turned to Sheila. "What in the hell is she doing?"

Sheila looked at Fred and smiled.

"Looks like she's gettin' ready to smoke some fools."

Jean stepped out of the Winnebago, routed her comms cable through the shoulder strap of the Spiritus Systems Micro Fight Chest rig, and connected it to the radio in the outer pouch. She made sure the Push To Talk was properly connected and tested it as she powered up her Peltors.

"How do you even know how to do all of that?" Fred asked as Jean lowered her nods.

The girl activated the DTNVS and quickly tested the CQB-L aiming laser as well as the night vision setting on the aim point red dot.

"Youtube," Jean replied.

Sheila laughed.

"This isn't funny!" Fred blurted, obviously in a low-level panic.

Sheila shook her head. "Okay," she ceded and turned to Jean. "She's kind of right. What are you even doing?"

"There's someone in the woods," Jean said simply. "They're heading for daddy and the boys and they're not gonna see them coming until it's too late."

"I'm coming with you," Sheila said.

"You're a liability," Jean replied quickly and then thought better of her wording. "I didn't mean it like that. It's just you don't know about patrolling or comms or any of this stuff."

"I can't let you go out there on your own," Sheila insisted.

"She's not," April called out from the darkness.

The woman had been pulling security on the machine gun mounted in the rear of the truck, a job for which she had also been outfitted with night vision, though it was a simple PVS-14 monocular device that only allowed her to see through one eye.

"I am," Jean shot back. "Look, I get it. You all just see me as a little girl, but I'm not. I can do this. I'm the *only one* that can do it. While everyone else was watching sitcoms or reading YA books I was learning how to use night vision, how to run comms, and how to patrol. If there are folks out in those woods with ill intent, we can't just tell our people to pull back. They're gonna be caught in the middle. They need intel."

Sheila stared at Jean for a moment.

"Shit," Sheila said. "She's right."

Jean turned to April. "I need you to swing that gun toward those woods and be ready. If I need back up, I'm gonna lead them right to you."

"I hate this," April said. "I hate that you're doing this."

Jean couldn't suppress a smile. "Well, that makes one of us." She looked down at April's leg. "How's your leg?"

April stomped it a couple of times on the ground.

"Like you said, cannibals heal fast."

As Jean stepped into the thicker darkness of the woods, the trees overhead blocking out much of the moonlight, she wondered if she had indeed bitten off more than she could chew. It was true—everything she had said about studying weapons and tactics for as long as she could remember. She'd even gone on some night time walks with her father under night vision, but that had been more to goof around and spend some time together than true training.

She felt discombobulated, like she couldn't feel her feet under her and she was tripping across the roots on the forest floor. She had no peripheral vision and could feel her sympathetic nervous system ramping up as she was now, in effect, living in tunnel vision.

No, she thought to herself. *You can do this. You know how to do this.*

Jean stopped and let out a breath, then took a few more. She let her eyes and her brain acclimate to the forty-degree white phosphor world she now lived in. No, that wasn't the right way to think about it. She owned it. She owned the night.

She practiced walking again, but this time kept her steps shorter and lower to the ground. Now, her boots tapped the roots and she easily navigated past them instead of tripping over them. There was an art to moving under night vision.

Jean manually relaxed her body and looked around, taking in everything she was seeing. She allowed herself a moment to rotate the NODs up and appreciate how dark it was around her. If the folks she was hunting didn't have night vision, they would be no match for her.

She rolled the tubes back down and watched the night melt away and the landscape come back into focus.

This was her time.

Jorge sat in a half-kneeling position across from Roland and Harris in the moonlight, waiting for Cotton to return. Up until that point, he knew Cotton was the real deal, knew the man had a reputation even within Devgru as being a notch above everyone else, but it hadn't really clicked. Yes, the SEAL had been ferocious in close combat at the farmhouse and had pulled off quite a hat trick at the rail yard in getting Dr. Fred out of the fix she was in, but was he really that much better than everyone else?

"I'm here," a voice said out of the darkness in front of him.

Jorge focused his eyes and realized he was face-to-face with Cotton. Finally, it connected. Now he understood what all the fuss was about. The man had moved up on him like a ghost in the darkness and Jorge had never even known he was there.

First Sergeant Jorge Ramirez was not some slouch, nor an average soldier that could easily be snuck up on. He had done things that even he still couldn't believe. Yet Cotton Wiley had taken him by surprise. Not only that, he had done it with ease.

"What's the word?" Roland asked.

"It's a platoon-sized element," Cotton replied. "Everyone has NODs but they're probably junk. Lasers on their weapons look like they're PERST's."

"So half of 'em don't work," Roland joked.

"Probably," Cotton affirmed. "They're heading north, but it looks like they're going to cross the road right where we're parked."

"Of course they are," Jorge said with a sigh.

Cotton's radio chirped in his ear. Running through his Peltor headset, no one but him would be able to hear it. He furrowed his brow for a moment, unsure who could be trying to contact him as the entire Recce element was within arm's reach.

"Go," he said quietly.

"Wool, this is lamb."

Cotton's eyes grew wide. It was Jean. Those were the call signs they had established long ago. Wool had been his call sign going all the way back to the SEAL Teams, as SEALs tended to not be terribly inventive with their nick names.

"This is Wool," he replied. "What in the hell are you doing?"

"I've got eyes on," Jean replied. "Looks like a Russian Recce unit. About twelve total."

Cotton felt his hands run cold. "You have eyes on?" he asked. "What are you doing out of the RV? Who's with you?"

"No one," Jean replied. "And I don't have time to explain. They're coming toward you. You'll be caught between them and whoever you're tracking." Jean hesitated for a moment. "I'm taking them."

"The hell you are!" Cotton snapped, a little too loudly for Roland's taste, who furiously waved his hands to silence the man. "You get back to the damn RV!"

"Negative," Jean replied. "I'm already committed. Going radio silent."

"Please don't do this," Cotton said quietly.

"I'm making a hole for you," Jean said. "Don't waste it."

"Don't shoot me," Colonel Maxim Lebedev said as he moved down the stairwell with Doctor Gregory Wilson behind him.

The Russian commando felt confident that, at a close enough distance, Gregory would be able to point his rifle, take off the safety, pull the trigger and kill someone within ten feet of him. However, he was not confident that the good Doctor wouldn't accidentally do all of these things directly behind him.

"I'll try," Gregory replied.

Lebedev stopped and turned to look at him in the darkness. His NODs were down and he had broken a chem light clipped to his plate carrier for the research scientist to follow.

"You'll try?" Lebedev asked.

"I'm doing my best!" Gregory snapped. "I'm not like Rambo or something."

Lebedev simply shook his head and turned back to his downward ascent, looking up at the sign on the wall that told them what floor they were on. There were still twenty to go.

"Tell me something," Lebedev said as they navigated the darkness. "How did you make it this long, not knowing how to fight?"

'Well, I guess there was always someone around to... to do the fighting."

"A uniquely American idea," Lebedev replied, the scorn in his voice obvious. "Not needing to be able to fight for yourself."

"It's not like that where you come from?"

"I was born in Siberia," Lebedev said. "In a village outside of the capital city of Novosibirsk. If you do not learn to stand up on your own there, you die."

"It sounds like a hard life."

Lebedev stopped again and turned to Gregory.

"It was an illusion, you know," Lebedev said. "The idea that you did not need to be able to fight for yourself, that someone would always come to save you. You see that now, don't you?"

"I'm starting to," Gregory affirmed.

Lebedev stopped at the ground floor and surveyed the large double doors that would take them into the lobby. "There's no other way?" he asked.

"Unfortunately, no," Gregory replied. "There are tunnels that run beneath the building, beneath the whole city, in fact, but I'm certain they're compromised. If we get caught down there with those things, we won't last long."

"Do you remember what I told you?" Lebedev asked. "About using the dot?"

"If they're within ten feet, aim for the forehead," Gregory affirmed. "I think. Right?"

"Yes," Lebedev said.

He had given the man the briefest possible course in mechanical offset in close quarters. The red dot aiming device was on a riser that set it nearly two inches above the barrel of the rifle and had almost certainly been zeroed at fifty yards. Because of this, in close quarters the round would impact well below the red dot.

"And remember," Lebedev said. "If I go down, my last act will be to kill you."

"What?" Gregory blurted. "I thought you were going to say something about how I should run and not look back!"

"That makes no sense," Lebedev chastised him. "We aren't friends. The only reason I'm keeping you alive is for intelligence value."

"Right," Gregory replied. "I guess I misread the situation."

"I'm sensing that is a trend in your life," Lebedev said.

"That's just hurtful."

The Russian did not respond and instead turned and pushed open the large double doors.

He hesitated for a moment and then put his targeting laser on the first one of the black-eyed cannibals that he saw. He dropped the creature with little fanfare, then moved to the next, then the next, and the next.

"Keep moving," Lebedev said calmly as he led

Gregory through the lobby, engaging targets of opportunity as they presented themselves.

There were at least twenty of the cannibals in the lobby, and while it was unlikely their night vision was as good as Lebedev's technology, they could clearly see the Russian and Doctor Gregory.

"Can they see us?" Gregory asked. "I can't see anything."

"Just follow my light," Lebedev said as he moved toward the front entrance. He had wrapped his chem light with strips of electrical tape, so while it still emitted a light that could be seen, it wasn't much, and it was also to his rear. It was a calculated risk, but the only play he had. "Just don't panic and you will be fine."

"I think I'm panicking," Gregory replied.

"I said *not* to panic."

Lebedev slowed to a stop and performed a tactical reload of his rifle. He knew he had taken at least twenty shots, but did not want to find out the hard way that it had been more. He also knew he had two more full magazines on the front of his plate carrier and three in his back panel, but the obvious question was: Would that even be enough?

On the street outside, he could see that there were dozens of them, and it was approaching a full moon. There was a chance they wouldn't see him, but it was not a guarantee.

"We're going to have to change tactics if we want to make it through ten blocks of this," Lebedev said. "I don't think fighting is an option."

"What do you mean?"

"Eject the magazine from your rifle and hand it to me," Lebedev said.

He watched as Gregory (unbelievably) properly ejected the magazine from the rifle and held it out. Lebedev took it and then took the rifle, which he quietly laid on the ground. He stuffed the magazine in a cargo pocket.

"Grab on to the back of my plate carrier, and whatever you do, don't let go."

CHAPTER 2

Despite having access to the IR aiming laser, Jean opted not to use it. Instead, she moved silently and kept the aim point on the rifle at the night vision setting.

Jean stopped suddenly. She could see a light up ahead and knew it was only a very dim, red-filtered light, but her night vision picked it up with the intensity of a signal beacon. She moved forward again and, after about twenty feet, could see them: twelve men moving in single file. Unbelievably, someone was using a red light to read a map, and they were whispering to each other in Russian.

It didn't make any sense. Why were they moving with such poor noise and light discipline?

Unfortunately, there wasn't enough time to

decode this mystery. Jean could see that they were indeed heading toward her father's position, either to link up with whoever he had found or to engage them. Either way, she knew she could not let that happen.

It was clear that the men did not have night vision capabilities and were relying on the moonlight to navigate through the trees. Jean moved forward again until she was about 30 yards away. She felt as if she were close enough to reach out and touch them. She moved her left hand to the forward controls and activated the aiming laser. There was no need to also activate her IR illuminator, as there was more than enough ambient light from the moon and the stars, and it was one less thing that might give her away.

Whoever these Russians were, they had gotten lazy with their patrolling. The rear man wasn't turning every few steps like he should have been to make sure no one was coming up behind him—a mistake he was about to pay the ultimate price for.

Jean took a half-kneeling position, slowed her breathing, and put her laser on the head of the last man in the file. She exhaled and broke the wall of the trigger. She heard the cycling of the bolt in the gun but not much else as the man dropped. Jean didn't pause to appreciate the result of her efforts as she traversed the laser to the left and broke the trigger again, and again, and again. After the fourth man had dropped, the rest finally realized what was happening.

There was shouting in Russian and Jean adjusted her tactic to further sow the seeds of chaos. She shifted to the first man in the group and put a round in him. This one wasn't as clean as the others, hitting him in the shoulder and spinning him hard before dropping him to the ground. Not perfect, but she would take the result either way.

Then she saw what she was looking for: a long set of antennae protruding from the pack of one of the Russians. She quickly shifted her laser to him and put a round through his head just as he was bringing up a handset to send a communication.

Jean briefly wondered who the radioman was going to make comms with, just before she felt the zip of a round passing dangerously close to her head. The girl dropped to the ground and rolled into the "urban prone," posted up her side to minimize her profile and still get her laser on target. She momentarily considered shutting down the CQB-L and moving to passive aiming with the red dot, but if someone out there was seeing her, it was most likely too late for that.

About one hundred yards away, she saw muzzle flashes and felt more rounds passing by her, but these were not nearly as close as the first one. That first shot had been luck.

Jean suddenly realized what she had walked into. It was not a squad-sized element, but most likely a platoon-sized one. This also meant there were possibly another forty men in the woods around her. Too many. With a group that size, it was also likely they had at least a handful of night vision devices, which would explain how they knew where she was.

There was only one play and she knew it.

Jean rolled back up to half-kneeling (confident that the men in the distance were not laying down accurate fire), turned, and unleashed fast suppressive fire against what remained of her first target set. She felt the bolt lock back as the magazine ran dry, performed a speed reload from the chest rig she was wearing, and proceeded to dump half of that magazine into the few remaining fighters in her close distance.

She turned and moved forward, toward the much larger force and dumped the rest of the magazine into them, bounding as she did so to avoid completely giving away her position. Then she turned and ran toward the road as she hit another speed reload.

"Is that her?" Roland asked in amazement. "That ain't a fucking squad she's taking on!"

"Damn it!" Cotton shouted as he spun and began running back the way they had come.

At this point, there was no need for noise discipline or tactical patrolling. The Chinese they had moved up on were either going to move to a far rally point to steer clear of whatever was going on, or they were going to move toward the sounds of gunfire.

Running at top speed, he knew it would still take at least three minutes to make it back to the road and the Winnebago.

Three minutes Jean didn't have.

"I'm coming in hot!"

April snatched up her radio from where she was sitting in the bed of the Toyota and hit the call button. It was Jean, and it was clear that she was moving fast. Probably toward the road.

"Out of the woods on the western side of the road! Fifty meters from your location!" Jean shouted.

April swiveled the M240 machine gun toward the point Jean had referenced and watched the strip of land through her night vision monocular. She did her best to control her breathing and stop her hands from shaking. There was no laser mounted to the heavy machine gun, so she had to keep her single night vision tube aligned with the red dot atop the gun. Without that alignment, she wouldn't be able to hit a thing.

She pulled the stock in tighter to her shoulder and continued to slow her breathing. It suddenly occurred to her that she had never fired the gun before. How hard would it kick?

"Do you see her?" Sheila asked.

"Yeah, she's wearing a party dress and leading a parade," April said sarcastically. "If I saw her, don't you think I'd say something?"

"Your attitude is not appreciated," Sheila said dryly.

The older woman didn't have night vision capabilities, but she still stood at the ready with her modified Knight's Armament rifle. Even if she couldn't see clearly in the darkness (particularly far away), she figured it would be a safe bet to just fire in the direction that April was, or failing that, fire at the muzzle flashes of the men shooting at them.

Then, April saw the girl. Jean broke from the tree line and pivoted fast, running down the road toward where the RV and the truck were parked.

"I see her!" Sheila nearly shouted as the radio beside April chirped.

"Russians!" Jean's voice resonated from the handheld. "Twenty yards to my rear!"

April didn't answer, but kept her night vision aligned with the red dot and her finger on the trigger.

Jean was only twenty yards from the truck and closing fast when April saw the first Russian soldiers emerge from the same tree line the girl had.

"Come on," April said quietly. "Come on."

Jean finally reached the truck, slid to a stop, turned and slammed her rifle up against the corner of the vehicle to create a stable shooting position. She was breathing like she'd just run a world class marathon time, but the fight wasn't over.

April put her dot on the chest of the soldier closest to her, out in front of the others. She could see him, but he could not yet see her.

"Welcome to America," she shouted, and pressed the trigger of the machine gun.

Simultaneously, Jean began firing and Sheila also

took up position, hammering rounds at the advancing Russians, even if she couldn't quite see what she was aiming at.

April traversed the gun as she engaged the Russian soldiers, following what quickly became their line of retreat back into the woods, but their efforts were futile. The Maxim Defense suppressor on the machine gun was making it next to impossible for them to pinpoint her position, and even if they could, they had only a matter of seconds to attempt to return fire with Jean taking accurate shots at them with her aiming laser.

In less than a minute, the men were retreating back into the woods. April walked her fire in after them and was still knocking them down when she finally lost sight of the platoon.

"Guess they had enough," April said as she sat up behind the gun and watched the smoke drifting from the suppressor.

"I don't think so," Jean said and leapt forward from her position beside the truck.

"What the hell are you doing?" Sheila shouted as Jean sprinted back the way she had come toward the tree line.

. . .

Jean moved quickly into the woods, still able to see the last man who had run from April's withering machine gun assault. Without hesitation, she slowed to a walk, put her laser on his back and dropped him with one of the heavy 220 grain rounds.

She continued moving quickly through the pitch-black woods until she saw another of the men who had slowed to a jog. In the moment of truth, he had allowed his fatigue to get the better of him. He paid for it with his life.

Jean picked up her pace again and found the final Russian soldier leaning against a tree, panting and trying to catch his breath. Even through the white phosphor night vision, she could see the terror in his eyes.

He turned and looked to her. He could not see the girl in the darkness, even with the full moon, but he knew she was there.

"Please," he said in heavily accented English. "Please."

Jean brought the 300 Blackout up and put her laser on his chest.

"You shouldn't have come here."

. . .

"Did you really say 'Welcome to America'?" Sheila asked as she, Fred, and April stood in the darkness, waiting for Jean to come back.

"I was freaked out, all right?" April protested. "I don't know, it just seemed like the thing to say."

Sheila laughed. "I'll have to remember that one," she said. "I have a bad feeling it's going to come up again."

"There she is!" Fred nearly shouted.

April and Sheila turned to see Jean walking down the road toward them, her clothes soaked through with sweat and her face splattered with blood.

"What did you think you were doing?" April demanded.

"Fixin' wagons," Jean replied as she walked to the back of the truck and pulled out a jug of water.

"What?" April asked in confusion.

Sheila laughed.

"What in the hell is so funny?" April demanded.

"It's an old saying," Sheila said. "Like 'you fixed their wagon good'. It means you fucked someone up."

April turned back to Jean. "What planet are you from?"

"West Virginia," Jean replied with a wink.

"I feel like I'm taking crazy pills!" April said. "Is no one else concerned by what just happened?"

"I eat people," Fred interjected. "Like, other humans. So her behavior is pretty low on the list of my concerns. And anyway, she seems fine."

"Have you ever met a twelve-year-old girl?" April asked. "Nothing about how she's acting is fine."

"What would you prefer I be doing?" Jean asked. "Writing hashtags and cryin' over a skinned knee? Well, that ain't the world we live in, so I'll settle for punching tickets and fixin' wagons. Anyway, didn't you just gun down half a platoon of Russian soldiers with a machine gun while shouting 'Welcome to America'?"

"Y'all aren't gonna let that go, are you?" April asked.

Jean turned and saw her father, Harris, Roland, and Jorge jogging down the road toward them.

"Jean!" Cotton shouted.

"I'm fine," Jean replied quickly, holding up her hands. "All in one piece. Which is more than I can say for some."

"What happened?" Cotton asked, turning to April.

"Why is this my fault?" April blurted.

"Russians," Jean said. "Just like I said. About a

platoon-sized element but we took them all out. No one's left alive."

"How can you be sure?" Roland pressed.

Jean locked eyes with him. "I'm sure."

Roland smiled.

"We've got incoming!" Harris said.

Everyone turned in the direction the men had come from and saw a single light moving toward them, but it was at a slow pace.

Cotton lifted his rifle and snapped up the magnifier to get a better look at who was coming toward them.

He lowered the rifle. "It's just one guy," he said.

"One guy?" Jorge asked.

"And he's gone white light,' Cotton added.

"What do you think?" Roland asked.

"Taking a risk," Cotton said. "But he might want to parlay. If we can avoid going head on with that Chinese Recce team, I'm all for it."

"Okay," Roland said and turned back to the group. "You all hold fast. We're gonna walk up on this man and see if we can work things out without further bloodshed."

"Sure you don't want another gun?" Jorge asked.

"Nah," Roland replied. "Don't want to spook him. We ain't trying to wage guerrilla warfare with the Russians and Chinese, despite what some folks may think." He looked over at Jean, indicating her adventure in the woods. "If Fred's right about this whole 'gears of the apocalypse' thing, we've got bigger fish to fry."

Both Cotton and Roland approached the man coming toward them with their rifles slung and hands in view. Once they were close enough to make out finer details, they saw that he was an older man, most likely about their age or even a little older. He was very clearly Chinese but was kitted out in American gear. That wasn't a big surprise, as everyone had known for years that the Chinese were smuggling everything from night vision to plate carriers out of the U.S. through eBay.

In fact, it had become almost a running joke that if someone on eBay bought your tactical gear and had a shipping address near an airport in Oregon or Washington, that stuff was going on the next plane to China or Japan. The stuff going to Japan was most likely ending up in the hands of Airsofters, which was no big deal. The gear going to China, however, was probably going to Chinese military special operations units, like a long-range Recce team moving deep into Texas in advance of a larger invasion force.

The Chinese soldier stopped about ten meters from them and raised his hands.

"I'm Xi," he said.

Roland looked at Cotton and then back to Xi.

"I'm 'he/him'," Roland said, pointing to himself.

"What in the hell are you talking about?" Cotton asked.

"I thought we were doing pronouns," Roland said, leaning in and lowering his voice.

"Ex-eye," Cotton said, spelling the man's name. "She."

"Oh," Roland turned back to Xi, "I'm Roland. This is Cotton."

"You ran the entire command," Cotton said wonderingly.

"Hey!" Roland snapped. "I'm not good with people, okay? Unless it's, you know." He mimed pulling a trigger.

"I am a Colonel in the People's Liberation Army," Xi went on, pretending the preceding exchange had not just occurred. "As you may have guessed, we are on a reconnaissance mission here."

"I don't want to tell you how to do your job,"

Roland said. "But you might have missed a couple of your recon classes."

Xi smiled. "American humor," he said. "I like it."

"Happy to be of service," Roland said with a smile.

"We have no quarrel with you," Cotton interjected, putting an end to the levity. "We just want to pass."

Xi nodded.

"Are the Russians dead?"

"Affirmative," Cotton said. "Looked like a platoon-sized element from what my scout relayed. They're no longer with us."

"Then you have done me a favor," Xi said. "For that you may pass."

"Mind if I ask a question?" Cotton ventured. "Curiosity is all."

"Of course."

"What do you get out of this? After it's all over, after you go at it with the Russians, what's gonna be left? What will the point of it be?"

It was a reasonable question, as Cotton understood that all-out war between the Russians and the Chinese on American soil, even without nuclear weapons, would be catastrophic.

Xi looked at the ground for a moment and then back to Cotton.

"That very question, my friend, is precisely why America failed. It was the lack of understanding that there is a whole world out there, a big one that has little concern for what happens to the United States of America. We like your movies and your blue jeans, much like the Soviets did, but we can do without both." Xi paused for effect. "Understand that this war is not about the conquest of America. Rather, you are only providing the battleground, and after the victor is decided, we will simply return home and leave in our wake a kingdom of ashes."

"You—" Roland began what sounded like an aggressive line of speech but Cotton put a hand on the man's chest and turned to him.

"He's not wrong," Cotton said. "Gettin' mad about it won't change anything."

Roland wanted to press on but decided not to.

Cotton turned back to Xi.

"Now, if it's all the same to you, we'll head back and be on our way."

Xi looked at Cotton for a moment, then reached into his pocket and retrieved a small card.

"Where I come from, we believe in the repayment of debt," Xi said. "You may not understand this, but by intercepting that patrol and doing what you did, you provided us aid. So, in return, I give this to you."

Xi held out the card and Cotton took it. He looked at the Chinese lettering on it and then back to Xi.

"What is this?" Cotton asked.

"I believe in the popular board game 'Monopoly' you would refer to it as a 'get out of jail free' card," Xi said with a smile. "It won't work on the Russians, but if you run into more of us that are not as understanding as I am, show them that card and they are likely to let you pass."

"Thank you," Cotton said with a nod.

"I don't like the way that went down," Roland said as the two men walked back down the road to where the Winnebago and the truck were parked.

"What are you talking about?"

"This is the fucking Super Bowl," Roland replied. "These guys... they're here and we're just letting it pass."

"You said it yourself," Cotton said. "We're not here to get in fights with the Russians and the Chinese. We have bigger problems."

"I know. It's still hard to take."

The two men walked back to where the group was waiting beside the big RV, and everyone was well aware that they were presenting a very large target in the middle of what appeared to be two converging enemy armies.

"Okay," Cotton said. "We're rolling out of here. I checked the map and there's a few towns down the road. First one that looks like it might be safe, we're going to call home for the night."

"We have to get to Houston!" Fred insisted.

"We've been fighting almost non-stop for two days," Roland said. "I get that this is important, but Cotton's right. We need some solid, uninterrupted sleep and a few beats to get our heads right. I know you all want to get this shit over with, but I also want us to make it out the other end alive." Roland surveyed the group. "Make sense?"

Everyone nodded, some waiting a few beats longer than others to register their agreement.

Bill Rampart rubbed his eyes as he stood at the coffee bar in his well-appointed apartment within what had become the de facto headquarters for Fluid Dynamics, New Orleans. Technically, the true headquarters building was still in New York City, but it had been overwhelmed by the Gen 2 cannibals forty-eight hours prior.

It appeared that New York was putting up quite a fight, a very different outcome from the way that Houston had seemingly imploded in a matter of hours. This most likely had to do with New York's ability to seal off individual Boroughs and retreat into the subways. They were still looking at eighty percent of their population going Gen 2 cannibal, but between the aforementioned tactics and some other surprises, they were waging what amounted to an all-out war within the City State.

Bill wondered which way it would ultimately go. If the Gen 1 cannibals managed to become the victors, would they start asking questions about what had happened and how it had happened? The obvious concern was that those questions would eventually lead back to him.

They would lead back to him, because ultimately, he was the cause of all of it, intentional or not.

"You're a man of many talents," Bill said as he took the steaming cup of coffee from his assistant Jared.

"I do my best, Sir," Jared said with a smile.

The much taller and younger man seemed perpetually uncomfortable, and this had not gone beyond Bill Rampart's notice. It wasn't that he was nervous, but rather that he knew he was a man out of place. This was not uncommon with military veterans, particularly Marines, such as Jared had been.

A gentle beeping emitted from Jared's pocket, and he retrieved his phone to read the text message that had come through with a frown.

"What is it?" Bill asked, sensing that he was about to be the recipient of bad news.

"They've lost comms with the strike team."

"Finley's men?"

"Yes, Sir," Jared said. "And the drones picked up an explosion from the top of the Fulbright building as well, just minutes after Finley was supposed to check in."

"I don't like that," Bill said, shaking his head. "I don't like that at all."

Jared scrolled through the message thread. "There's something else," he continued.

"Something else I won't like?" Bill asked.

"I fear that will be the case," Jared replied and then paused for a moment. "The drones sent back video feed from several minutes before the explosion, from the roof of the building."

"And?"

"There was a second helicopter parked there. Not one of ours."

"Whose is it then?"

"They've identified it as Russian."

"In Houston?" Bill blurted.

"We've known they were in Texas," Jared said slowly. "Just not that far east."

Bill looked confused as he took another sip from his coffee. "They're moving fast," he said. "Far faster than our calculations. Is it possible they know about Doctor Wilson?"

"In the current climate, Sir, I would say anything is possible."

Bill tapped a finger on the countertop. "Shit."

Jared waited, knowing it was best not to further offer his opinion if it was not solicited.

"Send an assault element," Bill finally said.

Jared's eyes blinked rapidly. "An assault element?" he asked, understanding that this was a platoon-sized force of just under fifty men.

"All we know right now is that Mister Finley is out of contact, there was a Russian helicopter on the roof of the building, and we do not know the whereabouts of Doctor Wilson," Bill said sharply. "Am I not correct?"

"You are correct."

"Well, that seems like a pretty big fucking problem, doesn't it?" Bill snapped.

"Yes, Sir."

Bill clenched his jaw for a moment and then let out a breath. "I'm sorry," he said. "I didn't mean to... act like that."

Jared said nothing. "Which assault element?" he asked.

"Alpha," Bill said without hesitation. "With Bravo on stand-by. I understand we only have four of these elements, but if the Russians get that code from Doctor Wilson, the chess board will be most decidedly tipped in their favor."

Colonel Maxim Lebedev took a well-aimed shot through his night vision and dropped the black-eyed cannibal that looked as if it had taken notice of him and Doctor Gregory Wilson. From there, he brought his rifle down to the low-ready and continued to move.

It was slow going through the city streets, even slower than he had anticipated. He'd seen that the streets were flooded when he'd flown in, but had not anticipated how deep the waters would be, in some places up to his hips.

After they had gotten clear of the Fulbright Building and the hordes of cannibals wading through the same waters on the street below, the crowd had thinned out quite a bit. For whatever reason, the majority of them seemed to be clustered around that building.

There were still plenty to contend with, but at least it now looked as if they had a chance of making it to their destination. Lebedev was very open to the idea of there being a fifty-fifty chance that at some point he would need to cut this man loose and focus on saving his own life. After all, he had seen what these things could do if there were enough of them and they were focused on a target.

However, he had also observed that these cannibals were not like the ones that he had encountered on that hilltop. Those cannibals had been strong and fast, hyper-aggressive and with at least some level of conscious intelligence.

The ones he now encountered in the streets of this city were nothing like that, almost zombie-like, for lack of a better word. The Alpha Group commander was not unappreciative for this small blessing, as he doubted he would have made it this far faced with the other variant.

Lebedev turned and tested one of the storefront doors. It had some give to it, so he pushed it open and moved inside. He flooded the space of the small liquor store with his IR illuminator and saw no obvious inhabitants.

Gregory was still behind him, holding fast to the length of 550 cord that Lebedev had attached to his belt. After the first block, it had become apparent that just having the man hold onto his plate carrier would not work, as the good doctor had almost pulled him over trying to avoid a piece of garbage on the sidewalk.

Once they were both inside, Lebedev turned and secured the door with a carabiner. He let out a breath and raised his NODs into the stowed position on his helmet. After his eyes adjusted, he could tell that there was just enough ambient light coming in through the windows from the moon above so that he could see.

"What are we doing?" Gregory asked.

"Just taking a moment," Lebedev replied as he walked down the aisles.

He stopped at the vodka section and tapped each

bottle in turn until settling on one he knew. He pulled it from the shelf, uncapped it, and took a swig.

"Are you sure that's a good idea?" Gregory asked.

"None of this is a good idea," Lebedev said before taking another swig and re-capping the bottle. "But this will make it a little less painful."

"I've never had it," Gregory said.

"What?"

"Alcohol."

Lebedev laughed out loud and then stopped and studied Gregory.

"Oh," the Russian said. "You were serious. I thought that was an American joke."

"I had other things to do," Gregory replied.

"Like destroy the world."

"I thought I was helping!" Gregory protested. "We all did."

"You mentioned an antidote to the vaccine," Lebedev said. "What is that?"

"You get me out of here first," Gregory said stoically. "Then I'll tell you."

Lebedev drew his fighting knife and held it in one hand, bottle of vodka in the other.

"I will cut out your eyes with this," he said, holding up the knife, "and then pour vodka into the bleeding sockets."

"You're an amazing negotiator."

"I've had a lot of practice."

"Look, I didn't work on the vaccine, okay? I just know about the antidote because we developed it here in Houston. Just in case. We were willing to try the Gen 2, but I pushed them to synthesize an antidote."

"Why do I feel like you knew something was going to go wrong?"

"Because something always goes wrong," Gregory said with a shrug. "Pharmaceuticals have side effects. That's the way it's always been, but no one ever reads the insert."

"Like turning people into white-eyed cannibals?"

"White-eyed cannibals that have super healing," Gregory corrected him. "When people took Pandemify, it didn't just stop the virus. It stopped cancer, diabetes, heart disease! I mean, it stopped nearly every disease state known to man in its tracks! But no one talked about that. They only wanted to talk about, well... the side-effect."

"It seems like a pretty big side-effect."

"What was the alternative?" Gregory implored. "That virus wasn't an accident. Come on, you must know that."

Gregory waited until finally Lebedev nodded.

"It was man-made. It didn't act like viruses are supposed to, and I believe to my core that it was going to wipe us out. So, we did the only thing we could. We developed a cure that cost us a piece of our humanity, but gave us our future back. What ended up destroying this country wasn't the fault of the vaccine, the fault lay in our response to it." Lebedev could see a sadness overtake the scientist's eyes. "It wasn't the vaccine that killed us, it was that little piece of humanity that remained, revealing its true nature."

INTERLUDE 1

June Kennedy walked through the darkness and stopped. She stopped and she listened. The darkness was at once around her and inside of her. The evolved were there as well, the shared consciousness that they had developed was impossible to define, yet ever present.

It took a great deal of effort for her to determine what their numbers were, to split this hive mind into simple math, but she knew they were several thousand strong, drawing more into their dark, swirling storm with every passing hour.

She stopped and took a breath, then leaned forward on her toes and peered into the black. There was something in the distance, something that wasn't just the black. There was a light.

June felt a wetness beneath her bare feet, almost like how she would imagine tar to feel against bare skin. She walked through it and could feel it heating up beneath her feet. Was this meant to discourage her? What was this light ahead, and why did the sentient darkness not want her to see it?

Finally, she could view figures in the dim light. They looked familiar.

June walked further through the swirling black, and beneath her feet she could feel the tar-like substance growing hotter and hotter. Finally, she stopped at what appeared to be the edge of the darkness. She was in the woods, and it felt like East Texas. It reminded her of her childhood growing up in Louisiana. Those memories seemed so foreign now that she had evolved, and yet somehow, they stayed with her.

She looked down at her bare feet. The tar was gone and she stood on a two-lane country road. She looked back and saw that the darkness was gone. She was somewhere else.

June walked forward again, and the people on the road gained clarity. They had an RV and a truck. Then she recognized them. It was the people from Oatmeal, and with them was the woman who had approached her outside the gate. The same woman she'd seemed to have some sort of connection with.

Suddenly, June realized what had happened. She wasn't really here. Somehow, she was projecting herself through this woman's consciousness. She took a moment to remember the woman's name: Sheila.

June walked closer to the group and stopped. It was true. They could not see her. She existed only within Sheila's mind. They were talking about something, but the words were garbled, almost as if they were speaking under water.

June stopped beside Sheila and stared intently at the woman.

"Who are you?" June asked quietly.

Sheila stopped mid-sentence and looked around.

"What is it?" Roland asked.

"Someone just walked across my grave," Sheila said, referencing the myth about shivers down the spine. "It felt like someone was standing beside me."

"Now you're proving my point," Roland said. "We definitely need to get some rest."

Had she heard her? June examined Sheila closely. The woman looked familiar, so familiar. What was it? Where had she seen her before?

Slowly, she reached out and tapped Sheila twice on the side of the head.

Sheila winced and put a hand to her temple.

"You okay?" Jorge asked, genuine concern on his face.

"Yeah," she said. "Just felt like someone tapping an ice pick against my head."

June stepped back and cocked her head to the side as she examined Sheila further.

In a sudden moment of clarity, she knew where she had seen the woman. The shape of her jaw, her nose, and the spacing of her eyes. Even the way she moved was intimately familiar.

"No," she said quietly. "It can't be. It can't be you."

June Kennedy recognized Sheila because she had seen her face in the mirror every day of her life.

Sheila was her daughter, the one she had given up all those years ago.

CHAPTER 3

COTTON PULLED in a deep breath through his nose as his eyes snapped open. That was usually the way it happened, the way he woke. He knew why it happened that way, it was because he had stopped breathing. He'd mentioned it to a doctor a long time ago, that he thought he stopped breathing while he was sleeping and would wake up drawing a breath of air. The doc had said something about having him do a sleep study, but it never went beyond that. The way Cotton figured it, so long as he kept waking up alive, it couldn't be that big of a problem.

He reached up to his mouth and pulled the piece of rigger's tape off. He took another, much deeper breath through his mouth and sat fully upright on the bench seat in the RV. That night had probably been the first in a very long time that he let himself drift into a truly deep sleep. The truth was that he hadn't really slept (at least, not like humans are supposed to) since everything had kicked off. Not since the cannibals had first emerged.

He thought about that for a moment as his eyes adjusted to the light. Not just the cannibals, but the variants. Fred and Jean had both mentioned something about that, about different strains. Someone else had called them "generations." Either way, he didn't like it, didn't like what he'd seen outside the gate back at Oatmeal.

That horde waiting out on the plains with the woman, June... well, he didn't like to admit it, but it had scared him. It scared him the way that the idea of a nuclear exchange always had. It scared him because he wasn't even going to have a fighting chance. If those black-eyed things decided that his time was up, then it was going to be up, and there wouldn't be a damn thing he could do about it. They would roll right over him like just one more inconsequential speed bump in the apocalypse.

That was why they needed to find another way around the problem. They hadn't really talked much about it, but there was an unspoken hope that this Doctor Wilson would know something that might help them in case that black-eyed swarm came back around their way. Never mind also making sure the entire world wasn't plunged into darkness.

"Here."

Cotton looked up and saw Fred standing over him, holding out a cup of what looked and smelled like hot coffee.

He reached out, took a sip, and nodded his thanks. "You really are a genius," Cotton said. "If you managed to brew hot coffee in the middle of this goat rope."

Fred smiled. "I think maybe, this is how we keep it together. You know? The little things. Even when the world seems like it's coming apart at the seams, the little things help us hold on to our sanity."

"The little things," Cotton said, and turned to look out the window.

They'd stopped in a small town that had seemed safe enough. It wasn't much to look at, just another little Texas speck on the roadmap, but it had all of the usual things you would expect from a small town.

"You want to 'what'?" Roland asked, the tone in his voice bordering on disbelief.

"Take a time out," Cotton repeated. "From the apocalypse shit. Just for an hour."

Cotton surveyed the group that stood before him. They were beat down, some still splattered with blood and carbon from close-distance gunfights and others still appearing dead on their feet even after the five hours of sleep they had just gotten. They needed more respite than just the sleep, and he knew it.

"No, we need to get back on the road," Roland protested.

"We need to be at our best," Cotton pressed. "And right now, we're not. Come on, you know I'm right. How many times did you stand us down when there was another target package ready to roll because you knew we wouldn't be at our best?"

"Not many," Roland countered.

"But you did it," Cotton said. "When you knew our fatigue level would hinder mission success. That's where we're at now. Remember, it's not enough to fight. You have to know what you're fighting for."

Roland grimaced. His own words coming back to haunt him. "So, what are we doing?" he asked. "Having a picnic? Square dancing?"

Cotton looked around the deserted town. "Meet

back here in two hours," he said. "Don't do anything dumb, don't go more than three blocks out and give a holler if anything goes south."

Roland nodded his head. "Okay," he said. "I know you're right." He looked at the rest of the group, finally seeing the same thing Cotton had. They didn't have another big fight in them, not in their present condition.

"And no weird tactical shit," Cotton said, seeming to address the order to Jean. "Field stripping rifles or cleaning gear is not relaxing."

"Why are you looking at me?" Jean asked, mildly indignant.

Cotton lifted an eyebrow. "If it quacks like a duck."

Roland watched as, one by one, the group split off. The idea was to find something in their immediate vicinity that would help them unwind.

He thought back to what Fred had said to him about dropping his armor if he wanted to legitimately make a connection with someone, that person specifically being April. He also thought about what Cotton had said, a reference to something he'd often repeated back in the Teams.

"Don't forget what you're fighting for."

Everything he had said about growing up in group homes and never having a family was true, and he knew that it had affected the way he lived his life as an adult. He remembered hearing once that most folks, by the time they're about thirty, don't ever really change again. All of their behaviors are set and they'll remain the same person until they die.

At the time he heard that, it didn't seem like that was a problem. He thought he was doing pretty damn good, and if he just kept things going the same way until his end of days, well that wouldn't be so bad.

Now he was starting to change his opinion on that matter. Maybe there was something else out there for him, something more than just being a soldier. What in the hell was he fighting for, after all? To just be able to fight more? The more he meditated on that idea, the more it seemed to not be the best path.

What was it about April that drew him to her? All the way back in the farmhouse, when he was first cutting her loose from that chair, he had felt it, some sort of a draw to the woman, as if something within her was pulling at something within him.

He watched her walk aimlessly down the street, scanning the surrounding storefronts.

"Go with her," Fred said.

"Jesus!" Roland started, nearly jumping out of his boots. He had been so lost in his thoughts that he had not seen the woman standing beside him. "You know, it's not cool to sneak up on people."

Fred just smiled.

Jorge pushed open the trap door at the top of the old clock tower and crawled through with his Recce rifle and a bottle of water. The wood plank floor was covered in dust, and it was clear no one had been up there for quite a while, maybe even from before the virus. He closed the door behind him and then unslung the rifle and lay it against the short, brick wall.

In the corner of the observation platform was a small, wooden stool. He brushed the dust off of it and smiled. There was a strong possibility that the stool was as old as the town itself, as it was clearly handmade and quite old. He flipped it over and saw that it was put together with wooden screws. He wasn't exactly a master wood worker, but he knew enough to understand that it was indeed very old.

He set it down beside the wall and sat down. Below him, the town was quiet. Everyone had already gone their separate ways and the only ones left that he could see were Roland and April. It looked like the former SEAL Master Chief was trying to catch up with her. He wondered what that was about? For a hot minute, he had thought there might be something going on between her and Cotton, which seemed strange, as Cotton wasn't exactly the president of the cannibal fan club.

Jorge shook his head at the thought that he was running and gunning in the apocalypse with a couple of SEALs. If he ever ran into another Unit member in this screwed up meat grinder that had once upon a time been the United States of America, he knew there would be no end to the amount of shit he would catch.

It wasn't that there was any real inter-service rivalry anymore, not like there used to be. Once the Global War on Terror had started and things got real, most of the petty bickering had gone the way of the buffalo. They all knew that when things got hot and you were in a pinch, it could be anyone coming to pull your ass out of the fire. Hell, he'd even had Air Force PJ's drop in out of nowhere and back him up in Afghanistan.

Even so, if he was being honest about it, he'd never really been that impressed with the SEALs he met. It wasn't that they weren't capable, it just seemed like the legend was greater than the reality. To be fair, he hadn't crossed paths with many of the Team Six guys, otherwise known as the Naval Special Warfare Development Group.

Until now. Cotton and Roland were clearly a different breed, much more in line with his experience working in Delta, and perhaps beyond even that. In many ways, he'd felt over the past couple of days like he was just trying to keep up.

Jorge reached into his back pocket and pulled out the battered, leather wallet that he always kept stowed there. Inexplicably, he still had some cash in it, just a couple of twenties and two singles. Several times over the past year, he'd thought about getting rid of them, but there was always this strange idea in the back of his head that he might need them someday. What if things somehow got back to normal and he'd just thrown away forty-two dollars? Or maybe it was a Schrödinger's cat type of scenario, and by throwing away the money, he would be dooming the world to never return from the apocalypse.

Both of those scenarios were unlikely and he knew it, so he pulled out the cash and laid it on the edge of the short, brick wall. The breeze gently lifted the edges of it. Maybe this was the way to do it. Let the wind decide.

Jorge thought about this for a moment and pulled a tattered photo from the wallet, holding it in his hand for a moment and staring at it. His wife and two daughters looked back at him as he remembered the day he had taken it. Cheryl and the girls all sitting together on the swings at the park. That had been a good day. Maybe it had been the last good day.

He turned the picture over in his hand and looked at the message on the other side.

Love you to the moon and back.

Jorge felt the tears welling up in his eyes. Maybe it was too much, too much to carry this around with him forever. After all, their deaths had been thoroughly avenged, not one, but three times. He would have preferred it had been done at close range, so he could look the son-of-a-bitch in the eyes, but from a mile away, the Accuracy International AX50 rifle had done the job just fine.

He turned the photo over again and looked into their eyes.

"Why can't I bring you back?" he asked quietly.

It was too much. Perhaps he should let the wind decide this as well.

He laid the photo down on the brick wall beside the cash, just as the wind lifted one of the singles and he watched it drift away.

Jorge sat back and stared at the photo.

The wind lifted one of the corners, then the other. Finally, the entire photo floated into the air and away from the clock tower.

"No!" he shouted and lunged forward without thinking.

He grasped at the photo with his fingertips and nearly fell from the tower as he finally reached far enough to grab it and pulled himself back over the wall.

"Shit," he said quietly as he sat back down on the stool and stared at the photo.

One by one, the remaining bills were lifted from the brick wall and floated away.

"Mind if I come with you?" Roland asked as he walked up behind April.

April turned and looked at the former SEAL Command Master Chief. She couldn't help but smile.

"What is it about me?" April questioned, cocking her head to the side.

"How do you mean?" Roland asked.

"Look, the world might be ending for real, and a lot sooner than we might like. A girl doesn't have time for bullshit anymore."

Roland laughed out loud. "You mean why do I like you?" he asked.

"Yeah."

"Seems like a girl like you would be used to guys goin' sweet on her."

"That's a good line."

"Maybe it ain't a line," Roland countered. "Look, in case you hadn't noticed, I don't do 'normal'. The stuff I do, the stuff I did, only a handful of guys in the world could do. That was all well and good, but it left a lot of holes. Holes guys like me end up filling with alcohol and maybe... I don't know. Maybe doing things that later we turn around and we don't know why we did them."

April relaxed her posture. Roland wasn't putting on an act, and she was starting to see that. Whatever he was asking, whatever he was offering, it was real. He was being vulnerable, maybe for the first time in his life.

She reached out her hand and smiled.

"It starts here," she said. "Keep it simple."

Roland took her hand, and the two walked down the main street together.

Cotton stopped on the main street in front of what he recognized as an old CD store. He allowed himself a smile at the memory of CD's and for a moment, dropped his own armor. He thought back to when he was a young metal head in West Virgina, listening to the hair metal of the late nineties before he moved on to Slayer and Pantera.

He reached out and pushed the door. It was unlocked and opened with a jingling of the bells tied to it. He wondered if that was a throwback to a time when a place like this would have had regular customers. For some reason, he doubted it was highly trafficked in the years before the virus.

Inside, the store was musty, and Cotton saw shelves full of CDs as well as some racks with old records on them near the back.

Then he caught something out of the corner of his eye and his head snapped to the right. It was the man who had owned the store. It must have been, or at least he thought it must have been. It was hard to tell what this figure used to look like. Most of his head was gone, and the rest of his body had decayed over months or perhaps even a year. Maybe he had pulled the trigger in the very beginning and no one had thought it was important to clean him up.

The shotgun the man had used to take his own life lay on the floor at his feet, showing signs of rust. For the most part, the town had appeared to be deserted. Perhaps most of them had been in the first wave to flee to Houston in hopes of salvation, but this man had opted to stay behind.

It was possible that he hadn't wanted to leave his CD collection behind. It was a strange idea, but it made sense to Cotton as he walked the aisles and went through the racks of discs. Many of them meant something to him, reminded him of important times in his life when that music had been playing and of people who had been important to him then. Those people were all gone now. He stopped at one of the albums and smiled, picking it up and turning it over in his hand.

It was Heartbreak Station from the band Cinderella. While Cotton had indeed left his hair metal days behind him when he moved on to the heavier stuff, he had pulled that specific album and the title track out of his past when he began dating his future wife, Sarah.

He looked around the store and realized there was no way to play it, until he saw an old Sony Discman sitting on the front counter, complete with headphones.

Cotton walked to it and leaned against the countertop, across from the dead man as he slipped the disc into the music player, closed it, and put the headphones on. It powered up, so he navigated to the song "Heartbreak Station" and hit play.

The familiar acoustic guitar riff filled his ears and triggered a memory—sitting on the beach with Sarah, watching the waves roll in at one in the morning, not even knowing or caring what time it was. They were both about to deploy to Afghanistan for the last time, but neither of them knew it. They knew they were each going to take that trip, but they had no idea it would be their last.

For Cotton, it would be decided by the command that he was no longer deployable to that region for personal reasons, and for Sarah Wiley, it would be because she had met her end in the mountains of that same country.

"Shit," Cotton said quietly as he listened to the music.

He leaned back against the counter and slowly slid down it onto the floor as the tears started to come. He felt as if his body were a long dormant volcano that was only now finally starting to erupt with emotion.

Cotton laid his head in his hands and let the images of his wife come flooding back in, the same ones he had kept suppressed for so long, because he knew they would have this effect.

"What happened to you?" Sheila asked as she walked down the Main Street beside Jean.

"What do you mean?" Jean asked as she surveyed the different shops and small houses that peppered the main drag, such as it was.

"Something made you this way," Sheila said.

"Not sure what you're gettin' at," Jean replied.

Sheila stopped and turned to Jean. "You're not a normal twelve-year-old. You must know that."

"You eat people and you've only got one arm," Jean countered. "Seems to me like a case here of the pot calling the kettle black."

"Fair enough," Sheila nodded and continued walking. "What do you want to do?"

"I'm looking for something," Jean said. "Just not sure where I'll find it."

"What is it?"

Jean looked up at Sheila and smiled. "Wouldn't be a surprise if I told you, would it?"

"Suppose not."

"Mind if I ask you something?"

"Might as well," Sheila said. "Way I hear it, we're on borrowed time. Might as well get to know each other."

"How'd you get like you are?" Jean asked. "Tough, I mean."

Sheila smiled. "I don't know if I'd called myself tough."

"Tougher than most folks," Jean said. "Hell, you ate your own arm."

Sheila looked down at the stump below her left elbow. She'd avoided looking at it too much because she still couldn't believe it had happened, that she'd had to do that and there wasn't ever going to be a way to take it back.

"I did what I had to, to survive," Sheila said. "Tough doesn't factor into it. You just have to decide if you want to live bad enough to do things other folks won't."

"Makes sense."

"I never had a mom or dad, not like you've got," Sheila went on. "Guess I had to start making those kinds of decisions early on."

"Did you ever know them?" Jean asked. "Your mom or dad?"

Sheila shook her head. "My dad died in prison, before I was born. Never met my mother either, but I knew she was out there. Maybe still is."

"Ever try to find her?"

"Once," Sheila answered. "Hired a private detective and the whole deal. Now, I don't even know why I did it."

"Did he find anything?"

Sheila nodded. "He found her, all right. She was working as an administrator or something at some lumber company in Baton Rouge. That's where I came from, out in Louisiana."

"You didn't want to meet her, did you?" Jean asked.

"By the time it got to that point, and it got real... I realized she didn't want to meet me. If she had, she would have found me on her own before then. The P.I. even had an envelope for me with all her information, but... I didn't take it."

Jean stopped and looked up at a building to her right. Above the door was a sign that read: Library.

"Found it."

. . .

"Isn't there something you want to do?" Fred asked.

"Not really," Harris shrugged. "Figured I'd just tag along with you, if it's all the same."

"Doesn't bother me," Fred replied. "I don't even know where I'm going."

"Kind of reminds me of the town I grew up in," Harris said as he surveyed his surroundings. "Just the one stoplight. Almost feels like progress left it behind."

Fred stopped in her tracks and looked around.

"Do you hear that?" she asked.

Harris stopped as well and listened intently. "Hear what?"

Fred's head jerked to the right. "That!"

Now Harris heard it. It was the sound of a dog barking. It was faint, but it was there.

"Okay," Harris said. "Now I hear it. But if there are dogs here, that ain't gonna be good."

"I don't know," Fred replied and shook her head. "Listen. It sounds like they're inside of some building. There's an echo."

"That's great, Doc. I still think it's none of our business."

No sooner had the words left Harris's mouth than Fred was heading for a side street.

"I'd like to file my strong protest!" Harris called

out after her as he followed. "That this is a bad freaking idea!"

"Noted," Fred replied curtly.

***

"I heard a story," April said as she sat across from Roland in the now long defunct soda shop. "That you cut a guy's hands off for stealing."

The line of questioning clearly took Roland by surprise. He leaned back in his chair and folded his hands on the table.

"I had my reasons for doing that."

"I'm not judging," April said. "Maybe pre-apocalypse cutting someone's hands off would have been a red flag, but we aren't pre-apocalypse. I've done things just in the last few days that I... that I still can't reconcile. All the same, I know they needed to happen."

"That's the key," Roland said. "When you start doing the things that need to be done. People always think there will be some grand epiphany. That the skies will open up and reveal the answer as to why they had to do what they did, but that ain't the truth. That's never how it goes. You just know it needed to be done, even if you can't understand the 'why' of it."

"So, you don't know why you cut that man's hands off?" April pushed.

"No," Roland said with a shake of his head. "I know exactly why I cut that man's hands off."

There was silence for a moment.

"I get that I'm pushing," April said. "But the thing is, I like you. I can't explain it, maybe like these things we do that you were just talking about. Maybe liking you is one of those things. But I need to know you're not a total psycho."

Roland smiled. April laughed.

"I'm serious!" she pushed.

"Okay," Roland acquiesced. "I get it. Just because the world ended doesn't mean we stop having good judgement. And just for the record, I like you, too."

"So, you know why you did it then?"

"I tried it once before," Roland said. "Building a society. Right after I took that shot, right after I became a known man in these parts, I started putting a town together. It wasn't really about trying to rebuild civilization. It was more about recruiting fighters, because I figured a fight was coming."

"You figured right."

"Seems so," Roland nodded. "I started it in a little town called Cranfills Gap. I mean, this town was a nothing, even before the virus. Maybe a few hundred people there. I figured it would be easy to defend. It had enough natural resources that we could grow food, purify water. All the stuff we needed. So, we made a go of it.

"The first mistake I made was that I trusted people. Not a lot of them, just a few, but enough that it was a problem. I also let shit slide. Folks did things they shouldn't have, and I gave them second chances. Then third chances. Too many."

Roland went silent.

"What happened?" April asked.

"There weren't many women in the town," Roland replied. "Tensions built. Thing hit a boiling point where some of the men decided they would just take what they wanted."

Roland let the silence hang in the air.

"You don't have to say it," April said. "I understand."

"The other men didn't necessarily support the ones that did it, but they feared them enough that they backed them. When I tried to pass judgement, tried to set things right, they rebelled. Told me I wasn't the 'rule maker' anymore."

"What did you do?"

"I told them 'okay'," Roland said. "Told them

they could be in charge. Headed back to my house and turned in for the night." Roland looked April in the eyes, and something about his face changed. "After night fell, I dropped my NODs, went out into the town and killed them."

"Who?" April asked.

"All of them," Roland responded bluntly. "With a suppressor under NODs it wasn't hard. Killed thirty-two men that night. Real 'wrath of God' Old Testament style. I didn't want to do it, but they pushed me. Didn't give me any other option. After I took out the sentries they'd posted, it was easy. Just went from house to house killing them in their beds. Took about three hours."

Roland waited a moment. He waited for the horror to register on April's face. He waited for her to stand up and walk out on him, just like so many had done in the past. Instead, she reached out and took his hand.

"You did what you had to do," she said. "You set things right."

"That story got out," Roland went on. "And after that, building the community at Oatmeal was easy. No one would even look cross-eyed at me, but they knew that the man who killed everyone in the town of Cranfills Gap would be able to keep them safe. So, that was why I cut that man's hands off. You can't give folks an inch, not if you want them to be civil. I know. I've seen it."

"See?" Fred asked as she walked down the side street and toward a building labeled 'Animal Control'. "I told you."

"This doesn't make any sense," Harris said. "There can't be dogs locked in there, they would have starved to death by now."

Fred continued walking despite his protests.

"Hey!" Harris shouted. "Stop!"

She did. Fred turned and looked at her compatriot with clear surprise on her face.

"I didn't mean to shout," Harris said, holding up a hand in a placating gesture. "But think about it, come on. You're smart. We could be walking into a bad situation here."

Fred hesitated another moment and nodded her agreement.

"Okay, you're right," she said. "I just... I have this thing about protecting animals."

Suddenly, movement down the street caught her eye. She turned to see a fairly large dog walking toward them, looking at the ground.

"See?" Harris said. "There's your dog. He's fine."

Fred narrowed her eyes to improve her distance vision as the dog stopped and looked up at her. He curled back his lips and glared at them with white eyes.

"That dog is not fine!"

"Doesn't it seem strange?" Sheila asked as she and Jean walked through the rows of tall shelves in the two-story structure. The library was clearly one of the oldest buildings in the small town. "That a town like this would have such a large library?"

"Not that strange," Jean said as she scanned the shelves. "Lot of these towns put a high priority on education, so they had these big libraries. Especially before the internet came around. It was the only way you could find things out. "

"The internet," Sheila laughed. "I think a few years ago everyone thought that was going to be forever. Now it's just a memory."

"City States still have it," Jean said. "At least, if they're not all a bunch of black-eyed cannibals by now."

"They do?" Sheila asked, surprised she'd never heard about this.

"Kind of," Jean replied. "Mainly they've just got Social Media and Wikipedia. When things first started getting bad and falling apart, a lot of the tech companies open sourced their architecture. So anyone could just go in and copy it. Build their own version. But you had to have enough manpower and actual hardware to support something like that."

"Like the City States," Sheila surmised.

"Exactly."

"What was the point? Doesn't seem like a good way to use what little resources you have."

"Unless you need to control the population," Jean explained. "If you need to control your population, seems to me it's the best use of your resources." She stopped as she caught movement out of the corner of her eye. She snapped her head to the left. Something had shifted between the bookshelves.

"Did you see that?"

"See what?"

Jean drew her Glock 19 and silently cursed herself for having left her 300 Blackout behind at the Winnebago. Sheila followed suit and drew the Sig Sauer P229 she had retrieved from the armory.

"I saw something move," Jean said more quietly as she advanced down one of the aisles.

Then, she saw the movement again through the

books on the shelves and pivoted toward it, drawing her gun into the low compress.

"This is bad," Sheila said. "We're trapped. We need to get the hell out of here!"

"I don't get trapped," Jean said as she continued to move. "I set traps."

"That doesn't even make any sense!" Sheila protested.

Then they heard it. A low growl coming from their left. Jean turned on the ball of her foot and drove her gun out, picking up the red dot, though it took a moment for her brain to process what she was seeing. It was a dog. It was a dog with white eyes.

"Why the hell does that dog have white eyes?" Sheila asked.

The dog continued to growl and bared its teeth.

"You can ask him if you want," Jean said. "But I don't think he's in the mood for conversation."

The dog began to trot toward them and quickly broke into a run. Jean didn't hesitate. She fired three rounds in rapid succession, controlling her recoil with the skill of a much more seasoned shooter and making all three rounds count.

The dog lost its footing and slammed into one of the bookshelves, finally coming to rest just a few feet from the two women, where it lay dead.

"Why in the hell does that dog have white eyes?" Sheila asked again, growing more panicked.

"You already asked that," Jean said. "And I still don't know."

Sheila looked over her shoulder and saw that there were two more dogs at the end of the aisle.

"We've got company," Jean said.

Sheila turned in the girl's direction and looked past her. There were three more of the white-eyed dogs standing at the other end of the aisle. None of them looked very friendly.

"There's too many," Jean said, looking up at the tall shelves. "We have to—"

She stopped herself and looked down at Sheila's missing arm. Sheila knew what the girl was going to say. She was going to suggest they climb the shelves to put some distance between themselves and this pack, but she knew that for Sheila it wouldn't be an option.

"Go!" Sheila snapped. "Get up the shelves, I'll hold them off!"

"Negative," Jean responded quickly. "It's just some dogs! We can handle this."

The same moment she said it, Jean saw more movement between the open spaces in the packed bookshelves. The dogs at either end of the aisle began advancing on them. She had the twenty-one-round magazine in her Glock and she knew Sheila had fifteen rounds plus one in the gun. It wouldn't be enough.

Jorge took a deep breath and smiled. It had been a long time since he had felt he could relax and do something as seemingly benign as feel the warmth of the sun and cool breeze on his face.

A crazy thought occurred to him. Could he just leave it all behind? Load up a rucksack, shoulder his rifle and walk into the woods? Why was he even doing all of this? So what if this whole mission failed? What would it really mean? A few million black-eyed cannibals and an EMP. Would any of that really matter if he was out standing on a mountain in Montana somewhere when it happened? Well, of course, that was assuming he could evade the Russians forever.

Then, all at once, it came to him. He thought back to that first conversation he'd had with Cotton, when the SEAL asked him if he had believed in the mission during the GWOT. If he wasn't all in for it back then, why the hell had he done it for so long?

It was the people. Maybe that was the same

reason he was doing this. Already, he was seeing another side to Roland. He thought he'd had the man figured out a long time ago, but a lot of people had thought the same thing about him.

Then there was the girl, Jean. The two had barely said a handful of words to each other, but already they had both fought together back at the rail yard in Marble Falls. She was a pipe hitter, no question about it, but he had the feeling she was eventually going to crack. Maybe it was important that he be there when she did. Cotton seemed like a good father, but he probably hadn't been there as much as he wanted to. Jorge wondered about his girls, and what they would be like if they were still around?

He pushed that thought out of his mind and turned back to the street below, where his eyes fixed on movement, causing him to lean forward on his stool.

"What the hell?"

It was Harris and Doctor Fred, tearing ass down the street with what looked like a pack of dogs on their tail, further prompting a horrible realization.

He hadn't turned his radio on.

In one movement, the man brought his Recce rifle up on the short brick wall and pulled the stock to his shoulder as he reached up with his left hand and turned the dial to power his radio up.

The net was going crazy. What in the hell were they talking about? They're being attacked by dogs? Then something caught his attention.

"They have white eyes!"

Jorge adjusted the throw lever on his scope and picked up the first dog with his reticle. He didn't like this. For whatever reason, he'd never had a problem killing people, mainly because if they were on the wrong end of his gun, they generally had it coming. Dogs, though, that was different.

"Damn it," he whispered as he broke the LaRue trigger on his rifle and watched the dog tumble to a stop.

From there, he made a micro adjustment of his barrel position and engaged the next animal, which was only a dozen feet behind Harris.

Jean and Sheila stood back-to-back in the aisle with their weapons up as more and more dogs clustered at the end of the aisles.

"What in the hell are they waiting for?" Sheila asked.

"Re-enforcements," Jean said. "They're pack

animals. They want overwhelming superiority before they move."

"Great," Sheila replied.

"Hey!" A voice called out from overhead.

Jean and Sheila looked up and saw Cotton standing atop one of the tall bookshelves, wearing a gas mask. He had entered the library quietly and moved through the large room by walking across the shelves, as each was topped with a hard, wooden plank strong enough to support a grown man.

"Daddy!" Jean shouted. Her face broke out into a smile. No matter how tough she was, she had known that, in this moment, she was outmatched.

Cotton held out two gas masks and dropped them.

"Get those on! Now!" He called out as he pulled large canisters of 'Clear Out' tear gas from his cargo pockets. "It's about to get thick in here."

Jean donned and cleared her gas mask, then looked at Sheila, who was just staring at hers. Jean pumped her arms, making the universal military sign for "gas" indicating Sheila should get her mask on.

"What in the hell are you doing?" Sheila asked.

"Get your mask on!" Jean insisted.

"Why in the hell would I know how to use a gas mask?"

"Kneel!" Jean ordered and Sheila complied, even if she wasn't sure why.

The dogs were now moving down the aisle toward them as Cotton released the gas overhead. He was clearly waiting to drop the canisters until Sheila was protected, but Jean knew he wouldn't wait forever.

Jean secured the mask over Sheila's head with the straps and then placed her hand over the vent.

"Blow!" She ordered and Sheila complied by pushing out a breath of air before Jean moved her hands to the filters. "Breathe in!"

Sheila complied again, creating a suction effect after having cleared the mask that secured it to her face.

"Hit it!" Jean shouted and Cotton replied by hurling the smoking cans of gas at both ends of the aisle. He then turned and threw another into an adjacent aisle, the same location Jean had seen movement in earlier.

The canisters of tear gas quickly flooded the space and the dogs began to whimper and flee as Cotton quickly climbed down the shelf he had been standing on.

"Move! Move!" Cotton ordered as he pushed

Jean and Sheila toward the rear exit. "This place is packed!"

"Come on!" Roland shouted as he swung the baseball bat at the first dog to charge him and April behind the counter of the soda shop. He'd found the bat behind that same counter after they had jumped it to evade the first two dogs that had come in the front door.

He connected with the beast, but it recovered quickly and charged again so he struck it a second time, hard across the face. He could see its skull cave in between those dead white eyes, but again it recovered and charged.

Out of his peripheral vision, he could see that April was in a corner, using a chair to keep one of the snarling things off her. This was bad. It was bad and he knew it. Why in the hell had he left his weapons behind at the RV? Because he was acting like a lovesick teenager, and now they were going to pay for that mistake with their lives.

He had already wrapped his left arm in his overshirt, and now he thrust it out at the attacking dog. The animal latched onto it, taking the bait, and Roland dropped his bat, drew his knife, and slammed it into the dog's head. This did the trick where the bat had not, and the dog released its jaws and collapsed to the floor.

There were now two more heading toward him, and he could see that the one April was fighting was rapidly getting the best of her.

"Get down!" a voice shouted.

Roland complied and dropped to the floor as shots rang out.

Harris stood in the doorway, firing controlled pairs into the white-eyed dogs, killing each one in turn before he pivoted to where April was fighting off the last one. He walked up to it, put the muzzle of his Glock to the dog's head and pulled the trigger.

"Jesus!" Roland shouted. "What in the hell is going on out there?"

Beyond Harris, he could see that someone was shooting even more of the white-eyed dogs in the street from an elevated position.

"Think we're gettin' the upper hand!" Harris replied. "Jorge's in the tower and Cotton's gettin' Jean and Sheila, but we need to get back to the RV."

CHAPTER 4

Bill Rampart sat in the semi-darkness of the conference room and scrolled through the messages on his smart phone. Many were alerts from individual department heads, with status reports for phases of the different projects he had them working on. Some were real, but others were simply busy work. It was important to keep up appearances, and it was even more important to keep people distracted as the gears continued to turn.

He stopped at a particularly stern message from the Governor of the City State of New Orleans, a man that Bill Rampart himself had put into place. Governor Newcomb seemed to be getting a little full of himself, and perhaps even beginning to *believe* the story that he was the savior of New Orleans.

Yes, the Governor had put a stop order in place to delay the distribution of the Generation 2 Pandemify until they had completed further testing, but of course Bill had been the one to order him to do that. The Fluid Dynamics Chief Executive Officer did have every confidence that the 2nd Generation of the Pandemify vaccine would do what he had promised it would, but he also had not predicted the side-effects of the first generation.

The message from Governor Newcomb had demanded a meeting with Bill and was also heavily implying that his title be changed to "President."

Bill looked up from his phone to where Jared stood in the corner of the room. The man had an almost unnerving ability to blend into his surroundings and go unnoticed. At least some of this, no doubt, came from his history, having been a Marine Corps Scout Sniper, working primarily in Iraq during the Global War on Terror. Despite looking like a malnourished librarian, Jared had over one hundred confirmed kills under his belt, and at least a few dozen more from after he'd exited the military and begun working for the Fluid Dynamics CEO.

"Why in the hell does Newcomb want to be the President?" Bill asked with more than a mild level of annoyance in his voice. "Doesn't he remember what happened to the last president?"

Jared smiled. "People get greedy," he said. "And greedy people seem to have short memories."

"I'm starting to think he's outlived his usefulness," Bill said, and Jared knew this was more than just a casual observation.

"How serious are we about this?" Jared asked.

Bill let out a sigh. "Let's do this meeting," he said. "Then we'll move on to new business."

Jared turned to the wall of monitors beside him and keyed the remote control he held. The screens flickered to life and bathed Bill Rampart in their sallow glow.

"Good morning," Bill said.

"Well," Bill watched as Jared slid the panel closed, covering the monitors, "that went poorly."

"They did seem upset," Jared offered.

"I don't know what they think I'm supposed to do here," Bill went on, as if Jared had not said anything. "They need to understand the level of chaos I'm dealing with here. You can't rush, well... this."

Bill met Jared's eyes and it was obvious that his adjutant was holding his tongue.

"Okay," Bill ceded. "What's on your mind?"

Jared shrugged. "The elite are the elite for a reason. They get what they want."

"And in this case, they want a fucking reset. A do over." Bill paused for a moment. "I mean, I've given them everything they wanted. Hell, we even shipped samples of the Gen 2 vaccine for them to study so that perhaps they could somehow fix their own broken vaccines."

"Sir, with respect... they are still dealing with the problem of the virus. That's all they can see."

Bill's eyes seemed to search for something for a moment and then he nodded. "You're right. Perhaps I just need to be more patient with them than they're being with me."

"No one else could have done this," Jared pressed on. "If any of them were in your position? America would have completely crumbled long ago."

"I appreciate that," Bill said. "More than you know."

"Would it make you feel better if I killed Governor Newcomb?" Jared asked.

"President Newcomb," Bill corrected. "And yes, that would make me feel better."

. . .

"Are we whole?" Roland asked as he and April arrived back at the RV.

"We're good," Cotton said as he laid his rifle in the back of the Toyota truck and splashed some water in his eyes in an effort to refocus his vision.

Fred disappeared into the RV and returned with a small bag. She clearly intended to head back into the town.

"What are you doing?" Harris asked. "We barely made it out of there with our lives!"

"I'm pretty sure they're all dead," Fred insisted. "And I need to know what in the hell happened back there and what was wrong with those dogs."

Roland looked hard at her for a moment.

"She's right. Just because they're dead doesn't mean the threat is," Roland said. "I think we can all agree that being attacked by a town full of dogs with white eyes is not normal. Get geared up. We're going back in."

"Are you okay?" April asked as she approached Cotton.

"I fucked up," he said bluntly.

"What are you talking about? You saved Jean

and Sheila. They'd both be dog food right now if you hadn't come when you did."

Cotton stared hard at her for a moment.

"I think I'm cursed," he said.

"What in the hell are you talking about?"

"There's this thing I do, when it seems like things are calming down. Sometimes I let myself relax a bit. I let my guard down. Not a lot, but just a little bit."

"That's normal. If you don't, you'll go nuts."

"But that's the thing, every time I do, something crazy happens. First time was when they launched the vaccine. After I got me and Jean to the cabin, I dialed it back a bit. Then folks started going cannibal. Now it happened again. I over-corrected and it almost ended us."

"You're not cursed!" April insisted. "At least, no more than the rest of us are."

"What's going on?" Roland asked as he approached the pair.

"Cotton thinks he's cursed," April said.

"That thing again?" Roland asked, the fatigue in his voice obvious.

"You know it's true!" Cotton shot back.

"We ain't got time for this," Roland said. "Kit up. We're heading back in."

"Roger that," Cotton responded, rote, as he

retrieved his rifle from the back of the truck and moved to join the others.

"How are you doing?" Roland asked April, genuine concern in his voice.

"I'm fine," April said curtly. "Couple scratches. Nothing to write home about."

Roland smiled. "You were fightin' like a damn wild cat with that chair."

April's face was blank. "I wasn't scared," April said.

"Good," Roland remarked with a nod.

"No," April said. "Not like that. I wasn't being brave. I just didn't have any fear left. I knew that whatever the outcome would be, that was going to be how it was." She paused for a moment. "Does that make sense?"

"More than you know."

"Okay, circle up," Cotton called out. He looked to Roland, respecting that the man was still the de facto leader. Roland responded with a nod of affirmation. Cotton had the reigns. "Pretty sure everything in that town is dead. Either it was dead when we got there or we just killed it. Fred, take Harris and Jorge and do what you need to do with the dogs. Jean, you and Sheila come with me. Roland, if it's all the same to you, I'll have you and April hang here and make sure we don't get any nasty surprises when we come back."

"Roger that," Roland replied.

"Everyone's on comms," Cotton continued. "Don't take any unnecessary risks. If something looks dodgy, call it in and we'll rendezvous back here."

Fred, Harris, and Jorge walked back into the town square where the bulk of the fight with the dogs had taken place. Looking around, they saw that there were at least a dozen dogs scattered around the street.

Fred shook her head as she walked through the scene.

"It doesn't make sense," she said.

"What's that?" Harris asked.

"Some of these aren't predators. At least, not in the sense we're used to." She pointed at one of the slain animals. "That's a damn Corgi mix. When was the last time you heard of a Corgi attacking anyone?"

"Nobody wants to say it," Jorge said.

"Say what?" Harris asked.

"They've got white eyes," Jorge said. "Just

like us."

"Cannibals?" Harris asked. "But wouldn't they be trying to eat other dogs?"

"They should," Fred said. She knelt down beside the Corgi mix and turned over the tag on its collar. "Unless that was never what we were."

She unclipped the tag from the dog's collar and held it up. It read: "Vaccinated / Lot 2"

Sheila stood beside the front door to the animal shelter and waited for Cotton to give her the command. He stood a comfortable distance back from the front entrance with Jean set up behind him. The idea was to make a soft entry and clear the building, then try to secure some intelligence as to just what had caused those dogs to act the way they did.

The whole thing was surreal, but everyone understood that even if the events of the last hour seemed beyond belief, they needed to know why it had happened. It was also worth considering that nothing about the attack of these white-eyed dogs was any stranger than the rest of the events of the past two years.

Cotton pointed a gloved finger to the door and

Sheila turned the handle and yanked it open. Cotton moved steadily and purposefully through the open door and into the dimly lit building. Jean again noted how his feet seemed to almost slide across the ground. She had watched plenty of videos of other men doing CQB, and sometimes they even seemed to be stomping around, but not her father. He moved like a ghost.

The building wasn't very large, so it didn't take much time for Cotton and Jean to move through the entire structure before they finally came to the kennels. Cotton stopped there and lowered his rifle.

"I didn't need to see that," he said quietly to himself before turning and giving Jean the 'all clear' sign.

"All good?" she asked as she put her weapon on safe and brought it to the low ready.

"Yeah," Cotton said. "All good."

Jean studied her father's face and knew it wasn't all good.

"What is it?" she asked.

"Shot 'em all," Cotton said as he reached back and closed the door that led out to the kennels.

"Why would they do that?"

"Don't know," Cotton said, shaking his head. "Doesn't make any sense."

"Typical SSE," Cotton said as they led Sheila into the building, indicating a Sensitive Site Exploitation. The woman had been waiting outside, as she understood that she would only slow Cotton and Jean down in this kind of scenario. "Bag anything that seems important, but we're probably looking for treatment records or any reports filed on those white-eyed dogs."

Sheila walked into what looked like the head office for the Animal Shelter and stopped as a box sitting on the desk in the center of the room caught her eye. She pulled it open and retrieved what looked like a manifest from inside.

"You're going to want to see this!" she called out.

Cotton and Jean entered the room, and Sheila held out the sheet of paper. It read: "Pandemify Generation 1 / Canine Variant."

"What in the hell?" Cotton asked as he took the piece of paper from her and scanned it.

"Remember?" Jean said. "In the beginning they were talking about animals spreading the virus? Then it turned out it was only certain types of cats, but they went ahead with a vaccine for household pets."

"That's what this is?" Sheila asked. "I didn't watch the news much."

"Looks like it," Cotton said. "So they shot these dogs up with the vaccine and they... went cannibal?"

"But they went after us," Jean said. "Not each other."

"Why this town?" Sheila asked. "Is it just our bad luck to land in a town full of cannibal dogs?"

Cotton continued to flip through the manifest and shook his head.

"Not just this town," he said. "There's a distribution list here. It's broken down county by county. It looks like they sent it all over."

"So, there are other towns full of these things," Jean surmised.

"Why?" Sheila asked.

"Flood the house," Cotton said.

"What?" Sheila said.

"Back in the day, if we were hitting a target that needed to get got, we'd flood the house. Hit them from the roof as well as the ground. Get as many guns inside as we could without it getting crowded and drive him to the ground with overwhelming force."

"That's what they're doing now," Jean said.

"This country is the house," Cotton said. "Whoever's got their hand on the wheel here is throwing as much as they can at the population to drive it down. Virus, vaccine turning people into cannibals, Gen 2 making cannibals on steroids, now cannibal dogs."

"And next is the EMP," Sheila concluded.

"That would probably be a safe assumption," Cotton agreed.

Sheila touched the side of her head and winced.

"You okay?" Cotton asked.

"Yeah... I think so. Just been getting these weird little headaches. Like someone's tapping on the back of my skull with an ice pick."

"You like it?" Roland asked as April sat behind the M240 Bravo machine gun in the back of the truck.

April allowed herself a smile as she sprayed some Breakthrough lubricant into the action of the heavy gun and worked the bolt.

"I guess," she said. "It makes sense to me."

"What do you mean?"

"It's simple. There's no... I don't know. There's no guile to it. It's just a never-ending stream of destruction. When I'm behind it, when I was firing on those Russian soldiers, I finally felt like I was in control."

Roland jumped into the back of the truck and cleared some of the spent brass casings out of the bed.

"Gotta keep your workstation clean," he said with a smile. "Last thing you want is to stand up and go ass over tea kettle slipping around on shell casings."

April turned, slid forward on one knee, put her hand on the back of Roland's head, and kissed him. She held onto him for much longer than she had intended and then finally let go.

He looked into her eyes.

"I'm not a good person," Roland said quietly. He wasn't sure where the words had come from, but he knew they were some of the only sincere ones he had.

"I don't think there are any good people left," April replied.

"What are you doing?" Harris asked as he watched Fred prepare a syringe and roll one of the dogs on its side.

"Doing a blood draw," she said. "I'll get samples

from at least three different subjects. Then if I manage to somehow find something that resembles a lab, I can get some usable information."

"Finding anything useful?"

Harris looked up to see Cotton, Jean, and Sheila walking toward them.

"Doc's getting some blood," Harris explained.

"Check this out," Cotton said and tossed the manifest to Jorge.

"What is it?" Fred asked.

"Shit," Jorge said under his breath. "Pandemify for dogs. And looks like this wasn't the only town on the list."

"Okay, this is it," Colonel Lebedev said as he crouched with Doctor Wilson behind one of the many smashed out vehicles that littered the roadways.

Less than a block down the street sat City Hall. It had taken them nearly seven hours to move ten blocks. Admittedly, the shots of vodka Lebedev had taken at the liquor store had not helped matters. The man was not quite the young bull he used to be.

There had also been several instances where they'd encountered small hordes of black-eyed cannibals and had to "go to ground," so to speak, and wait for them to pass.

Now, the sun had been up for a couple of hours already, and Lebedev could feel that he was losing water fast, sweating through his clothes beneath his plate carrier. He had already stowed his NODs and his helmet once dawn broke.

There were half a dozen cannibals between them and the door to city hall. Lebedev reached back and felt for the slap charge that was stashed beneath the back panel on his plate carrier. They would try the door first, but if it was locked, he would have to use the explosive breaching tool to force the issue.

He looked to the upper floors of the building and could again see lights on within the windows. There were definitely people in there, and they had power. Those two things were enough reason for him to know he had to get in there.

"Okay," he said, turning to Gregory. "We have to get in that door. If I try it and it doesn't give, I'm going to blow it."

"What do I do?" Gregory asked.

Lebedev reached down to the holster on his hip, retrieved his pistol, and handed it to Gregory. "There's a round in the chamber," he said. "All you have to do is pull the trigger."

"But I've never used one before!" Gregory protested.

"It won't be hard," Lebedev said, and putting a finger in his mouth, mimed pulling the trigger.

Gregory understood. The gun wasn't for him to fight cannibals with.

Lebedev emerged from the cluster of trees with Gregory in tow, and the two men moved quickly up the front steps of the building to the ornate, iron-wrought doors. For a moment, Lebedev wondered if the simple breaching charge would be strong enough to get through the iron. There was only one way to find out, but hopefully it wouldn't come to that.

The two men slowed down as they approached the door and finally stopped. Lebedev looked around. There wasn't a soul in sight.

"Does this feel wrong to you?" Gregory asked. "It's so quiet."

Lebedev didn't respond, and instead reached out and pulled on the door. It rattled but did not give.

"Step back," Lebedev ordered as he retrieved the slap charge and pressed it to the weak point on the door. "Get down."

Gregory did as he was told while Lebedev moved to a safe distance and triggered the charge.

The door exploded with (fortunately) a minimum of flying glass.

It was one of those moments where training takes over, and the muscle memory outruns conscious thought. Lebedev had already put rounds into the first three cannibals that came out the door before he fully understood what had happened, and more importantly what was about to happen.

The lobby of the building was packed with them. There was no way to know how many, but there were enough. Lebedev saw them streaming in from the adjacent hallways. They had not been in the lobby when he triggered the explosive, but had responded to the noise.

The Alpha Group commander stumbled back down the steps as he fired, nearly losing his footing. Then he felt a round snap past his head and strike one of the advancing black-eyed cannibals.

"I hit him!" Gregory shouted.

"Good!" Lebedev called back. "Now do it again!"

One of the beasts nearly overtook the Colonel, but he turned and slammed the stock of the rifle into the cannibal's head, knocking him to the ground. Gregory continued to fire, even if he wasn't having the same success he had enjoyed with his first shot.

Lebedev was mainly thankful that the man was not hitting him.

There were too many. He knew it, and it wasn't long before the situation escalated from bad to worse. He felt the click of his rifle and quickly slapped the bottom of the magazine and racked the charging handle. The bolt was locked back or a round was stuck in the chamber. There was no time. He drew his knife from the scabbard in his plate carrier and drove it forward into the closest cannibal.

"I'm out of bullets!" Gregory called out.

Shit, Lebedev thought. *You should have saved one for yourself. Maybe even two.*

They were all over him. He had seen from the helicopter while evacuating the hilltop what happened when these things swarmed a person, and it wasn't pretty. He knew that he could drive his knife into his own throat, he just had to summon the courage to do it. The sound of thunder snapped him out of this thought process and he felt a wetness on his face. It was blood.

"Get inside!" a voice shouted.

He looked up to see a short, blond woman in some kind of uniform holding a shotgun. There was a man beside her who was much taller and thinner, also holding a shotgun and wearing the same uniform. Gregory was already stumbling up the steps toward them as they continued putting slugs into the cannibals that were on the steps and in the lobby.

It was clear that they had a system. They understood cover and movement and how to reload fast.

Lebedev stumbled to his feet and moved up the steps. He hadn't felt like this in a very long time, that deeply-seated feeling that you are almost certainly going to die.

"Move it! Now!" the woman called out as she drove her gun forward and stepped into the doorway to cover the Russian.

The man was now moving backwards toward a bank of elevators as he fired his Mossberg shotgun, keeping the several cannibals that had spilled onto the front steps at bay, but it was clear he was starting to fatigue and was missing his targets.

Lebedev stopped in the lobby and looked at the chamber of his Kalashnikov rifle. He observed that there was a double feed, which was why his initial attempt to clear it had been unsuccessful. Now he dropped the magazine, pulled back the charging handle and slammed the stock onto the floor, breaking the double feed loose. He quickly pulled a magazine from his plate carrier, slammed it in, chambered a round, and stood back up.

In rapid succession, he used his red dot sight to take clean head shots at the six cannibals that were charging back up the steps. Once the bodies had dropped, Lebedev brought his rifle to the low ready and looked around.

The elevator to his rear dinged as the doors rolled open.

"Holy shit!" the man in the uniform called out. "That was some good shootin'!"

"Who are you?" Lebedev asked.

"Parks and Recreation," the woman replied. "Animal control."

"We do this shit all the time," the man added. "But I don't think this is the place for introductions."

"Every floor above us is barricaded," the woman went on. "You can stay here if you want, but I'd advise against it."

The elevator doors rolled open to reveal the top floor of the city hall building. It had clearly been the mayor's office once, but had been hastily converted into an open floor plan. There were cots in a sleeping area, an open kitchenette, and what looked like a comms station. There was also a makeshift armory with shelves that contained a few more shotguns as well as pistols.

Lebedev stepped out of the elevator and took a breath. The air smelled good, not like the stagnant air that mixed with the stink of the standing water in the streets below.

"It was you, wasn't it?" the woman in the uniform asked.

"What?" Lebedev replied.

"That sent up the flare."

"Damn it," Gregory said with a moan.

"No," Lebedev said. "We thought it was you."

The woman's face fell.

"Well, there goes that idea," the man said. He looked at Lebedev for a moment and then offered his hand. "I'm Jessie. This is Leslie. We thought you sent up the flare we saw last night, thought maybe you were some kind of rescue party."

"Sorry," Lebedev said. "No rescue party. I'm just trying to get this man out of the city in one piece."

"Why?" Leslie asked. "Who is he to you?"

Lebedev eyed her for a moment. "Do you know who I am?" he asked.

"It doesn't take a rocket scientist," Leslie shot back. "I just didn't expect you to get here so soon."

"Look," Jessie said. "We don't really care where

you're from and we don't care why you're here. I think we can all agree that we have bigger problems right now than a Russian invasion."

"Perhaps more than you know," Lebedev said. He looked around the building. "How do you still have power?"

"We won't for long," Jessie said. "This building was supposed to serve as the command center for the city. It's got generators in the sub-basement but they'll only hold for seventy-two hours. If that."

"We can't stay here," Lebedev surmised. "We need to get out of this city. We'll have to fight but we can do it."

"No," Leslie said, shaking her head. "We're staying put. We're going to wait it out."

"What do you mean?" Lebedev asked.

"I catch raccoons!" Leslie shouted. "And I'm bad at it! I didn't sign up for killing mutant cannibals!"

"Hey," Jessie said quietly and put a hand on her shoulder. "It's fine, okay?"

Leslie turned to the much taller man, her lower lip quivering. "I don't want to do this anymore," she said, and then shook off his hand and walked to the corner of the room, where she sat down on one of the cots.

"She'll be fine," Jessie said. "It's true. She was

really bad at catching raccoons. You know, I'm not cut out for this either. I'm not some... military guy or something." He looked at his watch. "This has only been going on a couple days and we're already having a tough time. We were both out when it started, and the only reason we didn't get killed in the first wave was that we came up in the service elevator from the parking garage. Went straight to the Parks and Rec floor."

"Everyone was dead," Lebedev concluded.

"It was bad," Jessie said. "That first wave wasn't like those ones we just went up against. They tore everyone apart. That's why we came up here. There was just too much... too much blood and meat on the other floors. So we barricaded everything off and stayed here. We figured if we just waited long enough, they would eventually, I don't know. Go somewhere else. Then we saw that flare go up." He looked to where Leslie sat staring out the window. "She really thought it was going to be over."

Lebedev examined Jessie.

"You're still human," he said, commenting on Jessie's clear blue eyes. "You're not cannibal. How?"

"We just kept slipping through the cracks," Jessie said with a shrug. "When the mandate first came down, we filed religious exemptions. Apparently, we're Zarathustrians now."

"Zoroaster is nothing to joke about my friend," Gregory cut in, showing real indignance at the idea that Jessie and Leslie had feigned religious belief to escape vaccination.

Jessie raised an eyebrow. "You're an actual Zarathustrian?" he asked.

"Zoroastrian," Gregory corrected him. "If you want to get technical about it, and yes I am."

Jessie couldn't help laughing.

"It won't seem so funny when your stomach is roasting in hell," Gregory shot back.

"Stop!" Lebedev shouted. He turned back to Jessie. "You said that you came up through the service elevator, from an underground garage?"

"That's right," Jessie confirmed. "But the garage is full of those things. That's why you're not seeing that many of them in the streets. Most of them went underground into the tunnels."

"The tunnels?" Lebedev asked.

"There are these service tunnels below the city. A whole network of them for moving supplies, electrical, you name it. Big enough to drive a truck through."

"That's how we get out," Lebedev said.

"I just told you it's swarmed with them."

"Then you had better reload your shotguns, because unless you know of some other way, it's the only option we have."

"There is another way," Jessie said. "Like I said, the streets were swarming with them when this started, but now it's thinned out. If we just get to our work van in the parking garage, it would probably be safer to just drive out."

Cotton did one final walk around the RV and the truck as Fred finished organizing what they had found and the rest did a final gear check. The reasonable assumption was that they would hit Houston by the afternoon and would almost certainly be in for a fight.

He stopped and watched Jean sitting in a squat, fiddling with her chest rig. He smiled. He knew exactly what was going on.

"Need a hand?" he asked.

Jean looked up. "It won't go," she replied.

Cotton took a knee and pulled out his knife. She had been trying to secure a pouch to the chest rig with the supplied MOLLE backing, but he knew once in a while those straps didn't want to play ball.

Jean watched as he slipped the knife in beneath the MOLLE straps and used that to guide in the strap from the pouch.

"It's the little things," he said with a smile. "Things like this you kind of figure out along the way."

"Thank you," Jean said.

"Just a trick," Cotton replied as he finished securing the pouch.

"No, I mean for back at the library," Jean said. "We were cooked."

"You would have found a way," Cotton said. "You always do."

"Maybe," Jean said, nodding her head. "But maybe not. I think I'm starting to get it a little more. The team thing. Why it's important."

"I'm always gonna be there," Cotton said. "You know? When you need me."

"No, you won't," Jean said bluntly. "You'll want to be, but you can't. You can't always be there. Maybe it's important for us to both know that."

"I'm not sure what to say to that."

"Nothing to say," Jean said.

Cotton leaned forward and put his arms around his little girl. He closed his eyes and, for just a moment, pretended that they were somewhere else. Jean rubbed her father's back and he laughed.

"Giving me gentle pets?" he asked.

Jean smiled. It was a throwback to when she was two and would pet the family dog, declaring she was giving him "gentle pets." Then, at a certain point, she'd decided daddy also needed gentle pets and it had kind of stuck. It became an inside joke with the family.

This time, they both understood it was her way of letting her father know that she was still the same girl she had always been, that she was still his daughter. Just different.

"You don't look so great," Jorge said as he watched Sheila getting her gear prepped.

"You really know how to sweet talk a girl," she replied.

He was right, and she knew it. Something was wrong. Her skin was ashen and she was blinking rapidly.

"Look, I know I'm not your favorite person, but can you let April look at you?"

Sheila stood bolt upright.

"I don't need a damn—"

She stopped mid-sentence, her eyes snapping wide open and her head twisting slightly to the left. Sheila's body stiffened and then dropped out from under her like a sack of bricks.

"Holy shit!" Jorge shouted. "I need help!"

Sheila lay on the concrete, her body at an odd angle and her eyes locked open.

"Get out of the way!" April shouted as she ran from the truck to where Sheila had fallen.

The group was already gathering around her and April knew this would not be helpful. They dutifully stepped back, except Jorge who kneeled beside Sheila, trying to perform some lifesaving maneuver.

April put a hand on his shoulder and looked him in the eyes.

"I need you to step back," April said. "So that I can help her."

Jorge's eyes were blank for a moment. Then he nodded his understanding, stood up, and backed away.

April went through her emergency assessment and turned to Roland as she started chest compressions.

"We brought the defibrillator with us, the one from the infirmary," she said. "I need you to get it right now."

Roland turned and ran for the RV while April turned to Cotton.

"IV bags and adrenaline. Get them." Cotton also complied as April turned to Jorge next. "I need you to take over for me."

Jorge moved to her and knelt on the ground. He took April's position, providing chest compressions. Roland arrived with the defibrillator and April took the device and began the activation sequence.

"What happened to her?" Jorge asked as he worked the chest compressions.

"I don't know," April said as she powered up the device. "There's no heartbeat, no breath, no nothing. It's like someone just turned her off. I'm going to have to hit her with this."

"Will it work?" Jorge asked.

April shook her head. "I don't know."

"I may have pulled too hard," June Kennedy said as she stood with Sheila on the hilltop. "I think I stopped your heart."

Sheila looked around. She was someplace else. She knew it wasn't real, but it felt real. A cool wind blew across her face.

"Where are we?" Sheila asked.

"Not far from where you were," June replied, looking at Sheila for a moment with her dead black eyes, then back into the small valley below. "It didn't take long to find them."

Sheila looked into the valley and saw what looked like an encampment with thousands of soldiers in it.

"The Russians," Sheila concluded.

"Food," June corrected her. "Call them by their name."

"Why am I here?" Sheila asked. "Why are we connected like this?"

June looked at her for a moment and then back into the valley. "You're my daughter," she said.

"What in the hell are you talking about?"

"It was a lifetime ago," June said. "I wasn't ready, and I gave you up."

"Effert and Sons," Sheila said suddenly, remembering the finding from the private investigator she had hired. Though she had decided not to learn her mother's name, she did know where the P.I. had found her.

"You do seem quite resourceful," June replied. "It doesn't surprise me that you got that far."

"You never tried to find me," Sheila said.

"It doesn't matter," June replied.

'It matters to me!" Sheila snapped.

"No," June said. "You misunderstand me. It truly does not matter. Everything from that life is dust. All that matters is this. This moment. Food."

Sheila looked back into the valley and watched the flood begin. Thousands upon thousands of what she could only assume were black-eyed cannibals poured into the encampment. Shots were being fired, but to little effect. It was a slaughterhouse.

"The cycle of the universe," June went on. "The consumption of matter and production of energy is eternal. That is what we are. We are the purest expression of the universal truth."

"You're insane," Sheila said as she took a step back.

"I am the future," June said. "You can be, too."

Sheila listened for the woman's thoughts, but it was clear that she was guarding them. Then there was a flash of something, like an image momentarily visible on a movie screen. It was an orange bottle.

"Get out!" June shouted, and the volume of the command pulled Sheila's skin tight against her cheek bones and blew her hair back.

She could hear the screams coming up from the valley floor like a dark tidal wave as she slipped out of the astral plane.

CHAPTER 5

Sheila drew a deep breath and her eyes opened.

"Get off!" she shouted as she shoved April aside and sat up on the ground.

"Calm down!" Roland snapped. "You had a freakin heart attack!"

"What?" Sheila asked, clearly disoriented.

"You fucking died!" Jorge nearly shouted.

"No, I didn't," Sheila said, shaking her head as she stood up. "That wasn't what that was."

"Okay," April said and held up her hands in a placating gesture. "I get it, you're in shock. But your heart stopped. I shocked you and brought you back. And you're, uh... you know."

April was gesturing to Sheila's shirt, and looking down, the woman saw that it was torn open.

"Oh."

Jean held out a new shirt, which Sheila took and quickly changed into.

"I was with her," Sheila said. "The Cannibal Queen."

"June Kennedy?" Jorge asked.

"Yeah. Except... I think she's my mother."

"What in the hell?" Jorge exclaimed.

"Why do you think that?" Cotton asked.

"She told me. And I don't think she was lying. She wouldn't have a reason to."

"That's why you can hear her," Jean said. "That's why you're connected."

"She's the destroyer," Sheila said.

"What?" April asked.

"Shiva," Sheila clarified. "The destroyer of worlds."

"Okay," Fred cut in. "I'm not trying to sound like an asshole, but why do you know who Shiva is?"

"One of the guys in the MC," Sheila said, ignoring the obvious slight. "He was really into mythology and wouldn't stop talking about it. He'd talk about Shiva a lot, about him being this destroyer of worlds."

"Well, technically Shiva was more about cleansing or 'destroying' the impurities of the mind

—" Fred stopped herself, recognizing that this was not the time for a lecture on ancient Hinduism.

"Okay," Roland cut in. "Everyone start speaking fucking English or I'm gonna lose my mind."

"She's going to kill all of us," Sheila said bluntly. "Maybe not right away, but she wants to spread those black-eyed cannibals around the world. She wants to kill everything that isn't her."

There was silence.

"Okay," Roland finally said. "You seem to know the most about this. What do we do?"

"I think I know how she became the way she is. We can get into each other's thoughts, and when I was in hers, I saw a flash of something."

"What was it?" Cotton asked.

"A bottle of Prozac. This will sound crazy, but I think her being on that stopped her from going the way that all the others did. I also think they're all connected, all the Gen 2 cannibals."

"What do you mean?" Fred asked.

"I think they're all in each other's heads. Like they're not thousands or millions of separate beings. They're just one."

"A hive mind," Fred concluded. "And to make matters worse, they found their queen. As I think about it... without her, they might have died out fairly quickly. Either turned on each other or run out of food. Probably wouldn't have figured out how to travel together as a group in time for it to matter."

"Wait a minute," Cotton said. "If this is true, we just have to kill her."

"You can't," Sheila said and shook her head. "She's too insulated. She's at the direct center of all of them. Literally and figuratively. You would have to fight through thousands of them to get to her, and on top of that, you would have to take her by surprise. It's impossible."

"We've all done the impossible before," Jorge said, looking directly at Cotton and Roland.

"He's not wrong," Roland agreed.

"It's suicide!" Sheila snapped. "You'll all die!"

"I think we're getting ahead of ourselves here," Cotton said. "One disaster at a time, please. We still have to get to Houston and stop this EMP from coming down the pipe."

"But if she's about to turn around and overrun us with those things, what does it matter?" Fred asked.

"There might be a way to buy some time," Sheila said.

"What do you mean?" Jorge asked.

Well... she and I are linked, but right now she's stronger than I am. Like, a lot stronger. I'm pretty sure I'm only getting in there because she's letting me."

"You're not building a great case here," Fred interjected.

"But we're related," Sheila went on, pretending Fred hadn't said anything. "Genetically we're kind of the same, right?" She looked at Fred for reassurance.

"Well, basically..." Fred paused for a moment, then her eyes grew wide and she looked at Sheila. "No!"

"I knew you were smart," Sheila said with a wink.

"Genetics are not destiny!" Fred snapped. "You can't guarantee what will happen if you do that!"

"What are we talking about here?" Cotton asked.

"If I take the Gen 2 Pandemify with a big dose of Prozac," Sheila said. "I may be able to get the upper hand."

"The hell you will!" Jorge shouted. He turned to Fred. "Tell her this is nuts!"

"It's nuts," Fred said. "It's beyond insane." She hesitated for a moment. "But that doesn't mean it won't work."

"You're not helping!" Jorge countered.

Then he felt a hand on his shoulder. He turned to Sheila.

"I'm sorry for how I treated you," she said softly. "And I'm sorry that you love me the way you do, but this has to happen. We don't have a choice."

"You always have a choice," Jorge argued.

"You're right." Sheila nodded her head. "And I'm making it."

"Can this really work?" Harris asked as he walked down the main street with Jean.

"What are you askin' me for? I'm just a hick from West Virginia," Jean said with a smile. "But I figure it could. If you suspend disbelief, it kind of makes sense."

"I guess," Harris said and then motioned to a small storefront at the end of the block that designated the building as a pharmacy. "If they didn't pick it clean, we should be able to find it here."

Harris stepped forward and put his hand on the door handle.

"Wait," Jean said and drew her sidearm. "I know the town seems quiet, but that don't mean it is."

"Right," Harris said, a little embarrassed that his tactics had just been corrected by a twelve-year-old girl. He drew his Glock 17 and then gave her a nod. "Thanks."

He pushed the door open and moved carefully into the front entrance. There wasn't much light aside from what came in through the dirty windows, but it was enough that they could navigate the space and would see if something was about to come at them.

The place was like a tomb.

"We should grab other stuff while we're here," Jean said. "If they're not cleaned out. Antibiotics and pain killers mostly."

"Roger that," Harris replied as he walked around the rear counter and up the steps to the pharmacy area.

He stopped and looked at the floor behind the cash register. Jean could see that something was wrong.

"What is it?" she asked, starting to walk toward him.

"Don't come back here," Harris cautioned.

Jean continued walking and then stopped and looked at what Harris had seen. It was a decomposed body that had been badly mauled. Blood stained the carpet all around it, and it was clear this man had fought for his life in his final moments only to lose the contest.

"The dogs," Jean said. "They did this."

She looked at Harris, whose eyes were locked on the body.

"Nothing you can do for him," Jean said. "But we have a job to do."

"Right," Harris said, snapping out of it. "I know."

"I hate that you're all helping her with this," Jorge said from the corner of the RV.

Fred tapped the IV bag she had strung up and then looked to April, who was checking Sheila's vitals. To the best of their knowledge, a conversion from Gen 1 to Gen 2 had never been done under controlled conditions. The goal was to give Sheila every possible edge in retaining her mind as her body crossed over.

"You're sure about this?" Roland asked as he sat across from her. "We don't know for certain that she's coming after us. We might have more time to figure this out."

"I'm not willing to take that risk," Sheila said. "Even if we wait, I can't see how we have any option other than this."

"Maybe that Doctor Wilson guy, maybe he's got—"

"Just— just let me do this," Sheila insisted. "And

you all don't have to be around for it. Just me and April."

Everyone looked around and nodded their understanding.

"And Jean," Sheila added.

"What?" Cotton asked incredulously.

"Jean, honey? Do you have your sidearm ready?" Sheila asked.

Jean tapped the Glock 19 on her hip and nodded in the affirmative.

"Good," Sheila said. "Because if I turn into one of those things, if I'm not myself anymore, you're the only person in this RV that I trust with absolute certainty to put a bullet in my head."

Cotton stepped out of the RV and looked at Jorge.

"I don't like this," Jorge said. "There has to be another way."

"I wish there was," Cotton said. "Because the last thing I want right now is my little girl doing... that. I don't want that put on her."

"You heard her," Roland said. "Jean is the only one she trusts. Considering what she's about to do, we need to respect that."

"Why do you think that is?" Cotton demanded.

"Why does she think Jean's the only one who will follow through?"

"It's not what you think," Roland said. "For whatever reason, I get it. She doesn't trust Jean to do it because she thinks your daughter is some kind of psycho, Cotton. She trusts her because Jean sees things in a way that we don't. Remember, she's still a kid. Her brain isn't full of past failures and second guesses. That's why she went into the woods after those Russians. She isn't reckless, she just knows what has to be done."

Fred tapped Jorge on the shoulder. He turned to her.

"Let's take a walk," she said with a smile. She took his hand. "Just you and me."

"What if it works?" Jorge asked as the two walked away from the RV.

"If it works, she'll still be herself. She'll just be different."

Jorge stopped in his tracks and turned back to the RV.

"I think that was the end," he said, as if the thought had just suddenly struck him. "Of whatever we were, I think that was the end of it."

"Don't you think maybe it ended a long time ago?" Fred asked. "And maybe you just didn't know about it?"

"I feel like a fucking idiot," Jorge snapped.

"That's how you know," Fred said.

"Know what?"

"That it was real," Fred replied. "At least for a little bit, the thing you had with Sheila. Only love can make us act like that big of an idiot."

Jorge laughed. "Maybe you're right about that."

April tapped the syringe containing the dose of Generation 2 Pandemify. Roland had brought a small box of it with them as well as some stock of the Gen 1. He didn't know why he had done it, but there had been a general agreement that there may be a need for it.

"Are you ready for this?" April asked.

For the first time since the idea had been floated, April could see in Sheila's eyes that she was nervous.

"I don't think I am," she admitted. "But we still have to do it."

April didn't say anything further; instead, she emptied the syringe into Sheila's right arm. The woman winced and then her eyes relaxed as she turned to Jean.

"Remember," Sheila said. "If I turn, you paint this RV with my brains."

"I'll do it," Jean said.

"I know you will." Sheila's skin flushed and she felt her breathing speed up. "That was fast."

"How do you feel?" April asked.

Jean drew her pistol and laid it on her leg, finger on the trigger.

"Hot," Sheila said. "Like I'm burning up. And I have to spit."

Sheila leaned forward and began repeatedly spitting on the floor.

"Okay, well that's weird," April said, growing nervous herself. She picked up the single pill from the counter and handed it to Sheila. "Chew it."

Sheila took the Prozac and chewed it up, swallowing hard.

"I can't believe this is the best idea I had," she said lazily. Her breathing had slowed down and seemed to be progressively shallower and more labored.

"Is she okay?" Jean asked.

Sheila's breathing slowed further and further until she leaned forward with her head almost in her lap and her breathing finally stopped. April and Jean looked at one another and then back to Sheila.

"Whoah!" Sheila shouted as she sat bolt upright, her black eyes locked on Jean.

Both Jean and April screamed.

"You scared the crap out of me!" the little girl shouted.

"I feel... everything," Sheila said slowly. She looked around the RV and then down at what remained of her left arm.

She stared at the stump for a moment. Viscous black tendrils began seeping from the stump where her lower arm used to be, intertwining and climbing over each other. In their wake, bones regenerated and were then covered by muscles, fascia, and finally flesh. Once they had finished their work, Sheila's left arm remained, as if nothing had ever happened.

Sheila waved her fingers around and then made a fist.

"Well," she said. "That's interesting."

"Your... arm just regenerated," April said, clearly stunned. "Are you okay?"

"I think I am," Sheila replied. "I just feel different. My skin feels alive."

"I have to do this," April said, holding up a thermometer and blood pressure cuff.

"Okay," Sheila replied, reaching over to the countertop to retrieve another doze of Prozac. "I feel like I might need more of this."

June Kennedy stood on the hilltop and watched as her army swarmed the Russian encampment. They were like a beautiful buzzsaw, shredding everything in their path. It wasn't even a fight, as the idea of one implied that both sides stood a chance.

A more honest assessment might refer to this as being a slaughter. Even more appropriately, it was the "culling" of a weak and diseased species that had already long overstayed its welcome.

Her forward scouts had already deployed far into the northern territories. It had taken some experimentation to understand their threshold for endurance, but June had figured out that they could run at a pace approximating a sprint for roughly eight hours before they dropped dead. So, she had throttled back their pace and directed them to slow down and walk for a few minutes each hour.

Those same scouts were locating the positions of the Russian invasion force, and she in turn would then direct her armies to those positions. The outcome would be no different than this one had been, or the two before it. The culling would continue, regardless of what the Russians had to say on the matter. They were inconsequential.

Screams rolled up from the valley below, and June smiled as her children devoured what remained of the Russian divisions.

Then, the ground shook beneath her and the wind suddenly intensified by a factor of ten. She felt a warmth on her skin and turned to the East, seeing a light steadily expanding up from the ground in the distance.

"What are you?" she asked quietly.

The door to the RV opened and everyone outside took a step back. There had been no screaming and no gunshot. There was no reason to think anything had gone wrong, yet the general tone among the group was one of caution.

Jean and April stepped out first, and immediately backed away from the vehicle to join the others.

Sheila stepped out and into the light. She looked at the others. She was separate from them now, and she knew it. Even if no one was going to say anything to that effect, it was clear.

Harris was the first one to notice it.

"Holy shit!" he shouted. "Your arm grew back!"

A few of the group clearly took another step back.

"I'm fine," Sheila said. "Just in case y'all are worried. I'm still myself."

"That doesn't make me less worried," Roland replied, only half-joking.

Sheila walked to a car that was parked near the RV.

"I want to try something," she said.

She reached out, grabbed the door of the car, and with little fanfare, ripped it off and threw it a dozen feet. She went to work, smashing the windshield and hammering fist-sized dents into the hood of the car.

Finally, she stepped back, her breathing only moderately labored. Steam was emanating from her skin.

"Do you see?" she asked, holding up her left hand.

Cotton understood.

"I get it," he said.

Sheila had just shown them, in a nutshell, what the black-eyed cannibals were capable of.

. . .

"So, do you think they can all regenerate?" Cotton asked, indicating Sheila's left arm.

"I think they can," Sheila said. "Maybe not as fast as I did, and maybe not a whole arm, but they definitely have accelerated wound healing."

"And they can tear a car apart," Jorge added.

"One more reason that trying to go toe-to-toe with them is not an option," Cotton said.

"She controls them," Fred pointed out. "The Cannibal Queen. She controls the black-eyed cannibals. Can you?"

Sheila shook her head. "I don't think so."

"How do you know?" Fred asked.

"It's hard to explain, I just do. I can feel that they're out there, but they're just beyond my reach."

"Is she?" Cotton asked. "Beyond your reach?"

"I'm not sure," Sheila said. "I think if I get knocked out again, I'll know."

"We have to go to Houston first," Roland said.

Everyone turned to look at him.

"Why?" Sheila asked.

"We did what we needed to here," Roland continued. "We got as much info on these dogs as we could, and Sheila had her little Exorcist makeover—"

"Fuck you," Sheila snapped.

Roland laughed. "Point being, if we need to

make a move against the Cannibal Queen, we can do it when we need to. It doesn't have to be right now." He turned to Sheila. "Am I right?"

"Yes," she nodded her agreement. "And I think my connection with her is stronger now. If she's coming at us, I'll know it."

"So, we go to Houston, then," Roland said. "And it won't hurt to have Sheila on our side if we run into trouble."

Roland sat on the tailgate of the Toyota truck with Cotton as the rest secured their gear for travel and did a quick maintenance check of the vehicles. Roland looked up at the position of the sun in the sky and then back to his watch.

"Night raid?" Cotton asked.

Roland smiled. "Only kind I know of," he replied. "Got some good white phosphor DTNVS NODs if you want to leap into the twenty-first century."

"You know I like the greens," Cotton replied.

"Yeah, that's weird," Roland laughed. He looked at the group. "They ain't ready for it. Jorge, probably. Maybe even Jean, but the rest..."

"Gotta learn sometime," Cotton said.

"Maybe we should have a rear element."

"I know where you're going with this," Cotton said. "And the answer is 'no'. We need every gun we can get. Can't afford to leave anyone behind."

Cotton could see that Roland was watching April, and he knew the two had shared a moment before everything went to hell with the cannibal dogs.

"Can't protect her," Cotton said, forcing Roland to look at his old friend. "You know that, right?"

"I don't think I've ever wanted to protect anyone before," Roland replied. "Not like this."

"It sucks," Cotton laughed. "Hard to explain. It's like your heart, or maybe just part of your heart is walking around out there without you."

Roland nodded. It was clear he understood, even if he hadn't quite come to grips with what it all meant just yet.

Bill Rampart stood over the table that had been built to resemble a perfect model of the city of Houston. They had them for all the City States, as there was always an assumption that interventions like this would eventually be necessary.

Part of the problem with the City States was that

they really believed they were independent entities. They thought that they had autonomy to make the decisions they wanted, which on occasion included pushing back against what they all at least acknowledged as being the "coordinating entity," the City State of New Orleans, and subsequently, Fluid Dynamics.

Colonel Fisker stood on the other side of the table, watching as Rampart mentally rehearsed the plan to hit the city and recapture or kill Doctor Gregory Wilson. Mike Fisker had been in command of the Charlie Assault Element since the beginning of the City State of New Orleans, and before that, he had been a platoon, company, and battalion commander in both Iraq and Afghanistan in the United States Army. He had never been a Special Forces soldier, but he had a black belt in closing with and destroying the enemy.

Current intelligence from the drones circling the city had communicated that the black-eyed cannibals roaming the streets were all what they now referred to as the "knock-offs", the lesser copies of the original Gen 2 cannibals. This was a significant relief, as these knock-offs did not seem to be that hard to kill, so long as you didn't allow them to overwhelm you. Going up against the originals would have been a problem. Possibly an insurmountable one.

"Why do we think they're at City Hall?" Bill asked, pointing to the building on the scale model.

"Drone intelligence relayed that a flare went up from near that location last night," Fisker replied dryly. "The only place we can one hundred percent rule out is the Fulbright Building. There's no way they would try to hold that location."

"What if they aren't at City Hall?" Bill asked.

"Then we have to make a decision about how to best use our resources. If new intelligence has surfaced by then, we can adjust to a new target." There was an obvious hesitation from the Colonel. "If there isn't, we do have the option of clearing the city. If it's that important."

"How would we do that?" Bill asked.

"All four assault elements and every other swinging dick we can scrounge up. We start on the periphery and work our way to the center, effectively back to the Fulbright Building."

"What are the odds of success?"

"Poor," Fisker said bluntly. "I've done something like this before. It didn't end well." He hesitated. "You know, there is another option."

A shadow passed over Bill's face. "No," he said

firmly. "I'm not willing to take it to that level. Not yet."

The door to the conference room opened and Jared walked in holding a bag.

"Is that what I think it is?" Bill asked.

Jared smiled weakly as he held up the bag and emptied its contents onto the table. The severed head of Governor/President Newcomb landed with a heavy thump on the wood surface.

Fisker looked at it but said nothing.

"You were right, Jared," Bill said with a smile. "I do feel better."

The door closed behind Jared, leaving Rampart and Fisker alone in the room.

"That guy gives me the creeps," Fisker said bluntly. "I remember what he did in Iraq. Who he was."

"He's very useful," Bill countered. "But I get it. The whole 'Ghost of Ramadi' thing freaks people out."

"So, what are we doing?"

Bill shook his head.

"I'm not sending our entire force into that city just to be potentially slaughtered."

"I don't disagree with that assessment," Fisker said. "At the very least I'd want to send some kind of recon element in ahead of us. At least have a fighting chance and know we're not just going on a wild goose chase into a meat grinder."

Bill looked back to the conference room door, then reached down and pressed a button on the table. "Jared, can you come back in here?" he asked.

In a moment, the door opened and Jared entered again. "Yes, Sir?" he asked.

"Jared, how many singleton missions did you do in Iraq and Afghanistan?"

"Oh, I wasn't keeping track, sir," Jared replied.

"Ballpark."

"Seventy-one." Jared paused. "Give or take."

Bill looked back at Fisker.

"Just him?" Fisker asked.

"You said it yourself. He's got the track record," Bill said with a shrug.

"I'm sorry, what are we talking about?" Jared asked.

"I want to drop you in the middle of the City State of Houston to gather intelligence on a possible location for our friend Doctor Wilson, ahead of Charlie Assault Element."

"Oh," Jared replied. "Okay."

Fisker looked at the tall man carefully. "Do you understand what we're asking of you?" he asked. "You might not make it back from something like this."

"Oh, I'll be fine," Jared said with a smile. "I've got all my shows on an old TiVo. I won't miss anything."

"You might die," Fisker clarified.

Jared cocked his head to the side. "I'm sorry, I'm not following."

"You'll almost certainly be eaten by black-eyed cannibals or killed by marauders."

"Probably not," Jared replied with a wink. "But I appreciate your concern."

After Colonel Fisker had left, Bill Rampart stepped into the hallway to find Jared at the reception desk on his tablet.

"Thank you," Bill said. "For stepping up like that."

"We all have to do our part," Jared replied. "For the common good."

"I have to ask you something," Bill said hesitantly.

"What is it?"

"You do believe me, don't you? That the Gen 2 vaccine wasn't supposed to cause this? That it should have turned people back?"

"Do you know that people think I'm a psychopath?" Jared asked abruptly.

"What?" Bill asked.

"I've heard how people talk about me. Like I don't have a conscience, but that's not true. I just see things clearly, maybe more clearly than most. Because of that, I have no qualms about doing the things that need to be done for the greater good. Things like this. I say all of this, because if you really intentionally created those things, if you caused all of this to happen for some reason, it would be you who would be the psychopath." Jared paused for a moment. "And if that was the case, I would then need to do what must be done. For the common good."

Bill understood the implied threat.

"But I didn't."

"Exactly," Jared replied. "So, I'm going to do this thing for you, in good faith."

"Shouldn't we wait until night?" Leslie asked as they secured their packs and checked their weapons.

Both she and Jessie had taped flashlights to their shotguns to help contend with the darkness of the parking garage. It wasn't a perfect solution (such as Lebedev's more securely and ergonomically positioned weapon light), but at least they wouldn't be running blind.

"Night is worse," Lebedev said. "At night, the cannibals will see any light we use, and we will most likely not be able to see them. At least this way, it's a level playing field. And if we can retrieve your vehicle and get out of the garage, we have the advantage of speed."

"I think I might stay," Leslie said abruptly and looked to Jessie. "Yeah, I think I might stay here."

Jessie leaned in to her.

"We talked about this," he said quietly. "You can't stay here. We're almost out of food."

It was true. No one had expected the city to suddenly be laid siege to by a swarm of black-eyed cannibals. Since the event had occurred, both Jessie and Leslie had essentially been surviving off food from the vending machines they were able to access in the building.

"I know," Leslie said. "But I've still got a little left and I think if I can just hold out for another day or two help will come."

"There's no one coming," Gregory said bluntly. "Trust me, I know. I was part of the city support structure. There's no one left to help. Not even Zoroaster can help us here."

"Reinforcements could be on the way," Leslie protested.

"Leslie, we can't leave you here—" Jessie started.

"Look, I can't do it okay?" she shouted. "I'm not going! I'm staying here!"

Lebedev took a step toward her. "This building will be your tomb," he said coldly. "After we leave, you will be here alone, and eventually those things will breach your defenses. They won't care who you are or what you have to say. They will eat you alive and you will die alone. Most likely in the dark."

Leslie stared at Lebedev, and he could see the tears welling up in her eyes. "I don't want to die here," she finally said.

"Then die out there," Lebedev replied. "With me. Fighting. Show the same courage that you showed down in the lobby when you saved us. Save yourself."

Leslie gripped her shotgun tighter and nodded.

"Okay," she said, letting out a breath. "I can do it."

. . .

The group had seventeen floors to get through from the top level to the sub-basement that housed the parking garage for city workers. In that garage, they would find the animal control department van that Jessie had the keys for and that they would then use to (theoretically) drive to freedom.

The problem was that Colonel Maxim Lebedev was not one hundred percent sure how the story would go from there. He knew what his training as an Alpha Group commander required of him. Once he had used these two to get out of the city, they would be left dead on the side of the road.

Now, though, as they were navigating this madness and plunging into the literal heart of darkness together, he wondered if that was the right move. It was a dangerous assumption that there would even be a Russian army left to rendezvous with once he escaped this rat's nest.

Based upon what he had seen on the hilltop when his unit was overwhelmed, these black-eyed fiends they had gone up against in the streets of Houston were simply weakened copies of the original Generation 2 cannibals. The originals were faster and stronger, and theoretically, there were millions of them roaming the American wasteland. If this was true, there would not be much of a Russian army left for long. Not against something like that.

So Colonel Lebedev decided he would not leave the two Houston City State employees dead on the side of the road. Not because of any human emotion getting in the way, but for the same reason that had driven the majority of human behavior for millennia: Survival.

As Leslie and Jessie had indicated, the doors entering the lower floors had been locked, and in some cases barricaded. They were unsure which floors housed cannibals and which did not, so they'd taken no chances.

Finally, after ten minutes of moving carefully down the stairs, they arrived at the much heavier double doors to the sub-basement. Jessie stopped, leaning forward to try to look through the glass, but there was only thick darkness in the parking garage. He turned back to the group.

"I've seen this movie before," he said with a weak smile.

"We're ready," Lebedev said firmly. "Just open the doors and we'll move."

"Right," Jessie said, turning and opening the door.

It was fast. They were fast. Three of the black-eyed cannibals ran through the door and tackled Jessie to the ground.

"No!" Leslie screamed.

She stepped forward and fired her shotgun into the closest one as Lebedev fired a round and then stepped into the fray, slamming the stock of his rifle into the head of the third cannibal. Two more came in the door and Leslie brought her shotgun back up and fired two more rounds in rapid succession. The heads of the two cannibals exploded as if they had been primed with charges.

Gregory finally snapped out of his shock and began firing into the open doorway.

"There's more!" he shouted as he continued shooting, seemingly without clear targets.

Lebedev stepped to the door and thumbed his weapon light to activate it.

"Jesus," he muttered as he began firing.

There were at least a dozen of them running through the parking garage. Why in the hell were they so fast? He went through his first magazine, then performed a speed reload and shot the rest only moments before they would have reached the door.

He turned back to where Jessie was laying against the wall. His face and chest were covered with blood and a piece of flesh was missing from his jaw.

"Shit," Jessie said quietly.

He started to reach up to touch his face, but Lebedev stopped him. He pushed the man's hand back down. He looked into Jessie's eyes. They were turning black. He looked around at the bodies of the dead cannibals. Their skin had a pink hue to it, and steam was still rising off of them. These were not copies, these were the originals.

"Oh my God," Leslie said, also seeing Jessie's eyes turning black.

Lebedev stood up and stepped back, well out of striking distance.

"What is it?" Jessie asked as the three stared at him. "What—"

His words were cut off as his jaw slammed shut so hard it cracked his teeth. His eyes went completely black and he whipped his head back into the concrete wall hard enough that it cracked the surface. Veins bulged from his skin and his mouth opened, blood covering broken teeth as he screamed in silence.

Then his body went limp, his posture drooped forward, and his eyes closed.

"Is that it?" Gregory asked.

Jessie's eyes snapped back open and he leapt to his feet, a deep growl emanating from within him as he lunged forward.

Leslie shouldered her shotgun and looked her oldest friend in his coal black eyes, in one instant understanding that he was no longer there. It was something else. Something she did not know.

She pulled the trigger and the slug hammered Jessie back against the wall. He stumbled and his eyes blanked rapidly, but then he lunged forward again. Leslie drove the gun toward him and fired three more times, racking the shotgun and pulling the trigger in rapid succession. Finally, he collapsed to the floor, his body shredded by the heavy slugs that had finally stopped his heart.

Leslie's eyes were blank as she looked at what remained of her old friend.

Lebedev put a hand on the shotgun and slowly lowered it.

"Are you okay?" he asked.

Leslie looked from Jessie's body to the Russian.

"I— I'm fine. I did what I had to."

"You did," Lebedev agreed.

Gregory was already examining Jessie's body, and Lebedev could see that something was on the scientist's mind.

"What is it?" Lebedev asked.

"It happened so fast," Gregory said. He had a small flashlight out and was pulling Jessie's eyes open to check the pupils. "It shouldn't have happened that fast."

"What do you mean?" Lebedev asked.

"He's right," Leslie said. "We saw it happening in the streets when this first started. People were being attacked, but they would be laying out for several hours before they finally got back up and became those... things. But it took him less than a minute."

"It's mutating," Gregory said. "That's the only explanation. It's learning and adapting."

"The virus?" Lebedev asked.

"No," Gregory said and shook his head. "The vaccine. I mean, technically not even really a vaccine. Remember? It's a technology. It bonds to your DNA and reprograms it to be more efficient at killing the virus."

"Even so, why would it change?"

"They couldn't have been that arrogant," Gregory said, almost to himself.

"*Who* couldn't be *how* arrogant?" Leslie pressed.

"There was talk, when they were in the development process for the Gen 2 vaccine. Someone had figured out how to plug A.I. into the technology."

"Artificial intelligence?" Leslie asked. "Wait. Into the vaccine?"

"Into the technology," Gregory once again corrected. "Something like that would never work on a classic inactive virus platform, but with a technology, in theory you could do it."

"I'm no scientist," Lebedev said. "But that sounds bad."

"It depends on which side of the argument you fall on. If you're a wide-eyed optimist, you could think it would cause the technology to evolve and save mankind."

"Or kill us all," Lebedev offered.

"That's also a possibility, which is why I argued against it, and was assured the matter had been put to rest."

Leslie looked again at Jessie's body. "I don't think it was."

"What about these ones?" Lebedev asked, motioning to the bodies littering the entrance and the interior of the garage. "Why are they originals?"

"That one's easy," Leslie said. "They were probably locked in the garage when this all started. But at least now you know what we're really up against."

"Damn," Gregory said quietly. "It's going to fix itself."

"What?" Leslie asked.

"The only thing saving us so far is that the copies are weak and slow. But if this theory is right and they did inject an A.I. into the Gen 2 vaccine—"

"They'll get faster," Lebedev concluded.

CHAPTER 6

THE SMALL CARAVAN had stopped just outside of Houston on State Road 290, and the decision was made to send Cotton, Jorge, Roland and Sheila into the city, much to the expected protest of Jean.

"I need someone I can trust out here, okay?" Cotton said to her. "This isn't like the other times. I'm not trying to sideline you."

"That's what it feels like," Jean replied.

"You know what the hardest part of Roland's job was, back when he was Command Master Chief?" Cotton asked. "Not going in the building."

"What do you mean?"

"When you're running the show, you can't be the first guy in the door. Hell, most of the time, if you're doing your job right you shouldn't even be on target.

Guys would try to do it. We'd see it all the time with the Army and the Marines. Some light colonel stacked up on a freaking door when he should be in the command center monitoring the ISR feed to make sure his guys don't get any nasty surprises."

"I'm not the leader," Jean said.

"Yet," Cotton replied. "But you're going to be. This new world, at some point it's going to need leaders to try to set things right again. Guys like us, we're probably not going to be around for that."

"That's not true," Jean said.

"You know it is. Even if you don't want to admit it. So, right now, in this moment, I need you to be a leader. I need you to hang back and be ready to step up if things go south."

Jean shifted her stance, finally nodding her understanding.

"Okay," she said. "I get it. Even if I don't like it."

A nighttime movement into the city had been ruled out, as the sun would still not set for several more hours, and it was generally agreed that time was of the essence. It was hard to know if this Doctor Wilson was holding position at the Fulbright Building or if he had already rabbited. If he was still there, it wouldn't be too difficult to extract him and get back out, assuming they didn't run into too many of the black-eyed cannibals.

"You all are QRF," Cotton said, addressing Jean, Harris, and April. "But only if we call for it."

"What if you're in trouble and you can't call out?" Jean asked.

"That's a risk we have to take," Cotton said. "It's not because I don't think the three of you can handle it. It's more about you coming in on accident and then we've got two groups separated in the city and we can't find each other. Even with a near rally point, there are too many ways that could go wrong."

"Understood," Jean replied.

Cotton knew full well that this was a pivotal moment. His daughter grasping what he was saying and putting her ego aside was important. He took out one of the city maps they had acquired and spread it out on the hood of the truck.

"This is the Harris County hospital," he said, pointing to the location on the map. "This is our near rally point. It's the most likely option to have everything we need if we have to strongpoint. Food, medicine, and possibly even power." He then looked up from the map and pointed toward the city. "There are drainage ducts on this side of the city, about three clicks down the road here that connect to the access tunnels below ground. They'll take you right to city hall. Roland said there are even directions stenciled on the walls in the tunnels."

"Under NODs?" Harris asked.

"Affirmative. You've already got a little time under night vision so it won't be hard. Just don't take big steps or you'll eat shit."

Harris laughed.

"But seriously," Cotton said. "Going into those tunnels will be bad. It's fifty/fifty that you'll be walking into a mess of those black-eyed cannibals and won't have a way out. Hell, odds might not even be that good."

"What about your odds?" April asked.

Cotton shrugged. "If we don't do this and what Fred's saying about all this stuff is right, our odds are zero."

Fred watched Cotton, Jorge, Roland and Sheila doing their final prep before the walk into the city. It was a complete unknown as to what might attract the black-eyed cannibals, how good their hearing was, etc., which meant that driving a vehicle in could immediately pull dozens or more of the things right down on top of them before they had a chance to do anything. Walking in was the only feasible option.

"What if he isn't there?" Fred asked.

"Wilson?" Roland replied.

"Yes. What if you get there and he isn't at the Fulbright Building. What then?"

"We'll search for intel and then move based on what we find. Same thing we used to do in Iraq."

"This isn't Iraq," Fred protested.

"I know that, Doc, but I don't have a better option at the moment. Do you?"

Fred's eyes wandered for a moment. "Damn it," she said. "I think I do."

"Gregory had an almost inappropriate relationship with his phone," Fred said as she fished hers out of her pack. "He will definitely have it on him."

"Why?" Cotton asked. "They don't work anymore, right?"

"They do in the City States," Roland said. "But you have to be—" He stopped mid-sentence as he understood what Fred was saying. "You're gonna call him?"

"No," she said. "That won't work. He's way too paranoid for that. This number won't be in his contact list, and if I try to call him from it, we run the risk of him ditching it."

"So, what do we do?" Jorge asked.

"We can ping it," Fred said. "I coded an app a while ago to get a fix on people I know. I can use it once I'm close enough to get on the network."

"Won't the network be down?" Cotton asked.

"When they put together the City States, they did a few things that they knew would be important to control the population. One of those things was that the network *had* to stay up. Remember the first time the internet went down?"

Fred was referring to the Fire Sale that had been initiated by hackers early on in their war with the Federal Government. The entire internet had gone dark for two weeks.

"It was chaos," Cotton said.

"That couldn't happen again," Fred went on. "So, the hardware for the network itself is buried in a concrete sub-basement that uses the pipeline around the city as a giant antenna. They then hard lined that into solar panels on top of several of the high rises. It will never, ever go down."

"That's kind of genius," April said.

"The only catch is, you have to be in the city to access it. The signal isn't strong enough to get more than a few hundred feet past the outermost antennae, and we're not even close to that."

"Okay," Roland said. "We'll take your phone in with us and ping him once we're in range."

"I have to go," Fred said.

"The hell you do!" Roland snapped. "This is a combat mission not a sight-seeing tour."

"Don't you think I know that?" Fred asked. "Believe me, this is the last thing I want to be doing, but can you learn this software and write a patch on the fly for it if it doesn't sync up perfectly to the network?"

"I might've missed that part of BUDs," Roland smirked.

"Well, I can. I'm the only one that can do it. I have to go with you."

"Can I have a word with you?" Cotton asked Sheila as he led her away from the group.

"What is it?" she asked.

Cotton stopped and turned to face the woman. Her eyes were so black, it was unsettling. Like looking into an abyss. He'd been close to the black-eyed cannibals he'd gone up against at Cypress Mill, but not like this. Not close enough to really study them.

"How are you feeling?" Cotton asked.

"Fine," Sheila answered. "Why are you asking?"

"If you're not yourself," Cotton said. "In any way, I need to know."

Sheila stayed locked on the former SEAL with her unblinking gaze.

"Nothing about me is the same," she finally said. "But I'm in control of it, if that's what you're asking."

"For how long?"

"Until I'm not."

"Not sure I like that answer," Cotton said with a shake of his head.

"Well, you're fresh out of options, friend," Sheila said. "Like it or not, you need me. I can do things none of you can, not the least of which is I'll know if those things are coming at us. I'm not quite fully synced up with them, but I'm still part of that hive mind. Knowing when you're about to get overrun and being able to get the hell out of the way isn't something you can do without."

"True," Cotton agreed.

"Look, I get it. You just want to protect your people, and like it or not, I'm not a person anymore. Not even the way that Roland and the others are. I'm not even one of the black-eyed cannibals."

"What are you?"

"Something else."

"Are you sure about this?" The pilot of the CH-46 helicopter asked as they closed in on the destroyed helipad of the Fulbright Tower. "Getting you back out of here will be tricky."

"You won't be getting me out of here," Jared said. "I'll call out with my location outside of the city. Don't worry, I'm not going to pull you into a hot LZ."

The pilot circled the building and then held position over the helipad.

Jared secured his pack and kicked the fast rope down through the "hell hole" in the center of the helicopter. There was no way they could touch down on the building, as the landing structure had been destroyed by the blast, so he would have to make his own entrance.

"I feel like you've done this before," the pilot said over the comms.

"Couple times," Jared replied as he pulled on the thick, leather gloves necessary for fast roping and then disappeared through the exit.

. . .

Colonel Lebedev walked ahead of Leslie and Gregory as they crossed the dark parking garage. He'd opted not to lower his night vision, since while the subterranean structure was very dark, it was not pitch black, and there was still just enough light to navigate.

"How far is it?" Lebedev asked quietly as they walked.

"Sorry," Leslie said. "It's at the far end. All the way across. It was this thing we did. We liked our job but we didn't like all the City Hall B.S. We made a point of parking as far away as possible so we could— so we could—"

Lebedev stopped and turned to her.

"I'm not good at the emotional stuff," he said. "So, stop it."

"Sorry," Leslie apologized.

Lebedev cracked a smile and Leslie laughed.

"I've lost people," he said. "People I cared about. Both in the military but also outside. It's never easy, but we honor their memory by pushing forward."

"I get it," Leslie said and reached into her pocket for the keys to the Animal Control van. She pointed to the end of the garage. "It's there—"

Three figures darted out from between two parked cars in the darkness. There was no question as to what they were, and in a moment, they collided with Lebedev, Leslie, and Gregory. They were too close for the Russian to engage with his carbine and so he released the weapon, drew his pistol from its holster and fired from retention.

The first two rounds didn't kill the black-eyed cannibal, but it pushed him back far enough that Lebedev was able to get the pistol up and fire another controlled pair into the creature's face.

There was a loud series of "booms" as Leslie made short work of the remaining cannibals, then activated the flashlight that was mounted on her shotgun and illuminated the area. Lebedev did the same. There was no more need for stealth.

She turned the light to where Gregory was leaning against a car, clutching his arm. He was bleeding and it was obvious what had happened. He looked down at the wound and then to Leslie. She racked a round into the shotgun and brought it up level with his head.

"No!" Gregory shouted. "Wait!"

Leslie didn't know why, but she did. Based on what had happened to Jessie, she knew they may only have minutes before Gregory began to turn.

Perhaps not even that. She watched as the man clumsily reached into the messenger bag he had been carrying and pulled out a small package with his shaking hands.

"What is he doing?" Lebedev asked.

"I don't know," Leslie replied.

Gregory ripped the package open and pulled out what looked like a small syrette. He pulled the cap and stuck the needle in his arm, then breathed a sigh of relief.

"What in the hell was that?" Leslie asked, though as she felt a chill race down her spine. She knew what it was.

"The antidote," Gregory replied. "To the Gen 2 vaccine. I figured it would work for this, too."

"You son of a bitch!" Leslie screamed and she stepped forward and rammed the stock of her shotgun into the side of Gregory's head. The scientist dropped to the concrete like a ton of bricks and Leslie pressed the barrel of the shotgun to his forehead. "You let him die!"

"I couldn't save him!" Gregory shouted. "It was too late! By the time we realized what was happening he was already gone! And it wasn't a sure thing!"

Lebedev reached out and gently pushed the barrel away from Gregory's head.

"He's right," he said. "You may not like it, but he is." Lebedev looked down at Gregory. "But why would you develop an antidote for a vaccine?"

"Because of what happened with the first one," Gregory replied.

"I think I'm dying," Fred said as the five trekked down side streets into the heart of the city.

"You're not dying," Roland replied without turning around.

"Has anyone ever died from walking too far?" Fred asked.

"It's barely been a mile," Jorge offered.

"This is why I was a powerlifter and not a runner," she argued.

Everyone stopped, then turned and looked at her.

"Say what now?" Roland asked.

"What?" Fred asked.

"You just said you were a powerlifter," Cotton said.

"Heavyweight class," Fred replied. "Texas state deadlift champion."

Roland looked her up and down. "Yeah, okay," he said. "I never noticed it before but you do have weirdly long arms. Like a gorilla."

"I bet you do really well with the ladies," Fred shot back.

"When were you a powerlifter?" Jorge asked.

"In the nineties," Fred said. "It's a math problem, so it appealed to me. Plus, it doesn't have running in it."

"I'm starting to think you don't like running," Sheila said dryly.

Roland looked around and then back to Fred. "Can you ping his phone yet?"

"If it'll stop this death march," she muttered as she pulled out her phone and powered it up. "I'll give it a try."

"Shit," Sheila said quietly. "We've got company."

The group all brought their weapons up.

"I need to be in the open for this," Fred said frantically. "I need line of sight."

"Where are they?" Cotton asked Sheila.

Sheila turned and pointed to a cross street.

"Right around that corner. And there's a freaking lot of them."

"How long?" Roland asked Fred.

"I don't know— um... five minutes?"

"We don't have five minutes," Cotton said as he watched the first of the cannibals rounding the corner of a building a block away from them. "They've seen us."

"Everybody keep your cool," Roland commanded. "We're gonna buy the doc the five minutes she needs."

The former Development Group Master Chief took a knee, set his firing position and began knocking down targets. The others followed suit and soon built up a steady and consistent rate of fire, shooting down the black-eyed creatures as they came around the corner and broke off toward them.

Jared moved through the Fulbright building with his 10.3" 300 Blackout rifle shouldered and his trusted Accuracy International sniper rifle slung across his back. He didn't have a side-arm because he was not (in his words) "a fucking loser."

The Marine stopped to hammer controlled pairs of the 220 grain ammunition into a small group of black-eyed cannibals that he'd found on the floor he knew had been previously occupied by Doctor Gregory Wilson. He stopped and looked down at the bodies, not understanding what all of the fuss was about. He knew these were not the original version that were supposedly stronger and faster, but he imagined that even those would respond similarly to a dose of sub-sonic persuasion to the face.

It was becoming rapidly apparent that the good doctor had fled the premises. Jared was about to exit the floor when he heard pops in the distance. They were suppressed rifles. Barely audible, but they were there.

He walked to the broken-out windows, feeling the cool wind across his face as he scanned the city. Then, he saw movement in the distance. How far was it? He had a pretty good idea but pulled his range finder from his cargo pocket and did his due diligence anyway.

They were two thousand three hundred and fifty meters away.

"Hm," Jared said. "Who are you, little bird?"

He set down the rifle he had been using and unslung the AX50 sniper rifle. He looked around and opted to set it up on a desk that had been bolted into the floor. This would give him the perspective he needed. Once he had properly set everything up, he looked through the Night Force scope and dialed in his view.

"Looks like we've got ourselves a street fight going on out there," he muttered whimsically.

He could not see as much detail as he would have liked, but it was clear there was some sort of heavily armed group of marauders fighting a fairly large group of the black-eyed cannibals, and they seemed to be holding their own.

Jared reached into his pack and retrieved a smart phone. He took a moment to log into the network and then observed the series of blue dots scattered around the city, indicating active signals. He set the phone down on the desk and then took his position behind the rifle.

"Sorry to be the bearer of bad news," Jared said as he chambered a round.

His Kestrel wind meter wouldn't be much use shooting from inside the building, and the reality was that for shots this long, it still wouldn't offer much help, as there was too much variability in the wind over two thousand meters.

Jared settled into his firing position, found his target, and began taking up the slack on the trigger.

"How are we doing over there?" Cotton called out as he changed magazines.

There were dozens of bodies littering the streets, and the group had spread out to improve the number of targets they could engage and avoid too much cross over.

"Almost there!" Fred said, the tone of her voice indicating that she was on the bleeding edge of being frantic. "Just one more—"

The windshield of the car Fred was standing beside shattered and the car rocked. She felt concussive force and dropped to her knees, the phone falling from her hands. Four more explosions hit the area around her, one after the other.

Cotton snapped his magnifier into place as he took cover behind a car and then turned and scanned the cityscape with it. He knew they were being shot at, but he had no idea where from. The rest of the group had also taken cover but were maintaining their fire at the oncoming cannibals.

Fred, however, was still sitting out in the open, clearly in shock.

"Get the hell out of the street!" Cotton shouted. "Someone's shooting at us!"

Then the shooting stopped and Fred's phone began ringing.

"What in the hell?" she muttered.

Fred felt a strong hand grip her arm and she

looked up. It was Roland. He was still shooting as he pulled Fred from the ground. In that last moment, she reached out and grabbed the phone she had dropped.

Everything snapped into focus. She realized what was happening. They were being overrun.

"We have to get inside!" Roland shouted. "Now!"

Cotton slammed the door behind them as Jorge grabbed a heavy desk in the corner of the ground floor office and shoved it up against the door. The windows were shattering as the throngs of black-eyed cannibals outside began smashing them, trying to break into the city utilities building the group had retreated into.

"Shit!" Roland snapped. "This ain't gonna work! We can't hold this building from the ground floor."

Cotton and Jorge began taking shots through the windows, knocking down the cannibals as they crawled through the broken glass.

"My phone keeps ringing!" Fred shouted.

"Are you freaking nuts?" Roland asked. "We're about to get eaten here!"

Sheila looked at the single flight of stairs in the

corner of the room and then back at Jorge and Cotton, who were doing their best to hold back the tide of monsters trying to get at them, but were obviously failing.

"Up the stairs!" Sheila shouted. "Do it now!"

Jorge and Cotton broke contact and moved to the stairwell.

"Okay," Roland said, understanding that the first floor was about to be lost. He tapped Sheila on the shoulder and took Fred by the arm. "Let's go."

"I'm staying," Sheila said firmly.

Jorge stopped on the stairs. "What do you think you're doing?" he asked.

Sheila looked at him from behind her coal black eyes and smiled.

"Something none of you can," she said and drew the battle knife she had fixed to her belt. "And if I were you, I'd get up those stairs because it's about to get downright biblical in here."

"Move!" Roland snapped and gave Jorge a push.

Jared opened the laptop he'd stowed in his rucksack and established his satellite uplink with New Orleans. He looked out the window to where he knew the three drones on station would be patrolling overhead. He selected the signal most proximal to his location and then toggled from the live video to the thermal option.

While they still did not know much about the black-eyed cannibals, they did know that both versions had very different heat signatures compared to Gen 1 cannibals or humans. The original black-eyed variant were super-heated, like an engine about to explode, and this was reflected in their thermal signature. The secondary infections, on the other hand, were very cool, even more so than regular humans.

These differences made it easy to discern just who and what the former Scout Sniper was dealing with in the former City State of Houston. Specifically, that there were several thousand of the secondary infections swarming the immediate vicinity of his location, several humans and Gen 1 cannibals trapped in the building at the location he had just opened fire on, and a handful of other humans near City Hall. It also stood to reason that the scientist he was looking for, this Doctor Gregory Wilson was in one of those two locations.

Jared picked up his phone, found the signal he was looking for, and dialed the number again.

. . .

"It's ringing again!" Fred screamed as Roland pulled her through the door at the end of the short hallway and into the large open space that occupied most of the second floor.

"Who could be calling you?" Cotton asked. "They have to be in the city, right?"

"Yes."

"And they have to know we're here," Jorge said, understanding what Cotton was implying.

"You think it's that son-of-a-bitch out there shooting at us?" Roland asked.

"Has to be," Cotton replied and reached out to Fred. "Give me that phone."

Sheila walked backward up the steps as she threw a forceful kick into the cannibal that was reaching for her and then followed up with a hard overhand strike with her Gerber knife at the next one in line who had decided to try his luck.

Her gambit had worked. She had bought enough time for the rest of the group to get upstairs, and she was more than holding her own against the Gen 2 cannibals breaching the ground floor. It helped that they all seemed to be the secondary infections and were not particularly fast or strong. Not like she was.

There were at least a dozen of them littering the ground floor, but there seemed to be no shortage of follow-up attackers as they continued climbing through the windows, clearly intent on turning her into dinner.

"I'm coming back!" she called out as she drew the big FN 45 pistol from its holster and started firing into the advancing cannibals who were moving up the stairs. The heavy .45 caliber slugs were doing just what they had been designed to. Namely, they were knocking the beasts to the floor. Even if she wasn't getting clean shots in the killbox, she was slowing them down.

The door at the top of the stairs opened and Jorge leaned out with his rifle, performing a mag dump into the remaining cannibals as Sheila turned and ran through the doorway. Jorge pulled his weapon back in and slammed and locked the door, after which Roland followed up by pushing a heavy wooden desk against it.

"You look like shit," Roland said.

Sheila was covered with cuts and bite marks, and it was clear the fight she had just been in had taken its toll. However, as they watched, the wounds closed and within a minute, the woman was restored to the same condition she had been in before the fight.

"That's a real cool trick," Roland said.

"Who is this?" Cotton asked.

'This is Jared Foster."

There was silence for a moment.

"What do you want?" Cotton asked. "Why are you shooting at us?"

"You're in quite a pickle," Jared said. "At least from what I can see. You should really look out your window."

Cotton lowered the phone, walked to one of the small windows and looked outside.

"Shit," he said quietly.

Where there had previously been a scattering of the black-eyed cannibals in the street, there was now an ocean of them. Fred walked beside him.

"Jesus."

It was clear that what this man had done was intentional. He wasn't trying to hit them, he was trying to trap them.

Cotton put the phone back do his ear. "Okay," he said. "I ask again, what do you want?"

"I work for a man named Bill Rampart. Are you familiar?"

Cotton looked to Fred.

"He's the CEO of Fluid Dynamics," she said.

Cotton turned back to the phone. "Okay," he said. "We know him."

"We just want Doctor Wilson," Jared said.

Cotton placed his thumb over the phone's microphone.

"He says they want Doctor Wilson," Cotton said. "Same guy we're looking for."

"Do not tell him that we don't have him!" Fred said frantically. "Right now, he's our only bargaining chip."

Cotton knew she was right. The building was surrounded by a horde of the black-eyed things and to make matters worse, even if they did somehow find a way out, this maniac was in an elevated position, ready to punch their tickets.

Cotton removed his thumb from the microphone.

"Okay," he said. "Let's make a deal."

"Come on," Jared replied. "Proof of life or we're not doing business. You know how this works."

Fred held up her hand and made a "give it here" gesture. Cotton handed her the phone and she put it to her head.

"This is Gregory," she said, altering her voice. "I'm awful scared. Are you getting me out of here?"

"Hi Doctor Wilson," Jared said. "I'm working on it. Please hand me back to the gentleman."

Fred handed the phone back to Cotton.

"You're sitting on top of one of the main intakes to the city access tunnels," Jared said matter-of-factly. "You can access it through the second sub-basement. Once you do, head a thousand meters east and I'll meet you at street level."

"Even if we could get to that sub-basement—which we can't—I'm supposed to just trust that you're not going to smoke us the moment we come into view?"

"Seems to me you're not long on options," Jared said. "And the bottom line is that I need Doctor Gregory."

Cotton hesitated for a moment.

"I know who you are," Cotton said.

"Good," Jared replied. "Then you know what you have to do. You have thirty minutes."

The line went dead.

Cotton turned to Fred. "When we worked together on projects, I used to imitate him," she said. "I was so good people on the phone couldn't tell it wasn't him."

"Well, we're in a fix now," Cotton said. "Not only do we have to fight our way back through the downstairs to meet this psychopath, but we don't have the guy he wants."

"You said you knew who he was," Roland said from where he was standing with Jorge and Sheila. "Who is he?"

"Jared Foster," Cotton replied.

"Are you shitting me?" Jorge nearly shouted. He looked around the room and then back to Cotton. "You know he's almost certainly got us on thermal."

"I don't think so," Roland said and shook his head. "If they just inserted him, he's got to be back at the Fulbright building. It's the only thing that makes sense. If that's the case, he isn't close enough to accurately hit us. Probably why he just started tearing up the neighborhood as a tactic to box us in."

"What in the hell is that?" Fred asked from where she stood, looking out the window.

Everyone turned to see a green flare exploding in the sky.

CHAPTER 7

"This ain't right," Jean said from where she stood atop the Winnebago with a pair of binoculars.

"Sounded like someone was tearing it up out there with a fifty cal," Harris said. "You know, sniper rifle. So maybe get off the roof."

Jean looked down through the makeshift sunroof of the vehicle to the inside, where April was working the short-wave radio that they were (in theory) using to stay linked up with the others.

"Anything?" Jean asked.

April looked up and shook her head.

"I had a connection," April said. "Then it dropped. Only thing I can think is they went inside a building and it's blocking the signal."

Jean put the binocs back to her eyes and scanned the city again.

"I can't see a damn thing," she said. "We have to go in."

"No!" Harris said insistently. "You heard what your dad said. We don't infil unless we get the call or they're out of contact for sixty minutes."

Jean looked at her watch.

"You know I'm right!" Harris insisted.

Jean clambered down the side of the Winnebago and looked around.

"Okay," she said. "But that means in twenty minutes we go hot."

"I can live with that," Harris agreed.

April walked to the doorway of the RV. "In daylight?" she asked. "I thought the plan was to go in at night if we had to?"

"No one thought it would go south this quick," Jean said. "We ain't got a choice. It's gonna be old school, scorched earth style."

"There are probably thousands of those things in that city," April said. "Maybe even tens of thousands."

"Then you better be fast on that machine gun," Jean said. "Because that's what's happening."

. . .

Doctor Gregory Wilson accelerated out of the parking garage and into the waning daylight. There were scores of the Wasted wandering the streets, but they didn't seem to notice the van that the three were fleeing in.

"Slow down," Lebedev said as Gregory accelerated away from City Hall.

"Are you nuts?" Gregory asked, the panic in his voice clear. "Those things are everywhere."

"I know," Lebedev replied as he held up a hand. "But none of them are coming after us. They don't even seem to notice we're here."

Gregory understood what the Russian was saying. He still didn't like the idea of becoming a sitting duck in the middle of the swarming horde of black-eyed cannibals, but he slowed the vehicle to a stop in the street.

Leslie looked through the side windows. "He's right," she said. "It's not just that they don't see us. It looks like they're going somewhere."

"Wherever that is," Gregory said. "I don't want to go there."

Lebedev turned to his right and looked out the window. A green flare was arcing through the sky.

"Is that what you saw last night?" he asked Gregory.

Gregory craned his neck to see the flare through the upper left part of the windshield.

"Yeah," he said. "Something else I don't want to find out about."

"Shit!" Leslie snapped. "I can't believe I forgot the color code!"

"What color code?" Lebedev asked.

"Oh no," Gregory groaned. "I forgot it, too."

"What color code?" Lebedev insisted.

"No one ever thought we would need to use it," Leslie said. "But when the city was first established as an independent state, there was a color-coded emergency flare system. Blue was for a natural disaster—"

"Orange was for an attack on the city," Gregory went on.

"Red was to abandon the city."

"And green was a call for mass rescue."

"Mass rescue?" Lebedev asked.

"If there was some kind of disaster or people were trapped and needed help to get out. That was green." Leslie looked at Gregory. "It's the hospital, isn't it?"

"We can't know that," Gregory said and shook his head. "We just need to get out of this city or *we're* gonna be sending up some damn green flares!"

"It could be a lot of people!" Leslie protested. "And they're trapped in this mess just like we are! We can't just leave!"

"He's right," Lebedev said. "We don't have time for this. We're leaving."

"Fine," Leslie said. She shouldered her pack, picked up her shotgun, and rolled open the sliding door of the van. "Leave."

Leslie stepped out into the street and she could feel her blood run cold. The Wasted were everywhere, but for whatever reason, they weren't paying any attention to her. They just continued heading down Bagby Street.

Lebedev watched her in the rearview mirror as she walked away from the van. She looked over her shoulder at him but continued to walk away.

"Damn it," Lebedev said. "Go get her. We can't leave her."

"The hell we can't!" Gregory nearly shouted. "You want to go to the hospital and join the buffet, that's on you! I'm driving this van out of here!"

Lebedev reached over, turned the ignition to the "off" position, and pulled the key out.

"No, you're not," he said.

"This is insane!" Gregory protested.

Lebedev stepped out of the van and looked

around. It was true. The black-eyed cannibals still weren't even looking at them. It was as if they didn't exist.

"Come back!" Lebedev called out.

Leslie stopped. She turned and looked at the Russian.

"We're going to the hospital," he said.

Sheila stood at the small window of the second floor and looked out at the ocean of black-eyed cannibals. By now there were thousands of them. They were everywhere, and they seemed to be coming toward them from every side street.

"Why are they all coming here?" Jorge asked.

"It's me," Sheila said quietly. "I'm drawing them in. Like a magnet. Just like the Cannibal Queen does."

"Can you control them?" Jorge asked. "Like her?"

"Not these ones," Sheila replied. "She can't either. These are like "read only." They can sense me... they know I'm like them but I can't control them."

"Seems like kind of a raw deal."

Sheila smiled. She had always appreciated the big man's sense of humor.

"You'll be the end of them," a voice hissed from behind her.

Sheila turned to see June Kennedy standing across the room from her. She flickered, almost like an image from a television with a poor connection.

"I'm pulling them in, aren't I?" Sheila asked.

"Who are you talking to?" Jorge asked.

The room fell away and Sheila stood in the darkness with June.

"Yes," June said. "They can feel your light. Just like they can feel mine."

"Then I have to leave," Sheila said.

"No," June shook her head. "You need to let them in. Let the grandchildren in."

"They'll kill my people."

"*They* are your people!" June snapped. "And what did these people ever do for you? Let you inject yourself with the vaccine? Let you turn yourself into a monster?"

"I'm not a monster!" Sheila shouted.

A smile slowly crept across June's face.

"You're right, my dear. You're not a monster. You are the future. They are the past." The darkness melted away and the room came back into focus.

June looked down the hallway at the door to the stairs. "So I say again, let them in."

"Wake up!" Jorge shouted.

Sheila's eyes snapped open and she looked around. She sat up and touched her face. Blood was pouring from her nose. Cotton handed her a towel and she used it to soak up the blood, pulling it away to see it stained black, not red.

"What happened?" she asked.

"You went into a trance and then fell over!" Jorge replied.

"I went somewhere else," Sheila said lazily.

"It was her again, wasn't it?" Cotton asked.

Sheila nodded.

"Open the door," a voice inside her head said. It was her voice.

"I don't know how much longer I can hold out," Sheila said.

"What do you mean?" Fred asked.

"I think she knows I'm a threat," Sheila said. "She's getting in my head. She wants me to let them in."

"The Wasted?" Fred asked.

"Yes," Sheila replied, looking at Fred. "And I'm going to do it, if this goes on long enough."

"Well, that seems like a pretty big problem," Roland said.

"We have to get out of the building," Cotton commanded. "And unfortunately, it looks like the only way out is by going right to Jared Foster."

"We can't just go a different way?" Fred asked.

Cotton shook his head. "Hard to know what we'd be running into without a map. Could be a dead end, could be an ocean of those black-eyed things. If Jared is sending us toward him, odds are pretty good he's already cleared a path."

"So, we just get the drop on him," Roland concluded.

"How in the hell do we do that?" Jorge asked.

"I feel like I'm being left out of something," Fred said. "Who in the hell is this Jared?"

"Jared Foster," Cotton said. "Also known as the Ghost of Ramadi. He was a Scout Sniper in Iraq who just decided he didn't want to go home. He was dishonorably discharged from the Marine Corps for unauthorized absence, missing a troop movement, etc. But his version of going UA was basically just going apeshit on Al-Qaeda in Iraq with his sniper rifle. There was a rumor that CIA or some other agency started funding him. Figured if they couldn't arrest him, they might as well hire him. He kind of went native, started living with the population and hunting the enemy from within."

"And now he works for Fluid Dynamics," Jorge concluded. "Shocking."

"Does anyone else have any bad news?" Fred asked, sounding like she was on the verge of a panic attack.

Cotton put a hand on her shoulder. "It's going to be fine," he said softly. "Trust me. If you had to end up in this situation, we're the three guys you want to be in it with."

"I'm staying," Sheila said.

"What?" Jorge snapped.

"You heard me," Sheila said. "I'm a magnet for those things. I go with you and they follow. And to make matters worse, I think at some point I'm going to start acting more like them and less like me."

"You don't know that," Jorge said.

"I do," Sheila said. "I thought I was going to be able to maintain control, but I can't."

Sheila holstered the pistol and watched the rest of the group line up in the hallway. Jorge looked at her.

She wanted to say something, but in what was left of her human heart, she knew there was nothing to be said. It was best to leave things as they were.

"Have you got him locked in?" Cotton asked Fred as she worked on her phone.

"Yes," Fred replied. "At least I think I do."

"What do you mean 'you think'?"

"Look, this isn't an exact science," Fred shot back. "I've got a handful of signals within an acceptable radius of the Fulbright Building. I know one of them is Jared but the other three... it'll be a guess as to who I'm calling. But if it isn't him, I just hang up."

"And you think it'll still work underground?" Roland asked.

"Yes, because of how they built the antennas into the foundation. It's not like trying to grab a signal from a cell tower or a satellite."

"Enough talking," Sheila said as she pushed past them. "We have to do this, let's do it now."

The plan was simple. Once the door to the lower floor opened, they would lay down suppressive fire and toss fragmentation grenades to clear out the current mass of black-eyed cannibals that had taken up residence below.

From there, they would move down to the lower floor, find the access door to the stairwell and then move to the sub-basement. This all assumed, of course, that Jared Foster wasn't full of shit and just leading them to their deaths.

"What do I do?" Fred asked in a panic, suddenly aware that she had not been given a specific role in the plan.

"Hold this," Roland said and pushed a fragmentation grenade into her hand. He slid the pin out and pressed her fingers tight against the spoon.

"Are you out of your mind?" Fred shouted. "Why in the hell am I holding this?"

"If we don't make it through this," Roland said coldly. "If they're on top of you, you let that spoon drop. That way it'll be quick for you and you'll take some of them with you."

Fred wanted to say something. She wanted to push back but she knew what he was saying was true. For a brief moment, fear clutched its icy fingers around her heart as she saw visions of being torn apart by the monsters downstairs, but she pushed the image out of her head. If she let herself be pulled into that line of thought, it would almost certainly become a self-fulfilling prophecy.

"Give them to me," Sheila said and reached out for the grenades Cotton was holding.

"Why?" Cotton asked.

"I can take a little shrapnel," she said. "I can get closer than you can, make sure they go where it counts."

Cotton handed the two grenades to Sheila. She clutched them tight and he pulled the pins, just like Roland had done with Fred's.

"All right," Sheila said, resolute. "Let's make it hot."

Jorge unlocked the door and shoved it open with his foot. There were at least a dozen of the cannibals on the main landing and he let loose with his suppressed rifle as Cotton and Roland fired from behind him. They cut down the demons quickly enough, allowing Sheila to walk through the carnage, heading down the stairs and into a veritable ocean of the Wasted.

She felt a sudden stiffness in her joints, and a feeling in her muscles as if they were about to cramp. Her movements became slow and disjointed.

"Don't do this!" June Kennedy's voice echoed in her head.

The woman was trying to physically control her.

"Fuck you," Sheila snarled.

Nearly at the bottom of the stairs, one of the Wasted lunged for her, and in one smooth movement, she released the grenades, drew the FN 45 pistol, and fired two rounds into it at point blank range. She continued engaging the cannibals shambling toward her and she could see that the men at the top of the stairs were also peppering the first floor with 5.56 rounds.

Sheila felt the concussive blast of the grenades hit her and slam her body against the wall. For a moment, she flashed back to the explosion at Oatmeal when she'd leveled Roland Reese's house and was thrown back into the windshield of the car across the street.

She went out for only a split second, then sat up on the stairs and looked at the chaos that lay before her, bodies and body parts everywhere. Some of the Wasted were still alive, but they presented no threat. The blast had not produced much effect out into the street aside from confusion, but she had done what she needed to.

"Move! Move! Move!" Cotton shouted as he pushed Fred down the stairs behind Roland and Jorge.

The men were all firing as they moved, and once they hit the ground floor, they hooked to the right toward the long hallway they knew would take them to the sub-basement access.

Sheila unslung her AR and started firing into the advancing cannibals as the group moved past her and down the hallway. She walked backwards behind them, continuing to fire as she moved. The plan had been for her to stay behind and lead the Wasted away from them, but she now understood that was impossible. There was nowhere else for her to go. There were too many of them and they blocked any other possible exit.

The phone in Fred's pocket rang.

"Give me that," Jorge said gently, and reaching out, took the grenade from Fred's shaking hand.

He turned and threw it as hard as he could into the street, producing another blast that slowed the advancing horde.

Fred fished the phone out of her pocket.

"It's him!" she said, holding the phone out to Cotton.

Cotton took the phone and turned to where Roland was pulling on the door handle at the end of the hallway.

"Damn thing's locked!" Roland shouted.

"Well unlock it!" Cotton yelled back.

Roland looked at the keypad beside the heavy steel door. "It's some kind of computer-controlled system. Only way through this thing is to blow it out."

Cotton hit the button on the phone to accept the call. "Kind of busy right now!" he said.

"You're falling behind," Jared said from the other end. "If you don't get underground right now, you're going to be overrun."

"The door's on a networked lock, we can't get it open!"

"Get creative," Jared said. "Adapt and overcome."

"You want this guy alive, right?" Cotton said. "How about I put a bullet in his fucking head right now?

"We have no time!" Jorge shouted as the Wasted began streaming into the ground floor.

"Please!" Fred said in her best Doctor Wilson impersonation. "They're going to kill me."

"Fine," Jared said. He navigated on his smart tablet to the networked controls for city buildings and found the locks for the city utilities building. "But remember that I did this for you."

The door at the end of the hallway beeped, followed by a heavy clunk as the lock disengaged.

"You're clear," Jared said. "But getting through that

door isn't going to be the problem. You need to make sure they don't follow you in there. If they do, you won't make it ten feet in those tunnels. See you soon."

The line went dead.

"I didn't like that guy in Ramadi," Cotton grumbled, "and I don't like him now."

"Okay," Jean said as she looked up from her watch. "We're going in."

April set her jaw.

"There are a dozen reasons they could be out of contact," she said, "None of which involve a need for us to go in there, guns blazing."

"Look, I get what I said about 'scorched earth'," Jean said. "We're not really going to do that. We're gonna move low and slow to the near rally point inside the city. We're not going to engage unless we absolutely have to. We're doing this."

"She's right," Harris said. "I don't like it any more than you do, but if they really are backed up against a wall and we're just sitting here…"

"Do you really think they don't need help?" Jean asked. "Or are you still trying to protect me?"

April didn't get a chance to answer before a

series of explosions rocked the edge of the city about a kilometer from their location.

"Discussion over!" Jean shouted. "Saddle up! We're moving."

April didn't protest as she moved to the truck and climbed in the bed behind the M240 machine gun, doing a quick check of her feed tray and that her ammo was properly set up. Then she reached back and grabbed a length of tubular nylon, which she secured around her waist to lock herself in place. This had been Roland's idea to keep her stable if she was firing while the truck was moving.

Harris took his place behind the wheel and secured his seat belt before firing up the engine. Jean planted herself in the passenger seat, her LMT gun between her legs, barrel oriented down and ready for action.

Harris stopped and looked at her. "You should buckle up," he said. "For safety."

"I hate this," Gregory said as he turned the corner that would take them to the main entrance of the hospital.

"No one cares," Leslie said flatly.

Lebedev leaned forward in his seat as the

hospital entrance came within sight. "What is he doing?" he asked.

"He looks like a Doctor," Leslie replied.

In front of the hospital, a lone man was standing in the white coat traditionally worn by physicians. He even had the stethoscope around his neck, but he appeared shell-shocked and his clothes were filthy. He looked as if he had just lived through a war, because by any reliable measure of the word, he had.

He turned and looked at the van moving toward him, but he didn't show any sign of fear or even apprehension, specifically because he knew that the black-eyed cannibals did not drive vehicles.

The van stopped, and both Leslie and Lebedev exited into the street. Gregory stayed in the van with the engine running. Leslie walked around to the driver's side window and held out her hand.

"I don't think so," she said, "Keys. Now."

"I'm not going to run!" Gregory insisted.

"Give me those keys or you're going to meet Zoroaster the hard way."

"Fine," Gregory said as he handed Leslie the keys. "But don't come crying to me when your face is being eaten off."

"Won't have eyes," Leslie said. "Problem solved."

"Are you the rescue party?" the Doctor called out.

Lebedev looked to Leslie, implying it might be better if the first voice this man heard had an American accent.

"No," Leslie said. "Is that what you're waiting for? A rescue party?"

The Doctor walked a few more steps towards them and then stopped. "I've been sending up the green flares since it started," he said. "I thought someone would come."

"There's no one left to come," Gregory offered. "Sorry."

"You're the scientist," the Doctor said. "The one on Youtube. Doctor Wilson, right?"

Gregory looked uncomfortable, but nodded in affirmation.

"You work for the City State," the Doctor went on. "So you must know what's going on."

"That's how I know that no one is coming," Gregory repeated. "They're all gone. Only reason I made it is my floor was sealed off by the security system."

Leslie looked at the man's name tag.

"Doctor Freer?" Leslie asked.

"Yes," Doctor Freer replied. "I— I'm sorry. I

don't understand. What do you mean they're all gone?"

"Everyone is dead," Gregory said.

"I don't understand," Doctor Freer said, his voice wavering. "How is that possible? Two days ago, this was a thriving City State. How on earth is everyone dead?"

"The vaccine... it— it caused another mutation. It turned people into those black-eyed things. Anyone that didn't turn, they killed."

"Killed and ate," Gregory added, "to be more specific. Or maybe killed them by eating them."

Leslie gave Gregory a dirty look.

"Either way they're dead," he finished.

"No, it wasn't the vaccine," Doctor Freer said. "They developed that to fix this, to get us back to normal. We were going to get back to normal!"

"I understand," Leslie said softly and held up a hand. "I know that's what we all wanted to happen, but it isn't. Okay?"

Doctor Freer looked as if he were about to emotionally come apart, but then he reigned it in and nodded his head.

"Okay," he said. "I get it. Honestly, after everything that's happened here, I should understand better than anyone."

"What did happen here?" Lebedev asked, seeing an opening to let the Doctor know who he was.

Freer recognized the accent and took a step back.

"It's all right," Leslie said. "He's here to help."

"I heard on the radio," Freer said. "It's not just happening here. It's everywhere, even your people."

"You heard Russians?" Lebedev asked. "On the radio?"

"We have an emergency communications relay set up," Freer explained. "We can listen pretty far away. Your— your people are being overrun."

Lebedev said nothing.

"What happened here?" Leslie asked.

"It's better to show you," Freer replied. He reached into his pocket and retrieved a handful of surgical masks, which he held out to the three of them.

"I don't think the virus is a big concern at this point," Gregory said.

"It's not for the virus," Freer said. "It's for the smell."

Leslie looked past the Doctor, and for the first time saw that the windows at the front of the hospital were covered in blood.

. . .

The four walked into the main entrance of the hospital and stopped in their tracks. The place looked like a scene out of a nightmare—walls painted red with blood and bodies everywhere. At least, what was left of the bodies.

"I wanted to clean up," Doctor Freer said. "I did, but... I didn't even know where to start. You believe me, right?"

Leslie looked around for a moment longer, her brain unable to process what her eyes were seeing. Even in photos she had seen of real war, it had been nothing like this.

"Of course," she replied.

"People thought they should come here, when it started. I don't know why. I mean, I know it was one of the designated disaster shelters, but when they established those, they were thinking of something like a nuclear attack or an organized assault by marauders. No one was thinking of this." Freer looked around for a moment and then to Leslie. "We had one of those infectious disease wings they put together when the virus really blew up. No one gets in and no one gets out. Re-enforced plexiglass and heavy locks on the doors. I got in there with some of my patients and locked it down."

"It this the first time you've been out?" Lebedev asked.

"Yes," Freer replied. "When I saw your van driving down the street, I came down."

"So, there are others?" Leslie asked. "Other survivors?"

Freer's eyes went blank for a moment. "Upstairs."

Freer pulled the doors to the infectious disease wing open and led Gregory, Leslie, and Lebedev down a long hallway to another set of doors. He pulled these open as well and led them into a long, open ward.

There were no true survivors, this was obvious. Instead, there were rows of bodies covered in sheets lying in beds.

"What happened here?" Leslie asked quietly. "I thought you said you locked yourself in with your patients?"

"I— I did. But they were all terminal, and when they saw what was happening in the streets, when they saw what those things were doing to the people they caught." Freer hesitated for a moment. "They said that they couldn't go on. They asked me to..."

"Assisted suicide," Gregory surmised.

"I didn't want to," Freer went on. "But they begged me."

Cotton knelt inside of the secondary hallway that would take them into the sub-basement, keeping up a steady rate of fire to cover the others as they ran in through the open door. He was going through ammo too fast and he knew it. He'd come in with four mags in his chest rig and one in the gun, but he was already down to two remaining. There were another three magazines in his assault pack, but those wouldn't last long either if this kept up.

The bigger problem was the bodies piling up inside the outer doorway. Cotton knew there was no way they were going to be able to close it.

"Shit!" He cursed as he stood up, performed another speed reload, and walked backward toward the secondary door.

Roland pulled the second door open and looked down into the stairwell. "This is it!" he shouted. "We have to get the hell out of here now."

One of the Wasted slipped by Cotton in the open hallway and Jorge killed it at point blank range. He looked back at Roland. "We ain't gonna make it," he said flatly. "Not like this."

He was right. They were coming too fast, and by the time everyone made it through the door, the cannibals would just be piling up inside of it again and wedging it open.

Roland looked at Fred. She could already see it in his eyes.

"If we fail, it's the end of everything, isn't it?" he asked.

"I'm sorry," Fred said. She could feel tears welling up in her eyes.

Roland turned from the door, brought up his AR and started firing at a steady pace into the flow of cannibals.

Cotton moved back, thinking Roland was just doing some version of cover and move. He ran to the sub-basement door but then turned when he realized Roland wasn't following him.

"Let's go!" Cotton shouted as Sheila darted by him and through the open doorway.

"Get the hell out of here!" Roland called out. "Or this is for nothing!"

"You can't—"

Jorge grabbed Cotton forcefully and shoved him through the door, then slammed it behind them.

. . .

There seemed to be a never-ending flow of the things coming down the hallway toward Roland Reese as he walked backward, doing his best to make every shot count as he lined up his Aimpoint red dot, going for shots to the head in a desperate last stand. They were getting close enough now that he had to employ a "mechanical offset," putting his dot slightly above where he wanted his rounds to go.

Before Roland even understood what he was doing, his left hand reached to his radio and locked the device into "talk" mode.

"I don't know if anyone can hear me," Roland said. "But I'm pretty sure this is it. I ain't no quitter, but there's too many of these things."

Roland took another few steps to his rear and felt his back hit the door the rest of the group had gone through. He hit another reload and continued firing into the seemingly never-ending wave of black-eyed cannibals surging toward him. The way they were piling up, he briefly thought they might create a barrier in the hallway, but he knew that wasn't going to happen. He understood the ultimate truth of his current predicament.

. . .

Jean slid the cabin window of the truck open and turned up the volume on the radio, looking over to where April was strapped into the bed of the truck.

April heard Roland's voice coming over the radio, interspersed with the sounds of suppressed gunfire and the growling of the Wasted. Her eyes grew wide.

"—not sure what I'm saying," Roland's voice came over the radio. "Not even sure how much longer I have left to say it, but I need someone to hear it."

"I'm sorry," Jean said.

Cotton stopped in the tunnel they had descended into and put the radio to his ear. The signal was broken up by the concrete, but they were still close enough to the exit to pick up Roland's broadcast.

He turned to Fred, Jorge, and Sheila.

Sheila parted her lips as if to say something and then stopped. Cotton knew that she wanted to go back for Roland, he knew they had been friends. He also understood that Sheila was their only link to June Kennedy and the hordes of black-eyed cannibals out there. If she sacrificed herself to save Roland, they would be left in the dark with no options when the time came to face down that threat.

"I don't think I was ever a very good person," Roland's voice crackled from the radio. "I did some good things, I know I did, but doing a few good things don't make you a good guy."

"There's nothing we can do, is there?" Fred asked.

Cotton shook his head.

Doctor Freer stopped at the end of the Infectious Disease ward and picked up the city network radio that had started broadcasting Roland's call.

"Who is that?" Lebedev asked.

"I don't know," Freer replied.

Roland's voice emanated from the handset.

"Maybe there's one thing I can do," he said. "One thing big enough to make up for all the other things."

"He sounds like he's in a hell of a fight," Lebedev said.

"He must be close by," Leslie said. "If he's on the radio he can't be far away."

. . .

Jared pushed open the heavy double doors in the sub-basement that would lead into the utility tunnels beneath the city. Carrying the heavy pack along with the AX-50 and the 300 Blackout gun was starting to take a toll. He hadn't done this kind of work in quite a while, and he also wasn't a twenty-five-year-old Marine anymore.

The door was closing behind him when the radio clipped to his chest rig started transmitting. He stopped, turned to the closing door, and stuck his size twelve boot in it. He knew that once it closed, the signal he was receiving was likely to be cut off.

He stood in the semi-darkness, listening to the radio. He didn't know who the man speaking was, but he knew it was one of them. It wasn't the man he had spoken to on the phone, but it was clearly someone from the same group.

"Why are you doing this?" he said to himself.

Jared Foster grasped the dire nature of the man's situation, and he also knew that all this man had to do was turn and run through the unlocked door. Why wasn't he doing that?

"I've always been out for myself," Roland said finally. "Even when I was on the Teams, I was always out for myself, I just happened to be on a team. Maybe this is finally my chance to change that, even if it is the last thing I do."

Jared brought the radio up to his lips and prepared to key it but then stopped.

The bolt locked back on Roland's AR for the final time and he hit the quick disconnect button, letting it fall to the floor as he drew his Glock and fired his remaining rounds into the advancing horde. Soon, the Glock went out of battery and he dropped that as well, replacing it with his battle knife.

It was dark. He hadn't realized that it was so dark until the Wasted completely filled the hallway to the point that they blocked out what little light had been coming in from the outside. Then he felt the first set of hands grip his arm and he struck with the knife, hard enough to knock the creature back, but then another set of hands replaced those, and then another, and another and another. Then the teeth. He felt a hot wetness on him and realized it was his own blood.

Roland slammed his head forward into the nearest target and felt teeth breaking against his skull just as others sunk into other parts of his body. He continued striking with his knife and his fists until his arms went numb, and he finally slipped into the darkness.

Seeing that the street they were on was safe, Harris slowed the truck to a stop and looked back at April.

The woman was staring off into the distance.

"You okay?" he asked.

April blinked her eyes rapidly and then rubbed at them for a moment before taking a breath.

"I'm fine," she said. "We can't just sit here. Whatever he was doing was important, and we need to make sure it wasn't in vain."

"We'll head to the hospital," Jean said. "That place they were at, they've left it now."

INTERLUDE 2

June Kennedy stopped in the woods she had walked into and stared into the darkness of the trees. The canopy was thick enough that it nearly blocked out the sun, and the darkness was cool on her skin. This was noticeable because the constant surging adrenaline kept her hot all the time.

Then she felt it. The eyes on her. She looked back and saw the seemingly endless ocean of her children, of the other black-eyed cannibals that had followed her. She turned back to the darkness of the trees.

"Who's there?" she called out. "Who is it?

A figured stepped out of the darkness, or rather, the darkness became a figure. She stood tall in the shadows, her hair falling in dark waves around her bare shoulders.

"Who are you?" June asked.

"More like you than not," the figure responded.

June tried to look into this creature's eyes, but could not seem to see them.

"I ask again," she said. "Who are you?"

"My name does not matter. What you do next, does."

"What I do next?" June echoed.

"You're busy playing war games with the Russians, when the real threat lies to the south. You let them go once."

"Sheila," June surmised. "And her people."

"Will end you," the figure in the darkness said. "If you let them."

"She isn't strong enough," June said.

"Not yet," the figure replied. "But her power grows. While you grow weaker."

"Weaker?" June asked, confused.

The figure held out her hand and then nodded to June's own.

June looked at the back of her hand, and more specifically the veins crawling across it. They were grey.

"What is happening?" She asked.

"You're like an engine that's been running too hot for too long," the figure in the darkness said softly. Look at your children, really look at them."

June turned again and looked at the horde that covered the landscape behind her. The figure was right. They had changed in the past day. Many of them appeared gaunter than they had, the pink hue of their skin giving way to a washed out grey.

She turned back to the figure. "How long do we have?"

"Not long," the figure said. "You're weaker by the hour. Even if you continue to find more food, as you feed, your ranks expand. Starvation is inevitable."

"Then... what is our purpose?"

"To feed the void," the figure replied. "To dwindle the ranks of man and replenish them with your grandchildren."

"Why the grandchildren? Why not us?"

"Don't you see?" the figure asked with a shrouded smile. "The role of the parent is to set the table for the children. You were never meant to be forever."

"I see," June said.

In a flash, it made sense to her. The Wasted did not require nearly as much sustenance as the original black-eyed cannibals. They were meant to be the new race, not her and her children. There was a brief moment of sadness coupled with this realization, but it quickly faded to be replaced by a new sense of purpose.

"She is the threat," the figure said. "Your daughter. She must be stopped."

June nodded her understanding.

"We will head south," June said. "And finish this."

"You will meet your destiny there," the figure replied, then stepped forward and revealed herself in the dim light of the woods.

June looked, and saw that it was a darker reflection of herself.

CHAPTER 8

"What in the hell is that?" Leslie asked as she stood at one of the windows, looking down on the main avenue approaching the hospital.

Lebedev, Freer, and Gregory Wilson joined her to watch the Toyota truck barreling toward the front entrance.

"Does that truck have a machine gun in it?" Gregory asked.

"I do believe it does," Freer said.

Harris pulled the truck to a stop beside what looked like a City of Houston Animal Control van.

They had still met no resistance. Not only that,

but once they had moved deeper into the city, they had not seen a single one of the Wasted.

"Where the hell are they all?" April asked. "I thought there were supposed to be thousands?"

"I don't know about you," Jean replied. "But I'm not anxious to find out."

The young girl opened the passenger side door and stepped out into the street with her rifle at the low ready. Harris and April followed suit, and the trio moved toward the front doors.

"Something happened here," Jean said as she saw the blood-smeared windows. "And it may not be over. Be ready."

"I got it," Harris said as he slung his rifle behind his back and worked his fingers into the small opening between the two sliding doors.

Putting as much strength as he could bring to bear into the task, he pried the doors apart until they created an opening that the three of them could slip through.

"Jesus!" April gasped as they entered the main lobby and saw the carnage that had unfolded there.

Across the lobby, the stairway door opened and Leslie and Doctor Freer entered the room.

"Stop!" Jean shouted as she brought her rifle up.

Leslie kept her shotgun lowered, but Doctor Freer raised his hands.

"We're not here to hurt you!" Doctor Freer called out. "We're on the same side!"

"What side is that?" Jean asked.

"The human side," Leslie replied.

Jean could see from the woman's eyes that she had never been vaccinated, and so she lowered her weapon. Being human didn't necessarily mean she wasn't a threat, but it was a good starting point.

Doctor Freer pushed the doors to the infectious disease ward open and Jean, April, Leslie, and Harris followed him in.

Lebedev turned to the group and met eyes with Jean.

The girl stopped in her tracks and brought her weapon up to the low ready.

"He's with us!" Leslie said quickly.

"He's a Russian!" Jean shot back.

"Siberian," Lebedev said. "Originally." He paused for a moment. "I'm no friend of America, just so we're clear. I've trained my entire life with the idea that I might someday be part of a movement strong enough and righteous enough to bring you and your people to their knees."

"Not exactly winning us over here," April said.

"But this is bigger than that," Lebedev went on, as if April had not spoken. "And I think you know that."

"You're talking about the EMP," Harris interjected.

Lebedev looked to Gregory Wilson and then back to Harris.

"You know about this?" Lebedev asked.

"Not all of it," April said. "But we know enough. We're just looking for some Doctor Wilson."

Gregory Wilson's face changed, and it did not escape Jean's attention.

"It's him," Jean said. "You're Doctor Wilson, aren't you?"

"You can see, right?" Fred asked in the darkness as they walked through the service tunnel.

"Yes," Cotton replied. He and Jorge had been navigating with their night vision units since descending into the tunnel. "And more importantly, I can also hear. Just like anyone else in these tunnels can hear you and find us if you keep running your mouth."

"What about you?" Jorge asked Sheila, albeit more quietly as they walked. "You can still see?"

"I can," Sheila replied.

After the door to the hallway had closed, Sheila had quickly realized that she could still see in the near total darkness, most likely with the same level of acuity that both Cotton and Jorge enjoyed with their night vision devices.

Cotton turned to the wall of the tunnel and saw that someone had stenciled the words "Fulbright Building" with an arrow on it. "Well, that's convenient," he said, pointing out the indicator for Jorge.

"How far you think?" Jorge asked.

"Jared said a thousand meters east," Cotton replied. "Figure we've already gone two hundred, so not long at this point."

The four moved forward for several more minutes, careful to move tactically and not be in a hurry to potentially meet their own demise. Ahead of them, Cotton could see the tunnel branching off into two different routes. Water was flowing through pipes overhead and the noise sounded almost as if they were standing beneath a waterfall.

He looked back to Jorge. "I'm pretty sure we go

right," Cotton said, moving ahead and pivoting to the right.

The former SEAL stumbled backward as he came face to face with a growling horde of the Wasted, but they were stopped by a chain-link fence.

"Belay my last!" Cotton shouted.

The rest of the group rounded the corner and saw what Cotton had.

"Definitely not right," Jared said from out of the darkness. "And before any of you starts thinking about getting squirrely, I've got a mag full of 220 grain and bad intentions."

Cotton knew that, even under NODs, there was no chance he could find Jared in the darkness, put his laser on him, and put the Marine down faster than he'd be put down himself. Instead, he let his weapon drop to sling retention and raised his hands. Jorge looked at him, and Cotton nodded that he should do the same.

Cotton looked at Sheila and saw her eyes narrow.

"Don't do it!" Cotton said. "We've still got a chance here."

"And what are you?" Jared asked, directing the question at Sheila.

"The future," Sheila replied, echoing June's words.

"I guess that would make the rest of us the past, right?" Jared asked. "The next step down on the evolutionary ladder?"

"Call it what you like," Sheila said. "But this isn't going to go the way you think it is."

"I'll give you that," Jared replied. "And yes, you may kill me, but not before I kill them. Is that a deal you're willing to make?"

Sheila said nothing.

"That's what I thought," Jared said. "This doesn't have to be a bloodbath. All you have to do is hand over Doctor Gregory." He paused. "But since I don't see him with you, I'm starting to think I've been had."

"He ran out of the building," Cotton said. "When we were overrun. I'm sure you heard our friend on the radio."

"I did hear him," Jared said. He hesitated for a moment. "Why did he do that?"

"Do what?" Cotton asked.

"He could have gone through the door with you after I opened it. You might have all made it. Why did he stay in the hallway?"

"This is bigger than him," Cotton said. "He

knew that. He also knew that if he stayed in that hallway to hold them off, we'd make it."

"You know about the EMP, don't you?" Jared asked.

"We do," Fred replied. "And Gregory might be the only person able to stop it."

Cotton had picked up Jared in the darkness about one hundred yards away, and now, he watched the man through his night vision.

Jared activated the laser on his 300 Blackout gun and put it on Cotton's chest. He reached for his push-to-talk and triggered it.

"This is Jared," he said. "Put me through to Mister Rampart."

"You don't have to do this," Cotton said. "We can find a way to make it work."

"I can take him," Sheila said quietly.

"No," Cotton replied. "This guy's too fast. He'll kill us all."

"Yes, Sir," Jared said. "I found them." In the darkness, he looked into Cotton's eyes. "But I lost them in the tunnels. They ran right into a horde. There's no way they made it, but I'll see if I can find the remains. Yes, Sir. Doctor Gregory, too."

Jared released the PTT and then powered down his radio. He walked toward the group.

"Why did you do that?" Fred asked.

Jared seemed to think about this for a moment before replying. "Everyone thinks I'm a psychopath, and they're right. But that doesn't mean I can't make my own decisions."

"Thank you," Cotton said.

"I wasn't always a piece of shit," Jared replied. "I thought I was working for the good guys. This whole time."

"Might not be any 'good guys' left," Jorge said. "Maybe just some of the monsters are better than others."

Jared smiled, pulling what looked like a small strobe from his chest rig, and walked to the chain link fence that separated them from the horde of the growling Wasted. He activated a small IR strobe, then threw it through the fence and into the churning mass of black-eyed cannibals.

"My distress beacon," Jared said. "They'll pick it up from the drone, see all the heat signatures around it and think I'm dead."

"Then what?" Jorge asked. "We can always use another monster on the team."

"You could do some good," Cotton added.

Jared shook his head. "Nah. Think I'll just hang out in the city for a while. Maybe go north and kill

Russians. Or south and kill Chinese. Hell, any direction I go, I figure there'll be some folks worth killing."

"Would it be pushing it to ask a favor?" Cotton asked.

"Shoot," Jared said.

"We've got a near rally point at the County Hospital. Can we get there from here or do we have to go to street level?"

"I'll take you," Jared said. "Just follow me."

"Why do you want him?" Colonel Maxim Lebedev asked April.

"All I know is this woman we're traveling with thinks he knows how to stop all this, or at least slow it down."

"What woman?" Gregory asked.

"Fred," April said. "Or, I guess, you would know her as Frederique Van Sant."

"You're with Doctor Van Sant?" Gregory asked, surprise on his face. "She's alive?"

"She was out in a town called Tow," April went on. "Now she says there might be an EMP coming and you would be the person to figure out how to stop it."

Gregory's face fell. "I'm sorry to be the one to inform you," he said. "But I'm the one that caused it."

"They're coming back," Harris said from where he had taken up position next to the windows.

"What?" Doctor Freer asked. He walked to the window and looked down to the street several stories below.

The Wasted were wandering back down the street toward the main entrance.

"Can they get in here?" Leslie asked.

"No," Doctor Freer said and shook his head. "Once the doors are closed, they're sealed. They tried before but they couldn't get through the glass. We're safe up here."

"You need to come with us," Jean said, addressing Doctor Wilson. "So you can help Fred stop this."

"I already told you," Gregory said. "You can't stop it. New Orleans has the package now, with the code they need to deploy the EMP."

"New Orleans?" April asked.

"That's where Fluid Dynamics is head quartered now. I've been working for the CEO Bill Rampart on this project to— to develop the EMP."

"Why in the hell would you think that was a good idea?" Leslie snapped.

"I'm sorry!" Gregory shouted. "He was very convincing. He said it was the only chance we had against the Russians and the Chinese."

Everyone looked to Lebedev, who then shrugged.

"He was probably right about that," the Russian said. "Up until very recently, this invasion was all but over. If Americans truly do have a weapon of this magnitude, it would change things. The prospect of shutting down the entire world's power grid would be unthinkable."

Gregory shifted his feet where he stood, clearly beginning to perspire. Lebedev looked at him more closely.

"What aren't you telling us?" Lebedev asked.

"It's about more than shutting down the power grid," Gregory said. "I'm good at building engines, but I always had trouble with the breaks, you know? That was why Fred and I were such a good team. When I built the EMP script for Mister Rampart I figured out how to chain together every satellite still active and send out a unified electromagnetic pulse, but I couldn't figure out how to throttle it."

"It only has one level," Jean said, understanding what he was implying.

Gregory nodded. "It won't just fry the power grid," he said. "It's way more powerful than that."

"How powerful?" Leslie asked.

"Your heart runs on electrical signals," Gregory explained.

Doctor Freer's eyes became wide. "Are you saying what I think you are?" the physician asked.

"It might stop a lot of people's hearts," Gregory said.

"Why would you make something like that?" April shouted.

"I didn't know all of this was going to happen!" Gregory protested. "I thought I'd fix it when I got to New Orleans! Sending the package was the only way I could get them to come pick me up!"

"Except they didn't," Lebedev reminded him. "They tried to kill you."

"Yeah," Gregory said. "I guess they did."

"We have a problem here!" Harris called out.

"A bigger problem than this?" April asked.

"Potentially," Harris replied.

April and the rest of the group walked to the bay of windows, looking down on the street leading to the front door, and saw a group of the black-eyed cannibals carrying what looked like a large flagpole.

"What are they doing?" April asked.

Gregory saw that they were also looking into the

windows of the van and truck that were parked at the front.

"Learning," he said.

The group of cannibals carrying the flagpole walked forward and slammed it into the glass of the front door.

"They're not zombies," Jean said. "We keep thinking of them like they're zombies, but they're not. They're still people, they're just slow. It takes them time to figure things out, but they can do it."

"That means they'll get in here," April said.

Jean looked to the woman.

"Which means we can't be here when they do."

"How many rounds in the 240?" Harris asked, indicating the heavy machine gun mounted in the back of the truck.

"At least two thousand, linked," April replied, but then shook her head. "No."

"I can make it," Harris said. "Look how we parked the truck under the awning. I can get on it from the second-floor window, then get in the bed of the truck and get on that gun. I can open up enough of a path for the rest of you to get to the vehicles."

"We can't leave," Doctor Freer interjected. "This is the safest place in the city and help still might come! I've been sending up flares!"

Colonel Lebedev turned to Doctor Freer and his eyes went cold.

"You don't get it, do you?" Lebedev asked.

"Get what?" Freer asked.

"No one is coming! Our only hope is to get out of this place!"

"No," Freer said, shaking his head. It was clear the man was not thinking rationally. "Someone will come. Someone always comes."

"How very 'American' of you," Lebedev said with a smile, as if he were trying to explain something to a dull child. "You always think that there will be some magical way to make everything okay. Perhaps that is why all of you are in this situation to begin with. Well, Doctor, I am sorry to be the one to tell you this, but there will be no Santa Claus coming to your rescue, no Cary Grant to ride with you into the sunset.

"Cary Grant?" Leslie asked. "How old are you?"

"Old enough to know that the world is not fair," Lebedev said, and then looked to the rows of patients in their beds. "And old enough to know that everyone dies. Some sooner than others."

. . .

Bill Rampart leaned back in his overstuffed leather chair and looked out his window at 2000 Opelousas Avenue, the former location of the 4th Marine Division. The base had served as the headquarters of the Marine Reserve Force, and once things had begun truly falling apart, Bill had moved to reposition the headquarters of Fluid Dynamics at this location. It was a far cry from the flagship building in New York City, but the world had changed and Fluid Dynamics had to change with it.

Outside, an armored vehicle drove by with a jeep behind it, and Bill silently wondered to himself how long this garrison with only a few hundred men to protect it could hold out if the Russians or Chinese found them.

That was why he'd needed the EMP that Doctor Wilson developed. It was brilliant, because it required no hardware. It would simply link up all of the satellites still orbiting Earth and use them to send a pulse so devastating that it would knock out every electrical device on the planet.

Including theirs. That had been a bit of a problem, but according to Doctor Wilson there was no way around it. An EMP of this magnitude, if you wanted it, was an "all or nothing" type of proposal. So, Bill Rampart chose "all."

While all the equipment on site had been "ruggedized" against EMP attack, Doctor Wilson had gone to great pains to make sure Bill understood it would not matter.

"This EMP will tear through everything in its path," Doctor Wilson had said. "Nothing will be safe."

With that in mind, Bill had begun retrofitting everything for the possibility of a true "grid down" scenario, including training their soldiers to fight on horseback. Every facility on the base even had a supply of kerosene lanterns.

If the invasion of America continued to progress as it had over the previous weeks, there would eventually come a point where Bill would conference call the Presidents of Russia and China, and deliver an ultimatum that he never in his lifetime thought he would.

Retreat or die.

The door to Bill's office opened, and Colonel Fisker entered. He stopped at the threshold, realizing that in his haste he hadn't knocked.

"It's fine," Bill said, waving away the potential disrespect. "What is it?"

"It's Jared," Fisker said. "I— I think we've lost him."

"Lost him?" Bill asked, obviously confused. "I just talked to him on Sat Com."

"I know," Fisker said and set a smart tablet down on Bill's desk with the active ISR feed for the Houston operation on display. "That's his IR beacon."

Bill looked at the screen and cocked his head to the side.

"What is that all around him?" Bill asked.

"Secondary infections," Fisker replied.

Bill looked up at the Colonel. "Does this mean what I think it does?" he asked.

"I know that you were close," Fisker said. "This can't be easy to hear, but I don't see how he could escape that. Even if he is still alive."

Bill looked back to the screen and lingered there for a moment longer. "We've lost so many people," Bill said. "I should be used to it by now."

"You never get used to it," Fisker replied. "I've lost more men than I care to count, going all the way back to the early days of Afghanistan. It never gets any easier. Because it shouldn't."

Bill looked back to the Colonel. "I'm not going to send your men into that city," he said. "Jared should have made it. Even on his own. If anyone was going to, he should have."

"Then what's the next move?" Fisker asked.

Rampart threw up his hands.

"I know it sounds anti-climactic, but we wait. I have a high degree of confidence that Doctor Wilson was either killed in the building or in that blast. If he somehow got out and it had anything to do with the Russians who flew that helicopter in, I don't see how they make it out of the city."

"There's another play," Fisker offered.

"Which is?"

"Rouge One."

Bill tapped one of his fingers on the desk and then looked out the window. "I've heard the rumors," he said. "That people think I may be becoming unhinged." He looked back to Colonel Fisker. "Do you think that's true?"

The Colonel was clearly surprised by the question.

"No, Sir. I don't."

"But you're asking me to task a renegade nuclear submarine, essentially a band of pirates, with launching an attack on American soil."

"What if the men on that Russian helicopter did, in fact, pull off the impossible and survive the explosion? It wouldn't take long for the Russians to extract the information they need from Doctor Wilson.

Then we would have a gun to our head that would be impossible to overcome." Fisker paused. "Rouge One has other options as well."

"Such as?"

"A conventional missile strike. It would not be as... extreme as a nuclear strike, but would get the job done. We would also have plausible deniability. The city is, after all, overrun by black-eyed cannibals. The public is afraid right now of what's happening."

Bill understood. "It will help us keep New Orleans in line," he worked out.

"Show them what happens," Fisker said. "When the people don't trust the government."

"Is that who we are now?" Bill asked. "There are almost certainly still Americans left alive in that city."

"I get it," Fisker said. "Really, I do. I'm not some crazy super villain in a comic book. What I am is a man who understands what happens in war, and the inevitable cost of ultimate victory. Make no mistake, we are at war. On multiple fronts. The odds of us just surviving the next week say nothing of victory are astronomical. Now is not the time to hem and haw about what is, in reality, a fairly minor amount of collateral damage." Fisker paused and then added, "With respect."

"I understand," Bill said. "And as always, I value your council. Perhaps sometimes, the truth is just hard to accept."

"This is a very bad idea," Doctor Freer urged as Harris crawled out the second-floor window and onto the massive awning that covered the front entrance to the hospital.

"I know," April replied. "But it's the best bad idea we've got."

Harris tested the length of tubular nylon that he had used to secure himself to a pipe inside of the room. He then looked down at the growing horde of the Wasted swirling below. As of yet, they seemed not to have taken notice of him.

"I'll be honest," Harris said with a weak smile. "I'm starting to rethink this, too.

"It'll work," April reassured him. "Just get that gun going as soon as you hit the truck. You only have to hold out for thirty or so seconds and then we'll be out the front door and getting the engine going.

"I agree with him," Lebedev said dryly. "This plan wouldn't even pass the logic test in the old Soviet Union, and that bar was set pretty low."

"Not helping!" April snapped.

"Sorry," Lebedev shrugged, and then became more serious. "I'll do my part. I'll keep those things off of you while you're getting to the truck. You can count on me."

"You a good shot with that?" Harris asked, indicating Lebedev's suppressed rifle.

"We'll find out," Lebedev replied.

"Remember," Jean said and looked at Doctor Freer. "Once he clears the way, we're going to make a break for it, find my father and the others, and then we'll come back for you."

"Will you, though?" Freer asked. "I'm not sure I'd come back for you, not through all of that."

"Let's hope we don't have to find out," Jean said as she performed a final brass check on her rifle and tapped each magazine that was secured in her chest rig.

"I'm sorry," Freer said.

"For what?" Jean asked.

"All of this," he said. "We screwed up. We all did. We pushed that damn vaccine through so fast... we should have known better."

"No one could have known this was going to happen," Jean said.

Freer shook his head. "I pushed it hard," he said. "I was really— I should have known better. If we had just left the virus alone, never in a million years would it have done what the cure did."

"No use cryin' over it now," Jean said. "And if you're looking for forgiveness, you're barking up the wrong tree. Only the man upstairs can give you that."

"I... I don't believe," he said. "I was just never the church going type."

Jean looked out the window at the ever-increasing mass of the Wasted.

"Well, if I were you, and you had a mind to start praying, I'd get crackin'," she said. "Because that down there sure looks like the end of days to me."

"We have to go," April said as Harris worked his way to the edge of the awning and gave them the sign that he was about to make his descent.

"This is it," Jared said as they rounded another corner and he pointed out the marking on the tunnel wall.

It read: HARRIS COUNTY HOSPITAL

Cotton turned to the man in the darkness.

"You don't have to go," Cotton said. "We really can always use another gun in this thing."

Jared smiled. "I don't fit in with people," he

said. "That's why I did what I did in Ramadi, and that's why I'm doing what I am now. I'm better on my own. I tried to fit in while I was working for Mister Rampart because I thought we could do some good. Maybe I should have just stuck with my nature."

"Apocalypses doesn't have much use for lone wolves," Jorge said. "If you want to survive, it's best to have people. Have a team."

"Says the man selling a team concept," Jared said with a wink as he turned and walked away. "It's only about a hundred more meters. You'll hit some access doors and come out in the hospital sub-basement."

"You think he's gonna make it?" Jorge asked as the four worked their way through the access tunnels toward the near rally point at the hospital.

"Jared?" Cotton asked.

"Yeah. I mean, I heard the stories just like everyone else did. I know the guy's a heavy hitter, but you think he can stay alive in this city on his own?"

"If anybody can, it's him," Cotton said. "For now, I'll settle for keeping us alive."

"It's a long shot, you know," Fred said. "That

Gregory's at that hospital. Just because someone's sending up flares doesn't mean he's with them."

Cotton stopped and turned to Fred. "You're scared," he said.

"Scared doesn't even begin to cover it," Fred replied. "I don't know what the hell I was thinking when I volunteered to come with you. Maybe I thought I was going to be a hero or something. Stupid."

"You were right," Jorge said. "If you hadn't been with us, we never would have connected with Jared. Even though he was trying to kill us, he got us out of that building in one piece. That was because of you."

"And odds are pretty good," Cotton went on. "That if I'm the first one this Doctor Wilson sees, he'll get spooked and run, at best. You're going to be a familiar face."

"We weren't exactly drinking buddies," Fred said, then shook her head. "I know you're right. I just... I just want to go home. I just want this to be over."

"This is how you get home," Sheila offered. "Just keep going forward."

Cotton turned and started walking again, then felt his boot hit something. He looked down and saw a blurred image through the intensifier tubes. He reached up, dialing his focus ring until the image became clear.

"Stop," he said.

Sheila looked down, then she peered deeper into the tunnel.

"Jesus," she said. "How many do you think there are?"

Cotton hesitated a moment before he answered, "Hundreds."

"Hundreds of what?" Fred asked, the panic rising in her voice.

Cotton gripped her arm in the darkness. "I need you to calm down," he said softly. "It's nothing that can hurt you."

"What is it?" Fred insisted.

"Dead bodies," Jorge answered. "It's hundreds of dead bodies, and we're going to have to walk through them to get where we need to go."

"I can't do this!" Fred said.

"Hey," Sheila said and touched Fred's shoulder. "I want you to walk with me, okay? You can close your eyes if you need to. It won't matter because you can't see anything anyway. You're going to feel some lumps on the ground, but you just have to move past them to get home again."

There was silence for a moment and then Fred reached out and took Sheila's hand.

Cotton looked at Sheila through his night vision, seeing that the woman was doing her best to keep Fred calm, and he watched the pair walk forward into the depths of the massacre.

CHAPTER 9

HARRIS HIT the bed of the truck hard, much harder than he thought he would. His shoulder struck the back of the cabin, and he felt something pop, but he endeavored to pay it no mind as he rolled up to a kneeling position and checked the feed tray on the heavy machine gun. It was loaded and ready to go.

Staying on track, he did just as he'd been instructed to, which included not getting too focused on what was directly around him, as it would only distract him from getting the 240 on target. Despite Lebedev's attempts at dry humor, Harris trusted that the big Russian would be watching his back, and this trust was soon rewarded with the sound of a 5.45 round zipping past his head and knocking back the black-eyed cannibal that had been about to take a bite out of him.

Harris traversed the gun to his left and worked the trigger, unable to hold back a smile as he drove the 7.62 rounds into the advancing horde, shredding them like a hot knife through butter. He'd never fired a machine gun before, and definitely not something as powerful as the 240 Bravo. It took a moment to get the hang of managing the recoil and staying on target, but once he did, he knew they were about to be home free.

"Are you ready for this?" Jean asked as she stood inside the main lobby with April. "It's about to get real."

"I'm freaking terrified."

"Good," Jean said. "Then you're not insane. Just stick to the plan. I'll keep them off your back while you get the engine going and then we're getting the hell out of here. Just ten more seconds."

Colonel Maxim Lebedev kept up a steady rate of fire from the second story window, and true to his word, he was knocking down every one of the Wasted that tried to get at the man in the back of the truck.

He sincerely hoped they were going to get this over with in a timely manner, as the way the horde in the street was building, he would run out of bullets before they ran out of numbers.

Click.

Lebedev's left hand slammed into the bottom of the magazine, he worked the charging handle and pulled the trigger again.

Click.

The weapon had experienced a catastrophic malfunction. Lebedev's blood ran cold as he realized there was no time to fix the problem. It was already too late.

Harris felt a hand grab his shoulder, then saw a cannibal crawl into the bed of the truck from the other side.

His cover fire was gone. He knew it was.

He dropped the grip of the 240, drew his Glock, turned, and fired two rounds into the Black-Eyed Cannibal he was now face-to-face with. Others continued crawling up the side of the truck as he began firing in seemingly every direction.

. . .

"Now! Now! Now!" Jean shouted as she ran to the lobby door and pulled it open.

One of the Wasted was already at the entrance and lunged for the girl as she worked, but was met by a round from April's AR.

Jean recovered quickly, brought her weapon up, and moved into the Main Street, already hitting targets as she walked.

"Stay calm!" Jean shouted. "Get him out of that truck!"

"What in the hell is happening?" Leslie shouted as she ran into the second story room to find Lebedev disassembling his rifle.

"I've almost got it fixed!" he shouted. "Start shooting out the window!"

"It's a shotgun!" Leslie protested, knowing her slugs wouldn't be particularly accurate at that range.

"I don't care if it's a potato gun!" Lebedev shot back. "Start killing those things!"

Leslie did as she was told, moved to the window, and began firing into the throngs of the Wasted.

. . .

Harris performed a speed reload as he stood in the bed of the truck and fired again but then felt a strong pair of jaws clamp down on his left arm. The pain was electric, and he felt a cold shot of fear race up his spine.

He turned, put the barrel of the pistol to the creature's head, and pulled the trigger. There were a dozen more right behind it. He fired every round he had left into the advancing horde and then felt the unmistakable sensation of the slide on his Glock 17 locking back.

That was it. No more rounds. He drew his knife and prepared to fight hand-to-hand. He knew that he had no chance of winning this, or even surviving, but he sure as hell wasn't going to just lay down and die.

"Get out of the truck!"

Harris whipped his head to the left and saw Jean and April charging toward him through the Wasted, firing as they moved, hitting their targets. The horde that was coming toward him were receiving the brunt of it, opening enough of a hole for him to jump out of the bed of the truck and into the road. He turned toward the hospital and started moving when he felt a sensation like being hit in the leg with a baseball bat. He collapsed to the pavement and looked down at his leg.

He had been shot.

"Oh my God!" Leslie screamed from the second-floor window. "I'm so sorry!"

"Are you freaking kidding me!" Harris shouted.

"Sit up!" Jean ordered as she approached Harris and handed him her rifle. "Keep them off us!"

April slung her own rifle and the two women each grabbed one shoulder strap on Harris's chest rig, dragging him toward the hospital entrance as he fired. He was leaving a trail of blood as he went, but he knew there had been no time to even apply a hasty tourniquet. He would just have to hope he had enough blood left in him to survive the next minute or two.

"They're not going to make it," Lebedev said from his shooting position in the second-floor room.

He had gotten his rifle back into action and begun firing back into the crowd of the black-eyed cannibals, but he could see what perhaps no one else could. They would be able to reach the lobby again, but they would never get the doors closed in time to stop the throngs of the Wasted from flooding the hospital.

"We'll lose the hospital," Leslie realized.

"Come on," Lebedev ordered. "We're heading down. Once they're inside, we have to get those doors closed. Do you think if we're close enough, you can avoid shooting any more of us?

"I hate you right now," Leslie said, trying to hide the fear in her voice.

Harris kept up a steady rate of fire as Jean and April dragged his two-hundred-pound frame through the main hospital entrance. His leg was throbbing, and his vision was beginning to blur as blood continued flowing from his left leg.

He didn't think it was an arterial bleed, as it wasn't spraying enough, but he also knew he didn't have long before there would be enough blood loss that he might even start to go hypothermic.

"We have to get those doors closed!" April shouted as they leaned Harris against the reception desk.

Jean took her rifle back and handed Harris her Glock 19. She then quickly applied a CAT tourniquet to his leg as he worked to control his breathing. Harris looked at the double doors and watched the Wasted walking through them.

He grabbed Jean's arm.

"I appreciate what you're trying to do here," he said, his voice strangely calm as he looked her in the eyes. "But you can't win this one. You need to get back upstairs and barricade yourselves in. I know what I have to do."

Jean looked at the gun in his hand and then back to the former insurance salesmen.

"No," Jean said. "That's not how this ends."

The girl stood up, turned toward the entrance, raised her weapon, and began taking what amounted to point blank shots at the Cannibals flooding the main entrance. Then, her shots seemed to suddenly multiply.

Harris looked over his shoulder and saw the Russian coming out through the stairway door and into the lobby with the girl, Leslie. He was firing rapidly into the crowded entrance along with April, who had taken up a firing position behind the counter.

Jean slung her rifle and grabbed the sliding door to her right, counting on the others to keep putting down the wave of cannibals coming at her, but she knew it was to no avail. They were falling all around her and there was no way she could pull the door shut.

She took a step back and then for some reason... she looked up.

A handle was hanging from the threshold: the security gate.

"I need a stool!" Jean screamed.

Harris looked up and saw the same handle that Jean had, silently wondering how no one had noticed it before. The man stumbled to his feet and walked forward, firing the pistol Jean had given him as he advanced on the swarm of black-eyed things coming at them.

"What are you doing?" Jean asked.

"You didn't leave me," Harris said. "I ain't leaving you!"

The man dropped down to his hands and knees.

"Get up!" he ordered.

Jean understood. She stepped up onto Harris's back. The load was almost too much for the man to bear in his injured state, and he had the distinct feeling that his left leg was about to break under the pressure of the girl's relatively minor weight.

Jean reached up, grabbed the handle, and then stepped off of Harris, letting her weight drag the emergency gate down until she fell on her rear end on the floor. Lebedev, Leslie, and April had run to the entrance to help, pulling the bodies of the

Wasted they had shot out of the way as Jean and Harris pulled the gate into position and secured it with the latches in the floor.

The five of them stepped back and watched as a tidal wave of the black-eyed cannibals collided with the emergency gate, but could not get through.

"That's weird," Jared said to himself as he stood atop the parking structure he had walked up to in order to get a better vantage point of the city.

He could see the black-eyed cannibals filtering back into the streets from wherever they had been. This obviously begged the question as to whether or not it had been a good idea to potentially back himself into a corner atop the parking structure.

Instead of worrying about things beyond his control, however, the Marine pulled out his small tablet as well as the mobile antenna and wired it together, then activated it in what the tech-heads had deemed "stealth mode." Now, he could be on the net with New Orleans and track what was happening without leaving any digital fingerprints.

<<NOCS ASSET PROTECTON>>

<<OUTGOING TARGET PACKAGE>>
<<RECIPIENT: ROUGE ONE>>>

"What the hell?" Jared asked himself.

A target package going to Rouge One could only mean they were going to launch on Houston. Nothing else made sense, not even going after the Russians or the Chinese. He had been the contingency, and when he had seemingly "failed," Bill Rampart had decided to do the unthinkable. At worst, Houston was about to become a mushroom cloud, and at best, it would be decimated by a flurry of cruise missiles. Either option wasn't something he should probably hang around to witness.

Then he thought about the four he had run into in the tunnels, and that they were heading to the hospital in an attempt to locate Doctor Wilson.

Jared pulled the phone from his cargo pocket and dialed the number for the woman, Fred. He still felt conflicted about having turned his back on Mister Rampart, but in his gut he knew it was the right thing to do. If he was going to help these people, he might as well be all in and tell them to get the hell out of the city.

He waited as the phone rang over and over again, but no one picked up.

"Why aren't you answering?"

"I can't believe I didn't bring some way to charge this," Fred bemoaned as she looked at the dead phone in her hand.

She hadn't accounted for how much power the calls through the city network would suck up, and when she retrieved it from her pocket to again attempt to pinpoint Doctor Wilson's location, it had effectively become a brick.

"Don't matter," Jorge said as they closed in on the heavy double doors on the right of the tunnel with the words "Hospital Entrance" stenciled over them. "We're here. If we don't find him at the hospital, it's time to cut our losses and get the hell out."

"What about the EMP?" Fred asked.

"We can only do what we can do," Cotton said. "We've already run into more resistance than we were counting on, and we've already lost a good man. I understand the importance of stopping this thing, but I'm not willing to lose more people over it."

"I can stay," Fred said.

"What?" Sheila asked.

"In the city," Fred said. "If we— if we can find a place for me to lay low and get some power to get my phone and my gear up and running, I can figure something out."

"What happened to being afraid?" Cotton asked.

"I don't know," Fred said and shook her head. "Maybe some things are more important than fear."

"Let's not put the cart ahead of the horse," Jorge said as he pulled the doors to the hospital open. "Let's just get—"

The black-eyed cannibal lunged through the open door and latched its jaws onto Jorge's neck. The big man winced, but the reaction didn't stop him from drawing his pistol and firing it into the creature still attached to him. Sheila reached forward and grabbed the thing, yanking it off of him and snapping its neck with a ferocious display of raw strength.

"No!" Fred screamed.

Two more of the original infection black-eyed cannibals ran through the door, but Cotton was ready for them and dropped them with two controlled pairs, causing them to hit the ground with a dull thud.

He shined his infrared light into the open stairwell and found nothing there, it had just been the three of them.

"Fuck! Fuck! Fuck!" Jorge cursed as he stumbled to his knees, his hands clamped over the wound on his neck. "I don't want to die like this!"

"It's okay," Sheila said softly as she moved to Jorge and put an arm around him. She guided the man to a sitting position on the floor of the tunnel and pulled him to her. "I'm here. It's okay."

"Did you see it?" Jorge whispered as he sat beside Sheila in the darkness. She could hear the blood gurgling in his throat. "What comes after?"

"I saw it," Sheila said. "I was there. Not long, but I was there."

"Will I see them again?" Jorge asked hopefully, knowing that his time was growing short. "I want to see them again."

"You'll see them again," Sheila assured him. She looked into Jorge's eyes and watched the flood of black overtaking his pupils. "You'll see them soon."

Jorge put his head on Sheila's shoulder as his body tremored. She looked up at Cotton standing over them, and nodded.

Cotton put his suppressor an inch from Jorge's head and pulled the trigger.

The man's body slumped, and Sheila gently laid him on the ground. No one said a word. Fred bit her lip to stop from crying, but the tears were flowing nonetheless.

Cotton laid his hand on her shoulder. "We're all going to die," she said quietly.

"No," Cotton said. "We're not. Not if we keep moving."

He could see by the look in Fred's eyes that she didn't believe him, but she complied and turned to the stairway. Cotton walked ahead of her and caught up with Sheila, who had already begun ascending the stairs.

"Was that true?" Cotton asked. "What you said about seeing what comes after?"

Sheila turned and looked at Cotton with her coal-black eyes.

"Yes," she said. "I was there. I saw what comes after."

"What was it?" he asked.

"Nothing," Sheila replied. "There was nothing there. Only darkness."

"I think I'm done," Harris said as the group ran up the stairs to the infectious disease ward where Gregory and Doctor Freer were waiting. "One of those things bit me, and we all know how that story ends."

"Not necessarily," Leslie said. "The originals, when they bite you or get their blood in your eyes or mouth it's fast, really fast, but the secondary infections take more time. And there may be something we can do."

They burst through the doors of the ward, and Freer met them at the entrance. He immediately assessed the situation and honed in on the bite on Harris' shoulder.

"Damn," he said. "That's not good."

"Thanks for the vote of confidence, Doc," Harris grunted.

"He has an antidote!" Leslie said, pointing at Gregory.

Gregory looked as if someone had kicked his puppy.

"It's— it's not a sure thing!" he countered.

"Seemed like a sure thing for you!" Leslie shouted.

"You have an antidote?" Jean asked.

"I only have two left!" Gregory protested.

"Got an antidote for a bullet?" Jean asked as she raised her rifle and pointed it at him. "Because if you don't turn over that medicine, you're gonna need one!"

"Whatever we're going to do," Doctor Freer said. "We need to do it right now."

The veins surrounding the bite on Harris' arm were turning black, and the pupils of his eyes were also darkening.

"Damn it!" Gregory groused as he reached into his messenger bag and retrieved another of the small syrettes carrying the antidote to the Gen 2 vaccine. "I would like to lodge my formal protest to this course of action."

"Noted," Freer replied. "Now stick him!"

Gregory pressed the syrette into Harris' other arm and then stepped back.

"We'll see if it works," Gregory went on. "It was designed as a counter for the vaccine in case something went wrong. Not sure how well it will work on a bite from a secondary infection. If anything, it should be more than strong enough, but you never know. Science is a lot more random than we like to think."

Harris winced and sat down on one of the beds lined up in the ward.

"I feel really freaking weird. Like... I don't know.

Like my brain is being scrubbed or something. My skin is crawling."

"Look up," Doctor Freer said as he pulled out his pen light. "Open your eyes."

Harris looked into Doctor Freer's light and the physician smiled, watching the black in Harris' pupils begin to fade.

"It's working!" Doctor Freer exclaimed. "It's really working."

"Maybe science isn't so random after all," Gregory quipped.

"Wait a minute..." Freer said as he watched the white in Harris' eyes also begin to recede, revealing a blue iris.

"Holy shit!" April shouted.

"What?" Harris asked, panic in his voice. "What in the hell is happening?"

Jean ran across the room, grabbed a small mirror from a table, and returned with it.

"See for yourself," she said, and held it up so that he could see his reflection.

Harris looked into his own blue eyes. "How is this possible?" he asked.

"I mean, it makes sense," Gregory said. "In a way. If the antidote was supposed to suppress the much stronger Gen 2 vaccine, it should easily knock down the effects of the first. When I took it, I was countering a bite from an original. For you it was only countering a bite from a secondary infection. So, it was strong enough to also override the effects of the first vaccine."

"We've got company," Lebedev said as he shouldered his rifle and squared up with the door.

Jean turned and saw her father, Fred, and Sheila heading down the hallway toward the entrance to the infectious disease ward.

"Wait!" she commanded and held up her hand. "They're with us!"

Doctor Freer hit the switch to release the locks on the doors.

"That's a freaking black-eyed cannibal!" Gregory shouted, pointing at Sheila as the three pushed through the double doors.

"She's okay!" April reassured him. "She's got it under control."

"Under control?" Freer asked.

"It's a long story," April appeased.

Harris turned and looked at Cotton as they approached.

"Holy shit!" Cotton exclaimed.

"That's what I said," April replied.

"You're human!" Cotton continued.

"I guess I am," Harris said. He was still clearly not used to the idea yet.

"He has an antidote," April said, indicating Gregory. "It can turn people back from cannibals to humans."

"Wait..." Freer began and then seemed to be lost in thought for a moment before he turned to Gregory. "You said you had two doses of that left? Before we gave it to Harris?"

"Yes," Gregory replied, clearly uneasy with where this line of questioning might be going.

"That's the cure! We can turn everyone back again! We have to get to the lab," Freer said, urgency in his voice. "We have to synthesize more of it!"

Gregory Wilson looked like a trapped animal.

"Gregory," Fred said. "You remember me, right?"

Gregory smiled awkwardly. "Of course. Hi, Fred."

"I know that look," she said. "I know you're about to freak out, but we need to do this. You understand what's at stake, right?" Fred walked toward him and held out her hand. "I get it," she said. "Selfless acts of sacrifice aren't your thing. It's usually the Gregory show, so I'm not going to ask you to help with this. But I do need you to hand over the antidote. Let us do the right thing here, even if you can't."

"I want to, you know," Gregory said. "Do the right thing. I want to be that guy."

"But you're not," Fred said. "And that's fine. Maybe we all just need to be who we are."

Gregory reached into his messenger bag and retrieved the last syrette. He handed it to her.

"I know I'm not the hero," he said. "But at this point I'll settle for just not being the villain."

"Why do people not answer their fucking phones?" Jared cursed to himself as he jogged down Bissonnet Street toward the hospital that he knew the group had been headed for. "What is the point of having a phone if you don't answer it?"

To make matters worse, he'd had to stash his AX-50 sniper rifle in the back of an abandoned car, and he sincerely hoped he would be able to retrieve it before it was evaporated by some missile strike.

In the distance, he could see the upper floors of the hospital between some buildings. He checked his watch. There was no precise timeline for when the strike might occur, but he knew it wouldn't be long. Typical time from transmission to target acquisition and then to launch was rarely more than an hour or two at most.

. . .

"You came," Cotton said to his daughter as the rest of the group coordinated their next move.

"You ain't cross?" Jean asked.

Cotton shrugged. "Don't see how I can be. You followed directions. Yeah, I'm not happy you're in the middle of this city surrounded by a million black-eyed cannibals instead of at a safe distance, but it is what it is."

"We thought you might be in trouble," Jean said and then looked across the room to April. "We heard the transmission when we got into the city. Roland's transmission."

"Shit," Cotton said. "I was afraid of that."

"I don't see Jorge," she added.

"I— he didn't make it."

Cotton's eyes were darting back and forth and Jean picked up on this.

"Ain't your fault," Jean said. "But you know that."

"Knowing and understanding are two different things. All the men we lost in the war, it never went down like that. He was bitten."

"And you had to do it, didn't you?"

Cotton looked at his young daughter, but saw the

eyes of a much older woman staring back at him. He saw her mother's eyes.

"I did," he said.

"Then there ain't nothin' more to say about it," Jean concluded. "So we best stop talking about it."

April approached the father and daughter. Cotton turned to her. "Look, I know you heard—"

April held up a hand.

"I can't talk about that right now," she said. "We have things we need to do and I have to keep my head straight."

For the first time, Cotton seemed to notice the rows of bodies covered in sheets lying in the beds. "What happened here?" he asked.

April looked to Doctor Freer and then back to Cotton. "They were terminal," she said. "When things started going south, he did what he had to."

Cotton studied the woman's face.

"But?" he asked.

"I don't know," April said and shook her head. "I just feel like something is off with him."

"Has he given you any reason not to trust him?"

"No," April replied. "Just something in my gut."

"Then you need to trust that. For now, let's just make sure someone's watching him."

Cotton turned to see Lebedev and Leslie approach him.

"You are the leader?" Lebedev asked.

Cotton took a step back and his right hand shifted to his pistol.

"No," April said and stopped him. "He's with us. For now, at least."

"Russian?" Cotton asked.

"Colonel Maxim Lebedev," he replied and thrust out his hand.

Cotton shook it. He decided to apply the same lesson he'd taken so long to learn about humans and cannibals working together and apply it to the Russian.

"What's your business here?" Cotton asked.

"The same as yours, I imagine," Lebedev said. "Saving the world."

"But that wasn't what brought you here."

"No," Lebedev said. "I commanded an Alpha group. You are familiar?"

"Yes," Cotton replied. "I was with Development Group."

"Ah," Lebedev said, obviously impressed. "That explains why you made it this far."

"I don't want to sound indelicate, but a group is usually more than one person."

"We encountered resistance," Lebedev said. "Of the black-eyed variety. I alone survived. Our intelligence suggesting a potential greater event led me here."

Cotton looked to where Gregory Wilson was standing. "And to him?" he asked.

"Yes."

"And now?"

"I think," Lebedev said. "The rules have changed, and the playing field has shifted. I have seen these things and what they can do. I labor under no delusion that many of my countrymen, at least out here, have survived. It seems to me, that for the moment, you and I share a common goal and a common enemy."

CHAPTER 10

"Okay," Cotton said as he addressed the group standing before him. "The lab we need to get to is in the first sub-basement. There's no guarantee we're alone in this building, so we should expect to meet some resistance. We've split into two groups. My group will take Doctor Freer and Fred to the lab to synthesize more of the antidote. Lebedev's section will head back the way we came and secure the access door back into the tunnels."

"And if we meet resistance in the tunnel?" Leslie asked.

"There's no easy way to put this," Cotton replied. "You've got to hold your ground. We should still have comms staying on the city network, even if you're underground. If you really can't hold, come back inside and secure the door, but understand we'll be trapped, and there may not be a way out."

"We'll hold," Lebedev said firmly. "No matter what."

"Well, 'no matter what' seems kind of—" Gregory started.

"Shut it," Leslie snapped. "No one cares about your opinion."

"Some people might," Gregory objected.

"No," Sheila said, glaring at Gregory from behind her black eyes. "I don't even know you, and I don't care what you have to say."

"I'll take the lead," Sheila said as her section entered the stairwell and began navigating downward into the relative darkness. "I'll still be able to see when it gets dark. If I call out, hit your lights."

"I'm starting to re-think this plan," Leslie said as she followed Sheila.

"You'll be fine," April insisted. "Just breathe."

"You sound like you've done this before," Leslie said.

"A couple times," she replied.

"Does it get easier?"

"I'll let you know after we're done," April returned with a smile.

Lebedev took up the rear and watched the stairwell above them, which seemed to ascend endlessly into the darkness, even though he knew it was only seven stories.

"How many floors down is it?" Gregory asked.

"Just three," Sheila replied. "We'll be there before you know it."

"Radio check," Cotton said into his mic as they moved down a parallel stairwell toward the second sub-basement and the lab they needed to access.

"Check," Lebedev's voice came back. "All clear."

"Roger that."

Cotton was "NODs down" to navigate the darkness of the stairwell, but as they approached the doorway to the second sub-basement, he saw flickering light coming from beneath the door.

"When was the last time you were down here?" Cotton asked.

"Never," Freer replied with a shrug. "At least, not since everything went south." He caught himself. "The first time. They were trying to come up with a cure for the vaccinated, so no one but project staff were allowed in. That's how I knew they'd have what we needed to synthesize more of the antidote."

"I don't like this," Fred said. "This is bad. This is like 'midnight movie on Cinemax' bad."

"Cinemax?" Jean asked. "How old are you?"

"Can the chatter," Cotton said as he stowed his night vision and brought his weapon. "Sorry Harris, but you're the breacher."

"Figures," Harris groused. "I finally turn back to human and I'm about to get my head ripped off by some crazy monster in a creepy sub-basement lab."

Despite his objections, the man moved to the head of the stack and grabbed the door handle.

"Don't test it," Cotton warned him. "Just grip and rip." Cotton turned to Jean who had moved up in the stack behind him. "You're on me. The rest of you hang back until we clear this place."

Harris nodded, then turned the handle, and pulled open the door.

There was nothing. Just a long hallway with doors on either side. The cheap fluorescent lights flickered overhead as Cotton moved inside of the hallway with Jean and Harris behind him.

Harris looked down at the floor and saw long, bloody streaks seeming to go in every direction.

"What in the hell happened here?" he asked.

"Not sure I want to find out," Cotton replied.

Jean turned to one of the doors and pulled the clipboard from the holder beside it. "They were trying to turn them back," she said. "But it looks like they killed most of them instead." She put the clipboard back, staring at the door.

"I know what you're thinking," Cotton said. "But if something's in there and hasn't left by now, that means it's locked in. Let's leave it alone."

For a moment, the girl seemed like she was in a trance. Cotton had been waiting for something like this. As tough as she was, and as much as he had seen she was still human, every human had a breaking point.

He put his hand on his daughter's shoulder. "Why don't you hang back with the Doc and Fred?" Cotton asked. "Keep an eye on 'em while we clear this place."

"I'm fine," Jean said. "I don't need to go back."

"Do it for me," Cotton said. "Please."

"Okay," she said. "Just as long as you know I can handle it. If I have to."

"I know, baby bear," Cotton said.

He watched as the girl turned and walked back to the entrance.

"How come I don't get to go back?" Harris asked with a smirk.

"Man reasons," Cotton said and gave him a good-natured punch in the shoulder. "Now let's get on with it."

Sheila stopped on the stairwell as she felt a "whoosh" past her head followed by a dull thud below in the darkness.

"What was that?" April asked.

Then it happened again, but this time, the dull thud was against the railing of the stairwell, and a black-eyed cannibal pulled himself up on the rail he had caught falling from an upper floor. Sheila turned, gripped him by the throat, and threw him back over the edge to the floor below.

Overhead, the group heard the clattering of footsteps and the sound of deep growls. No explanation was required as to what was happening. The creatures were on the upper floors, and were now heading for them.

"Go!" Lebedev shouted as he turned and took several shots at the movement he could see on the floor above them.

"I can't die like this!" Gregory said. "I'm important!"

"Shut up!" Leslie said as they moved more quickly, but still carefully, down the stairs.

April moved to the rear with Lebedev. She couldn't see much in the darkness, but she knew that she could at least fire in the same direction he was.

"How many?" she asked as they moved sideways down the stairs, firing into the upper levels.

"At least a couple dozen," he replied. "We need to get through that door and into an open space where we have a chance."

Sheila found the access door and pushed it open, leading the rest into the tunnel.

"You stay with me," she said to Gregory, grabbing him by the arm and pulling him away from the door.

Lebedev stowed his night vision device and activated the white light on his rifle. April and Leslie both did the same, and they lined up facing the doorway, reminiscent of British soldiers on a Revolutionary War battlefield.

"We're going to trap them in a funnel of fire," Lebedev said calmly. "They don't have firearms so there's no need for maneuver. Once they hit the door, give it everything you've got."

The man turned and saw that Leslie's hands

were shaking. He placed one of his hands on hers and looked her in the eyes.

"You are not afraid," he said. "You were born for this."

Something about the way the Russian spoke to her and the look in his eyes caused a strange wave of calm to pass over the woman. She gripped the shotgun with a new level of resolve and turned to where her light was shining on the open access door.

Then, the first of the demons came into view. He lunged through the door toward her, but strangely Leslie was transfixed for just a moment by the tattoos that covered his arms. For some reason, it reminded her that he had once been a man, just like any other. A man who had decided to get a tattoo, and then another and then another.

This hesitation lasted for only a split second before she pulled the shotgun more tightly into her shoulder, put the front sight on the man's face, and pulled the trigger. His head came apart like a piñata, but she had no opportunity to linger over the carnage as two more of the black-eyed things immediately took his place.

They were flooding into the tunnel, and the number was far higher than Lebedev's original assessment.

. . .

Cotton reached the end of the hall and gently pushed the final door open with his foot.

He looked at Harris. "Not exactly textbook CQB. But I'm old and tired."

Harris laughed and moved ahead of him, picking up the cue that he should make entry. Behind the door was a large, open laboratory, but nothing more.

"Guess we should get the others," Harris said.

Doctor Freer and Fred moved through the lab, checking that the equipment they needed was functioning properly.

"Got what you need?" Cotton asked as Fred turned on a machine and removed a lid from it.

"Depends on what they used to make this," Fred replied as she carefully opened the last remaining syrette, poured a small amount into the machine, and then closed the lid. "If it's a fairly simple structure we should be good."

"How long does it take to do something like this?" Harris asked. "To copy it, I mean."

Fred and Doctor Freer shared a look.

"Are we not going to like this?" Cotton asked.

"Again," Fred said. "It depends on what they had to do to make the antidote. Could be minutes, could be days."

"We don't have days," Cotton said. "Minutes at best."

"Science doesn't care about time," Fred said as she watched the read out on the computer connected to the machine they were using to break down the chemical structure of the antidote. "It will take as long as it takes."

She pulled off her backpack and retrieved a small paper-wrapped package from it, then removed two vials from that.

"Is that from the dogs?" Harris asked in surprise.

"I almost tossed it," Fred said. "I didn't actually think I'd find a working lab to analyze it. But I figure since we're already here..."

She moved to another equipment set up and began the process of analyzing the blood.

The first computer screen seemed to be pouring out an endless stream of information, until suddenly, it stopped.

"It stopped," Cotton said. "What does that mean?"

"Could be good or bad," Fred replied as she moved back to the first station and scanned the code, with Doctor Freer doing the same over her shoulder.

He pointed at the screen. "That can't be right," he said. "Is that right?"

"Oh my God!" Fred nearly shouted. "That makes total sense."

"Hey!" Harris snapped. "I barely finished high school. Enlighten me."

"Cyproheptadine," Fred replied. "It's a serotonin and histamine antagonist."

"Commonly found in most labs," Doctor Freer went on as he walked to a large cabinet and pulled the doors open. He reached inside and retrieved two jugs with white labels on them. "This is your cure."

"You said it made sense?" Cotton asked.

"Serotonin," Fred said. "Everyone thinks it's the happy hormone, including most physicians and researchers, but the foundational science behind that theory was flawed because it was based on the idea that LSD makes you insane."

"Which it doesn't," Freer said. "The overdose does."

"LSD is an antagonist to serotonin. So, the idea that serotonin makes people happy was based on a faulty premise. Serotonin is a primitive adaptive stress hormone. Whatever they did with the Gen 2 vaccine probably jacked everyone's serotonin levels through the roof."

"And their brainstem hijacked their Neo-cortex?" Doctor Freer asked, seeming to be thinking out loud.

"In theory," Fred said. "Either way, the only thing in that syrette was cyproheptadine in a DMSO solution."

"Can it make April human again?" Jean asked from the doorway to the lab.

"I... I don't think so," Fred replied, and it was obvious the woman understood that it also could not make her human again.

The computer at the second station also stopped running code and Fred walked to the screen, hitting the button to print the results and waiting as the papers emerged. She looked at them again and shook her head.

"What now?" Cotton asked.

"It's the blood I took from the dogs," she said. "There's something in it that shouldn't be there."

"I'm almost out of rounds!" Leslie screamed as she walked backward from the access door, firing her shotgun as she moved.

Lebedev stepped to the side, drew his pistol, and handed it to her while Leslie slung the shotgun, put the red dot of the pistol on her first target, and pulled the trigger.

The group was becoming too spread out as they fought, and April knew it. She was now a dozen feet from the others and her opposition was piling up fast. For just a moment, she looked to her left and saw Sheila going hand to hand with the black-eyed cannibals, and by any estimation, the woman was getting the better of the exchange.

April had only looked away for a moment, not even a second, but that was all it took. She felt one of the cannibals hit her like a freight train and knock her to the ground, pinning the AR to her and effectively rendering it useless.

Without thinking, she drew her pistol, pressed it to the animal's head, and pulled the trigger. He collapsed on top of her, but it was to no avail. Two more joined the attack and she felt the first bite, heavy jaws clamping down on her left bicep. Her eyes went wide and adrenaline rushed through her body. Then there was another bite. This one was on the opposite leg just above her knee. Hands were on her throat and she could see more movement out of the corner of her eye.

In a matter of seconds, there would be another half-dozen on her. This was it; she knew it. She was going to be eaten alive. It had always been a possibility, that it would end like this, but it had never seemed real. She hadn't really thought it would happen to her, but she also hadn't imagined it would happen to Roland.

Wasn't she supposed to be the hero? Heroes don't die like this.

She felt her heart rate slowing down as the bites went deeper and her breathing switched from fast and panicky to slow. It was her life force leaving her. She knew it.

Then she heard pops. They were quiet, even more so than Cotton's suppressed AR. She felt some of the pressure release from her body, then another pair of hands on her, but they were different, they were human.

She opened her eyes with a flutter and saw a man kneeling over her.

"What?" she asked lazily.

Jared stopped what he was doing, brought up his rifle, and took several more shots at advancing figures.

"Cover me!" Jared shouted at Lebedev. "I'm working here!"

April looked down and could see that he was applying tourniquets to her arm and leg where she had been bitten.

"You're fucked up," Jared said. "You're fucked up real bad but you're not dead. Do not quit on me and you'll make it through this."

April lay her head back down and looked up at the ceiling of the tunnel as the sounds of gunfire seemed to slow down, until finally they stopped.

"What are you doing to her?" Sheila shouted.

"Saving her life!" Jared countered as he tightened the last tourniquet. He looked into April's eyes and saw that they were already starting to turn. "But I don't know for how long."

"There's an antidote!" Lebedev said.

"What are you talking about?" Jared asked.

"It's true," Leslie said. "The rest of our group is in a lab just upstairs trying to synthesize more of it.

"Stand up," Jared said as he picked April up and put her on her feet, the black veins already starting to spiderweb away from her bites.

"I'll take her," Sheila said quickly. "Call it in, tell them I'm coming."

"We good?" Cotton asked.

Jean had taken up post beside the entrance while Doctor Freer and Fred collected what they needed from the lab.

"So far," Jean replied. "But I hear noises down below. Exfil in that direction may not be an option soon."

"Roger that," Cotton replied and moved back to the lab. "We have to go. Now. Science or no science."

"We're ready," Fred replied. They had acquired two one-gallon jugs of the Cyproheptadine as well as the laptop they had used for the initial sequencing.

"How many people will that work on?" Cotton asked.

"Most of this city," Fred said. "It probably only takes a few drops."

Cotton's radio crackled to life.

"April's been bitten," Lebedev's voice said.

Cotton felt his blood run cold.

"Sheila is on her way with her," Lebedev went on. "If you've got the antidote meet them on the way and administer."

Cotton hit his push to talk. "Confirmed. We're en route."

"Let's go!" Jean shouted and turned to the doorway.

"Wait!" Freer protested. "Didn't she just say they're below us?"

"No choice," Harris said and patted the physician on the shoulder as he passed him and followed Cotton and Jean out the door. "No one lives forever, doc!"

"I'm not asking to live forever," Freer said. "But I'd settle for ten more minutes."

"You don't have to do this!" Sheila said as she carried April up the flight of stairs with Jared behind her, wielding his 300 Blackout gun. "I can make it on my own!"

April was already limp in her arms and she could feel the woman's heart rate haphazardly slowing down and speeding back up again like an engine being throttled.

"Yes, I do," Jared replied. "Now shut up while I work. I don't do well with distractions."

Through his night vision, he could see well past Sheila, and he spotted the first of the black-eyed cannibals coming toward them in the darkness. He put his NGAL aiming laser between its eyes and pulled the trigger, sending a 220 grain hollow point through the creature's face. Three more were stacked up behind it and were executed in turn with three clean trigger pulls.

Another of the black-eyed cannibals seemed to come out of nowhere to Sheila's left and she turned and threw a hard front kick into the creature lunging for her, nearly dropping April in the process, but it created enough space for Jared to pivot and kill it.

"Still think you don't need me?" Jared asked.

"I'm in the process of rethinking your utility."

Cotton, Harris, and Jean went NODs down as they descended into the darkness with Fred and Doctor Freer behind them. Cotton activated a green chem light hanging from the back of his belt that he had mostly wrapped with electrical tape. It emitted very little light, but it was enough that Fred and Doctor Freer could follow them without the benefit of night vision.

"I hate this part," Fred said.

"Which part?" Freer asked.

"The part where we plunge into darkness."

"Does this happen a lot?" the physician asked.

"More often than I'd like," she said. "But I think I might be getting used to it."

"Stay quiet," Cotton admonished the two. "We

don't have far to go, and we don't want to attract more attention than we need to. Maintain fire discipline. Remember that friendlies are coming at us from below. Only shoot if you've got a laser on a target."

As if on cue, targets began to present themselves. Cotton, Harris, and Jean began sighting in with their aiming lasers and putting on what anyone would consider an impressive display of fire discipline and accurate shooting under pressure.

"Here!" Sheila called out as she arrived at a door two floors up. "We have to cross over here to get to the other stairwell."

She pushed her way through the door and walked into a large open space with another door leading to the adjacent stairwell on the other side. Jared entered behind her, weapon up and scanning the room for potential threats. Finding none, he brought his weapon to the high ready and secured the stock of the rifle under his arm, stowing his NODs in the "up" position and rotating the Surefire light on his helmet up and switching it to "white light." This created the effect of throwing an umbrella of white light across the previously pitch-black room.

"Shit," he said. "She looks bad."

The black veins that had been spreading out from the bites April sustained in the tunnel now covered her entire body, and her eyes had gone almost completely black, her breathing even faster than before.

Sheila snatched the radio from her belt and hit the "talk" button. "We're on the next landing down!" she said. "We can't go any further! You have to get here now!"

"En route," Cotton's voice came back. "One mike."

Sheila looked down at April lying on the floor. "I don't think we have a minute," she said to herself as she watched the muscles in April's body begin to tense.

The woman looked up at Sheila.

"Kill me," she said with a gravelly voice not her own. "Or I'm going to kill you."

"Better men than you have tried," Sheila said as she checked the tension on April's tourniquets. "And failed. You ain't gonna be the one to punch my ticket."

Jared looked at Sheila and nodded to his rifle.

"No!" Sheila snapped. "I'm not doing this again! I'm not losing anyone else today!"

"You may not have a choice in a minute," Jared said as he watched steam starting to pour off April's body.

"What in the hell?" Sheila asked. "She should just be a copy. Why is she turning like this?"

As if in answer to this question, April sat up and lunged for Sheila. Sheila grabbed the smaller woman by the shoulders, turned, and slammed her into the sub-basement wall hard enough that the impact of her body cracked the concrete.

"Stop!" Sheila shouted. "If you're still in there, if you can hear me, we're going to get you help!"

April hammered a fist into Sheila's ribs and the woman felt a crack. She had never been hit so hard in her entire life, and it caused her to loosen her grip. April slipped out of Sheila's grasp and ran for Jared.

"Don't!" Sheila called out, indicating for him to hold his fire.

"Damn it!" Jared cursed as he turned his rifle around and slammed the stock into April's face as she charged him.

Her head whipped back, blood gushing from her nose where he had broken it.

Behaving as if the assault had not even happened,

April turned and leapt atop Sheila, reaching around behind her head with one hand and throwing overhead hammer strikes into the side of her skull. Sheila responded by grabbing April around the ribs, lifting her higher and then slamming her into the ground with every ounce of strength she had. Again, the impact was hard enough to crack the concrete floor.

This was finally enough to shock April long enough for Sheila to get on top of her and pin her wrists to the ground. In a second, Jared was also on top of her, and used a pair of zip ties to hog tie her with Sheila's assistance.

The door across the landing opened and Cotton entered with the rest of the group.

The first thing he saw was April, hogtied and clearly insane with rage, her black eyes locked on him as he walked toward her.

"We're too late," he said.

"No, we're not," Fred countered as she dropped the pack they had brought from the lab. "She's just going to need a hell of a lot more of this than we gave to Harris. Hold her down."

Doctor Freer handed Fred a syringe that she then filled with the medication. It took nearly everyone working together to hold April still enough for the injection. Fred hesitated as her mind flashed back to the moment she had pointed the gun at her friend Celeste in Tow and took her life. It seemed like so long ago.

"Not again," Fred said under her breath, and she carefully inserted the needle into April's arm as the woman thrashed wildly. She depressed the plunger, withdrew the needle, and stepped back.

"Are you sure this will work?" Jean asked as she watched April.

It was clear that seeing her friend like this had shaken the young girl. For the first time, Fred could see that Jean had dropped her armor.

"I don't know," she said, and left it at that.

April arched her back and gritted her teeth.

"She's seizing!" Freer shouted. He reached for his medical bag and pulled out a bite block, then turned to Harris. "Help me get this in her mouth."

"You want me to put my fingers in her mouth?" Harris asked. "Are you out of your fucking mind?"

"Do it!" Freer ordered as he grabbed April's jaw and manipulated it in a way that forced her mouth open.

Harris worked the block in-between her teeth and Freer let go.

"If she kept that up, she'd break her own jaw," Freer said.

Everyone stepped back and April continued to thrash on the floor.

"It's not working," Jean said.

Cotton looked down at his daughter, and saw the same vulnerability that Fred had. "Go outside," he said. "You don't need to see this."

Jean's lower lip quivered as she watched April suffering. "I don't want to do this anymore," she said, reaching out to find her father's hand.

Cotton felt a lump in his throat as he watched what was happening. He knew that he couldn't let this continue.

"I'm doing it," Cotton said as he raised his rifle and stepped forward. He turned to Sheila. "Get Jean out of here. Now!"

Sheila reached for Jean's arm and the girl pulled away.

"No!" Jean shouted. "There has to be a way!"

Cotton put his EOTech reticle on April's head, exhaled as he took the rifle off "safe," and started to take the slack out of the trigger.

He stopped. Something caused his finger to freeze.

April continued to thrash and had now rolled on

her stomach, still hog tied and beginning to slam her head into the concrete.

Jared placed his hand on Cotton's rifle and gently pushed it down. He looked the former SEAL in the eyes.

"I'll do it," Jared said. "Maybe that's why I'm here. So you don't have to."

"I— I'm sorry," Cotton said.

"Nothin' to be sorry about," Jared replied. "She's your friend. This should be hard."

Everyone looked around as April thrashed, and there was a silent understanding of what needed to happen. The group exited the landing without another word, and finally the door closed, leaving Jared alone with the thing that used to be April.

CHAPTER 11

Colonel Fisker entered the office of Bill Rampart and quietly shut the door behind him. Bill stood at the office window, looking out at what had previously been the drill field for the 4th Marine Division. Fisker said nothing.

"It's done," Bill said, looking at his watch and then back out the window. "In roughly thirty minutes, Houston will be sitting beneath a mushroom cloud."

"Nuclear?" Fisker asked, clearly surprised.

"A mentor of mine once said, do it right the first time and you won't have to do it again. We just can't risk Doctor Wilson escaping that city and passing what he knows on to the opposition."

"I don't disagree," Fisker said and decided to leave it at that.

"And I checked with meteorology. We won't get any of the radiation here."

"You read my mind," Fisker responded.

"We're walking on a tightrope here, Colonel. If we're not perfect, if our execution is not perfect, we will fail. If we fail, America dies. Perhaps humanity as well."

Rampart turned to face his military commander and nodded to the papers the man held in his hand. "I'm guessing that's not good news?" he asked.

Fisker shrugged. "Might depend on your perspective," he said. "We're getting reports of an outbreak of black-eyed cannibals in India, China, and the U.K."

"What?" Bill asked. "How is that possible?"

"I thought you might know," Fisker said. "We did send samples of the Gen 2 vaccine to other countries, didn't we?"

"Well, yes, but not to use! It was supposed to be for lab study only."

"I'm no scientist, boss," Fisker replied. "But it looks to me like someone decided to use it."

"I'll have to look into it, but at this point, it's safe to say that genie is thoroughly out of the bottle."

"What about distributing the antidote?" Fisker asked.

"It only works on Gen 1 cannibals that were infected. If it's spreading over there it's jumping people straight from humans to Gen 2 cannibals."

"I see," Fisker said. "We have another problem."

"Because things have been going so well?" Bill asked with an unconvincing smile.

Fisker stepped forward and handed Rampart a tablet, showing a live ISR feed that included Infrared overflight imagery.

"This is live," he said. "It's coming from one of the far recon drones currently on station in North East Texas."

"What am I looking at?" he asked. "Are these... people?"

"Yes, Sir. More specifically, it's a horde of black-eyed cannibals. We have a classification system now. Anything under a hundred is a cluster. One hundred to a thousand is a swarm."

"And a horde?" Bill asked.

"Up to ten thousand, and we think this group is pushing the upper limit of that. Maybe they're already beyond it."

"Where are they heading?" Bill asked, afraid that he already knew the answer.

"We're mapping their trajectory, but it's hard to say. At this point, any estimates we offer would be pure guesswork."

"Then guess for me."

"At the least, they're heading for our area."

"Jesus," Bill gasped. "How long do we have?"

"Based on their current speed?" Fisker considered for a moment. "A week. Maybe less."

"How is that possible if they're on foot?"

"Based on the drone footage, we've clocked them running at a moderate speed, and they seem to be maintaining that pace."

"They can't keep that up, can they?"

"You've seen it yourself. They're not mindless, but they're... they have no sense of self-preservation. They only know one thing."

"Hunger," Bill concluded.

"That's about the size of it."

"But it doesn't make sense. They're not supposed to— to band together! Why would they do that? They have no direction, no leader!"

The look in Colonel Fisker's eyes told Bill Rampart everything he needed to know. The poor man had no idea why the black-eyed cannibals had coalesced into a group and were now on a collision course with Fluid Dynamics.

. . .

Cotton stood with the group in the stairwell outside of the landing as they waited. No one said anything. They all knew what was coming. Already they had lost both Roland and Jorge. Sheila would never be the same again and Harris had also changed, even if for the moment, it seemed to be for the better.

"How long do we wait?" Doctor Freer asked. "Not to be indelicate, but aren't we sitting ducks here?"

"As long as we have to!" Jean snapped.

No one else said anything.

They all heard the door latch working and turned toward it. They knew that Jared would join them and then it would be time to head home, whatever that meant anymore.

The door opened.

April stared out at them from behind crystal clear blue eyes. Her nose was broken and there was a gash in her forehead from where she had been pounding it against the floor. Her face was covered in blood, but her eyes were human again.

"April!" Jean shouted, running to the woman and throwing her arms around her.

"Ow," April said with a grimace, but returned the hug. "Ribs might be broken."

"Sorry," Sheila said. "I probably did that."

"Better than the alternative," April replied.

Jared walked out behind April.

"Figured I wouldn't shoot her," he said. "What with her changing back to human and all."

"Good call," Cotton said, then turned to April. "I'm glad you're okay."

"Me too," she said.

"I don't want to sound indelicate," Harris spoke up. "But we need to get the hell out of here."

"You don't now the half of it," Jared said.

"What exactly do you mean by 'they're going to nuke the city'," Doctor Freer asked as the group entered the main tunnel through the access door.

"What's up with this guy?" Jared asked, as he had already thoroughly explained the most probable scenario.

"I'm sorry!" Freer said. "I'm new at this, and I'm having a hard time with the idea that the people I de facto work for are about to drop an atom bomb on Houston!"

"Look," Cotton said as he turned to face the

group. "I know most of you are messed up, some worse than others, but if what Jared's saying is true, we don't have much time to get out of this city."

"What about going to street level?" Leslie asked. "Getting some vehicles?"

"No," Jared said and shook his head. "Wherever those things were hibernating when I got here, they're awake now. The streets are flooded. We wouldn't make it five feet."

"The outer sub-stations," Jean suggested. "Remember on the maps? Out at the edge of the city. It would make sense that these tunnels lead there."

"And if they don't?" Gregory asked. "What if they're just a dead end?"

"Then we're dead," Cotton said abruptly. "But it's the only option, unless someone else has a better idea."

Everyone was silent.

"How long do you think it is?" Cotton asked his daughter, knowing she had studied the map to the greatest level of detail.

"Thirty minutes," she said. "Jogging at a moderate pace."

"Jogging?" Harris asked and then looked down at his leg. "Princess sunshine over here shot me."

"I didn't do it on purpose," Leslie said and then

paused for a moment before continuing. "Do you really think I look like a princess?"

"Here," Freer said, reaching into his pocket to retrieve a small bag of pills and then handing two to Harris. He gave two to April as well. "It's oxy."

"Why are you giving me oxy?" April asked, sounding slightly indignant.

"Because you look like you tried to French kiss a train," Freer replied. "And my understanding is that we need to be moving fast."

"I feel freaking amazing!" Harris called out as the group jogged through the tunnel.

"Don't get used to it," Freer replied. "It's a pain killer, not a lifestyle."

"That's not what I heard," Harris shot back. "You've been hanging out in the wrong trailer parks."

"Stay on task," Cotton reprimanded them. "We're only ten minutes in and we don't know if we're alone down here."

"I think I'm going to throw up," April said.

"Sorry about that," Freer said. "Some people have that reaction. Hard to know which one you are until you try it."

"I've got movement!" Sheila called out.

Cotton, Jean, Lebedev, Jared, and Harris were all running under night vision, while Sheila could see in the dark. This left April, Leslie, Gregory, Fred and Freer all following the chem lights attached to each of them in the total darkness.

Cotton picked up the movement in his green phosphor night vision, put his laser on it, and fired two shots. He hoped to hell it was a black-eyed cannibal and not some innocent wandering around in the tunnels.

In a moment, he got his answer as they passed the body; it was clearly one of the Wasted.

"I doubt he came down here alone," Cotton said. "Keep your heads on a swivel."

"There are more," Sheila said.

"Can you see them?" Cotton asked, unsure if her natural night vision might be better than their man-made versions.

"No," Sheila said. "I can feel them."

Then Cotton had a thought that seemed absurd, but he realized it was exactly what they were doing. None of them were running their IR illuminators. This would be standard practice in most combat scenarios. You wouldn't want to be walking around, flooding the area in front of you with infrared light for no reason. Even though it can only be seen by those wearing night vision, you would be taking a big risk on no one out there having that capability. Even in Iraq and Afghanistan, it was known that some of the insurgents or foreign fighters had captured night vision devices.

Going up against black eyed cannibals, however, there was no such concern.

"Activate your IR lights," Cotton called out. "Flood the tunnel."

Almost simultaneously, all five of them activated their IR devices.

"Holy shit," Harris said.

They were surrounded by black-eyed cannibals —hundreds of them—but they had been standing just beyond the point where they could be seen by night vision without additional illumination.

"What is it?" Fred asked.

"Stay calm," Cotton said. "We're surrounded by them, but they aren't attacking."

"What are they doing?" Fred asked.

"I don't know," Cotton said. "They're just kind of... standing there. Watching us."

Cotton scanned the hundreds of cannibals and confirmed that indeed they were just standing in silence watching them. Then, one raised a hand to his mouth and coughed. Another did the same thing.

"They're sick," Gregory said. "There was one in my building doing the same thing. I think if they're sick long enough, they'll probably die."

"We don't have that kind of time," Cotton said. "We have to walk through them."

Without another word, Cotton began walking forward. He could see a clear path through the creatures, as they seemed to be gathering along the walls.

"Can you still feel them?" Cotton asked Sheila as she walked alongside him.

"Yes," she said. "They're talking to each other, like they're on some kind of network, only it's not a language I understand."

"Something's happening," Lebedev said. "They're moving."

"He's right," Jean said. "They're moving into our path. What do we do?"

"Sheila?" Cotton asked.

"I— I don't know! I can hear them but it's just noise."

"Damn it!" Cotton snapped. "Okay, start clearing our path, but only take the targets you need to. We don't want to stir up a hornet's nest that we're standing in the middle of."

No further communication was needed. Cotton watched lasers begin lighting up targets, followed by the subdued crack of suppressed rifles. The group was exercising good fire discipline and was indeed clearing the path forward. Thus far, the rest of the black-eyed cannibals on the periphery did not seem to have any interest in attacking.

"I've got light ahead," Jean said.

Sure enough, in the distance, light could be seen, which meant they were nearing the end of the access tunnel that would empty out near the outer substation Jean had seen on the map.

"Okay," Cotton said. "Stay cool. We're not there yet."

"Shit," Sheila uttered.

"What is it?" Lebedev asked.

"Their— their thought process. It's changing. They know we're here now."

"She's right," Harris said. "They're all starting to move in."

"We may have to run," Cotton said. "If you don't have NODs, just follow my light. No matter what you hear, don't slow down and don't look back. Lebedev, Harris, take up the rear and watch them."

Cotton picked up his pace until he was running at a decent clip. There was no point in checking his six to see if the others were keeping up—this was going to be a sprint to the finish.

Then he started hearing rounds zipping past him and realized what was happening. Lebedev and Harris were picking up heavy resistance as the black-eyed cannibals that had been occupying the periphery were now closing the gap and getting dangerously close to them.

Once again, there was no time for him to turn and see how the others were faring, as both he and Jean were now running and gunning through the tunnel. He heard the clatter of a polymer magazine hitting the ground to his right and he knew that Jean had already performed a speed reload on the move.

"How are you doin' Baby Bear?" Cotton called out.

"Full of joy," Jean replied as she dropped target after target. "But it'll be good to feel the sun on my face again."

"Almost there," Cotton encouraged.

Then he heard a voice call out behind him, but it was in the distance. He suddenly realized that their radios may not be working properly in the tunnel, and the voice he was hearing was Harris.

"Stop!" Cotton ordered, and he and Jean came to a halt. He turned and saw the rest of the group nearly eighty yards away in the darkness. "Damn it!"

"What do we do?" Jean asked.

"Keep going," Cotton said. "Get out of the tunnel and make sure we have a clear path. "I'm going back."

Jean complied without question and resumed her sprint to the end of the access tunnel.

Cotton ran back into the very hornet's nest he had been afraid they would be trapped in. The things were everywhere. It was absolute chaos. Up until this point, they had known that the black-eyed cannibals could see in the dark, or at least that they could see better than a normal person. Now he realized that while they could see in the tunnel better than he could with his naked eye, it wasn't that much better. He still had an edge over them with night vision.

Lebedev, Jared, and Harris seemed to be shooting in every direction while April, Leslie, Gregory, Doctor Freer, and Fred were effectively helpless.

"Go white light!" Cotton shouted. "They already know we're here!"

Cotton stowed his NODs and waited two beats before activating his Surefire. Within seconds, the tunnel was lit up with multiple weapons' lights, allowing April and Leslie to engage the horde that they could now see surrounded them. Even Fred drew the pistol she was carrying.

"I don't have a gun!" Freer screamed.

The man was panicking. For the first time, he could see just how many of the black-eyed cannibals there were surrounding them and how close they were. Cotton turned and saw that the opening Jean had run through to get to the exit was already flooded with dozens of the things.

"Danger close," he quietly said to himself, and then gripped one of the fragmentation grenades he had secured to his chest rig. He raised his voice. "Frag out! Now! Or we're all gonna die!"

Cotton turned as he pulled the pin on the grenade and hurled it into the churning mass of the Wasted. Lebedev, Jared, and Harris all followed suit, each man sending out two or three grenades a piece. The explosions resonated throughout the tunnel, but they were getting the job done, cutting down vast swaths of the cannibals.

Then, Cotton heard a sound he should not have. It was a very distinctive "clang": the sound of a grenade ricocheting off a pipe. His head snapped to the right, toward the sound and watched something fall at Doctor Freer's feet.

Almost as if it were happening in slow motion,

Cotton watched Doctor Freer look down at the device lying on the ground.

"What—"

The grenade detonated and the blast sent Freer back across the tunnel, directly into a mass of the black-eyed cannibals. Within seconds, they were on him. Cotton felt his body lunge forward but then he stopped himself. The rest of the black-eyed things were being drawn to the injured man. He was easy prey and they knew it. Cotton could see Freer's arms moving, at least what was left of them. He knew that the man was still alive, but he also recognized that there was nothing he could do.

"Move! Move! Move!" Cotton shouted. "Get out! Now!"

The rest of the group ceased fire, turned, and ran behind Cotton as he headed for the tunnel exit.

Jean moved through the substation grounds, clearing the exterior of the small building as well as the fence line. She reached into her sustainment pouch and used the small 3x optic she had stored there to glass the surrounding fields and make sure there weren't any nasty surprises waiting for them out there.

There was nothing. As near as she could tell, she

was alone. She checked her watch and thought about the possible timeline Jared had given them. They only had a maximum of twenty minutes to get the hell out of dodge. If this man Jared worked for really did intend to go nuclear, they would then still only have about thirty more minutes to get clear of the potential fallout.

The girl stopped for a moment and felt her eyes glaze over, staring at a single tree in the distance. She felt transfixed by it. Everything hit her all at once, what was happening, what might happen, and what it all meant for her future. Just as quickly as she had fallen into the trance, Jean snapped out of it.

She heard the sound of movement, and turning one hundred and eighty degrees, she saw her father emerge from the access tunnel. A smile broke out across her face.

The rest of the group quickly came out behind Cotton. For the most part, they were covered in blood. Some had clearly caught some shrapnel from the grenades and looked as if they had just run an ultra-marathon.

"I... never... want to do that again," Harris said.

Lebedev walked to the tunnel, threw a slap charge on the upper edge of the entrance and then stepped back.

"Clear?" he called out.

"Clear," Cotton replied.

Lebedev hit his detonator and the charge brought the tunnel entrance down, stopping any of the Wasted from following them out.

A few of the group sat down on the ground to catch their breath.

"I assume we're good?" Cotton asked as he turned to Jean.

"All clear," she said. "I didn't go inside the substation, but it's padlocked from the outside."

"Good." Cotton motioned to Gregory. "You're the reason we're here. Do you have a hard copy of that code? The one for the EMP?"

"I need protection!" Gregory said.

"Think we've done a pretty good job of that so far," Cotton said. "But yeah, you'll get protection. As long as you do your part. There aren't any free rides anymore."

"I get that," Gregory said. "But I'm clearly not like you. If I'm going to give you this, I need to know you're not going to hang me out to dry."

"I only speak the one language," Cotton said. "If you also need me to say it in Chinese or something, you'll be waiting a long time."

"Fine," Gregory said. He dipped into his messenger

bag and pulled out a small plastic case with a data card in it. Fred reached out and he handed to her.

"I'll verify it," Fred said as she pulled the laptop she had taken from the lab out of her bag.

"Verify it?" Gregory asked, his indignance clear.

"Nothing personal," Cotton said. "But I don't know you from Adam, so I definitely don't trust you."

"It's all there," Gregory insisted.

Fred watched her screen for a moment and then looked up at Cotton and nodded.

"See?" Gregory asked. "I told you."

"Everything you need to stop the EMP is on there?" Leslie asked.

"Yes," Fred replied.

"Good."

The woman turned, brought her shotgun up to Gregory's head, and pulled the trigger.

"Jesus Christ!" Cotton shouted as Gregory's headless body dropped to its knees and then fell sideways into the dirt.

Everyone brought up their weapons as Leslie dropped hers and raised her hands.

"He killed my friend!" she screamed, tear already forming in her eyes. She turned to Lebedev. "You were there! You saw what he did!"

Lebedev lowered his rifle and sighed.

"It's true," he said. "It wasn't direct, but he was responsible."

Cotton glared hard at Leslie and then shook his head.

"We'll deal with this later," he said.

"No," Lebedev said. He brought up his rifle and fired a round into both Jared and Sheila's heads, then turned it on Cotton. "We deal with this now. Lower your weapons."

"What in the hell are you doing?" Leslie shouted.

"I needed all of you to get through this," Lebedev said. "Even a man such as myself knows my limits, but my loyalty is not to you, it is to the Russian people."

Cotton looked to where Sheila and Jared lay in the dirt, both with a neat hole directly in the middle of their foreheads—dead.

"Do as he says," Cotton said.

Harris, April, and Jean all lowered their rifles.

"You can walk away from this," Lebedev said. "I have no desire to harm you."

"Why them?" Cotton asked.

"They were the most direct threats," Lebedev

said. "You, on the other hand, are a man I can talk to."

"What do you want?"

"I think you know," Lebedev said with a smile, and held out his left hand to Fred as his right kept the stock of his rifle secured in his shoulder. "The data card, please."

Fred looked to Cotton, who nodded his affirmation. She stood up and handed the card to Lebedev.

"It's for the best," he said. "With this, we will once again even the playing field."

"She was my friend," Jean said, her voice flat and devoid of emotion.

The girl's voice took Lebedev by surprise. Since meeting her he had frequently forgotten she was even there. He smiled at her, and something about it seemed genuine. "I am sorry," he said. "But this is what happens in war. This is not a game for children. Perhaps this is a lesson for you."

Out of the corner of his eye, Cotton could see that Jean was holding her rifle by her side, her hand reverse gripping the pistol grip and her thumb on the trigger. He turned back to Lebedev and saw a visible red laser on the man's forehead. Her distance from him had meant she only had to cant the barrel ten degrees up from being parallel to the ground to align it with his forehead. She had done it so slowly that the Russian had not noticed, because he rarely noticed her to begin with.

Jean smiled.

"Maybe it's a lesson for you," she said.

There was a subdued pop and then Lebedev's head snapped back as the 220-grain hollow point from Jean's rifle took his life.

"Holy shit!" Harris screamed. "That was freaking awesome!"

Fred turned, dropped to a knee, and vomited on the ground.

"Okay," Cotton said. "You get a gold star for that one but we still need to get the hell out of here before we're all glowing in the dark."

He grabbed the data card from Lebedev's hand and stuffed it in his pocket—then stopped as he heard the sound of groaning coming from his right. He turned and watched Sheila rise to a sitting position in the dirt. She reached up and touched her forehead where the bullet had entered, her hand coming away with blood.

"That probably should have killed me," she said slowly.

Fred's eyes rolled back in her head, and she collapsed to the ground.

"Is she okay?" Harris asked.

April checked the woman's vitals and nodded.

"I think Sheila coming back from the dead might have been a bit too much for her," April said.

"We're almost there," Jean said from the head of the line as the group walked to where they had parked the Winnebago. "Just a few more minutes."

Harris watched April limping beside him as they walked and could tell that despite the dose of oxy she had received from Doctor Freer, she was still suffering.

"How are you holding up?" Harris asked her.

April tried to smile, but it was more of a grimace. At this point, after three days of hard fighting and being repeatedly injured, the woman looked like she had been run through a blender.

"I'll make it," she said. "I just feel... weak."

"Yeah," Harris said. "I feel the same way."

"Like you used to be super human and now you're just..."

"Human again?" Harris asked. "Because that's what happened."

"I was only a cannibal for less than a week. All I could think about was how much I wanted to be human again. How much I hated Randall Eisler for doing that to me."

"And now?" Harris asked.

"I don't know," April said and shook her head. "I get it, you know? I get that what we were, it was horrible. We had to eat other people to survive. But now I just feel like a shadow or something. It's hard to explain." Then she caught herself. "Well, I guess not to you."

Harris laughed. "Life has its ups and downs," he said. "You give a little, and you get a little. I've been a cannibal for a long time, basically since the beginning. Long enough to know what it was I missed about being human."

"What was it?" April asked. "Because I'm having a hell of a hard time remembering right now."

"Frailty," Harris answered simply. "I never liked the Superman comic books, because he couldn't be stopped. It wasn't interesting because I always knew he was going to win. Batman, though, Batman was different. There wasn't nothing special about him. He was just a man. He could get hurt, even killed. So, when he beat the bad guy, at least to my way of thinking, it really meant something."

"So, you never wanted to be Superman," April surmised.

"I think survival means more, when you're seeing it through human eyes," he concluded.

"You're a lot different than you were when I met you," April said.

"Well, yeah," Harris said with a warm grin. "I'm Batman now."

April laughed and almost immediately choked on some blood in her throat.

"You sure you're okay?" Harris asked.

"No," April said and then stopped long enough to spit a fairly shocking amount of blood onto the ground. "Mind if I ask you a strange question?"

"Go for it."

"Back at the farmhouse, you told Cotton if he sent out me or Jean, you'd leave."

"Oh," Harris said, and the shift in the tone of his voice told the story of his regret. "Yeah. That."

"What were you going to do? If he did?"

"Well, we knew he wasn't going to send out his daughter, so I figured it would be you. We weren't gonna do nothing crazy, like, well... you know. I just thought it would be nice to have a woman around."

"Like a den mother?" April quipped.

Harris laughed. "I'll be honest. I wasn't thinking a lot of stuff through at that point in time." He stopped and turned to her. "But I wasn't going to hurt you. Not like you're thinking I was. It's important that you know that."

"I do," April replied. "Now."

"So, what's the deal?" Cotton asked as he walked with Sheila, the two of them following Jean. "Are you immortal now?"

Sheila touched the spot on her forehead where the bullet hole had been. Over the past several minutes it had slowly closed up.

"I don't know," she said. "I hope not."

"What do you mean?"

"Look how much crazy bullshit I've already been through in just forty years," Sheila said. "I was kind of looking forward to there being an end to it."

Cotton laughed. "This does beg the obvious question," he said. "If something about your genetic code or whatever gives you this supercharged healing, does that mean the Cannibal Queen has it, too?"

Sheila thought about it for a moment.

"Only one way to find out," she said.

"What's that?"

"Try to kill the bitch."

CHAPTER 12

"Thank God," April said as they approached the RV. "I was expecting it to be gone, or burned, or full of zombies."

Cotton walked around the vehicle and checked through the windows to make sure it was unoccupied before circling back around and unlocking the door. He drew his pistol and entered the Winnebago, doing a quick sweep of the interior before holstering his weapon.

He grabbed a case of water and a bag of the food they had brought with them from Oatmeal. The thought suddenly occurred to him that they now had four human mouths to feed instead of two, and humans needed a steadier food supply than cannibals did.

He stepped back outside and saw that everyone had already collapsed on the ground, both Harris and Fred literally laying in the dirt. He looked at his watch and then shared a look with Jean, who was doing the same thing.

"Think we're far enough away?" Jean asked.

"Yeah," Cotton said. "If they go nuclear, the blast radius from even a good sized one isn't really that big. Direct radiation and fallout are the bigger problem. That being said, if it's coming from a sub, it will be a tactical nuke. Even less of a problem if you're a decent distance away."

"We shouldn't try to drive a little further out?" Harris asked.

Cotton checked his watch again.

"No time," he said. "We're already past Jared's drop-dead time."

April coughed into her hand, unease crossing her face as she looked into her palm and the mess of blood in it. "Damn it."

"You need a doctor," Cotton said.

April shook her head.

"It'll pass," she said.

"You sure about that?" Fred asked, real concern in her voice.

"I'm sure," April said confidently. "For now, I'm

going to go in the RV and lay down. I figure I'll know if that nuke hits."

Jean had positioned herself on a small folding stool she'd retrieved from the storage area beneath the RV and was now reading a small, worn paperback. The rest of the group had scattered about and were allowing themselves a moment of rest.

"What have you got there?" Sheila asked, approaching.

Jean looked up at her. She held up the book. Sheila could only laugh.

"Sweet Valley Twins?" she asked.

"Daddy said something about 'Sweet Valley' back at the rail yard, so I figured I'd look it up at the library. Found this book."

"What do you think?" she asked. "I used to read those when I was a little girl."

"It's okay," Jean said. "Except for there ain't one cannibal in this whole book."

The door to the RV opened and April stepped out. Everyone turned to look at her, and more specifically, into her milky white eyes. The wounds she had sustained over the past three days were all nearly completely healed and she had an energy about her that had not been there before.

"What in the hell did you do?" Cotton gasped.

"What I had to," April replied. "To make it through this. I couldn't live like that. Roland kept some Pandemify in the storage locker. I used it."

"I don't understand," Fred said. "Why would you want to be like this?"

"Do you remember being human?" April asked. "Being weak? Slow? I don't think I had long left. My face was smashed in, ribs broken, and who knows what else was wrong with me. The moment I felt the vaccine flowing through my body, I knew I was healing. Did it ever occur to anyone, to any of you that the vaccine did exactly what it was supposed to do? Yes, we're cannibals. Yes, we eat people to survive, but what do we get in return? We evolve."

"I'm not liking where this is going," Cotton said.

"You don't have to like it," April said stoically. "But it's what's happening."

Cotton was ready to push back but then he felt the earth rumbling beneath his feet. He looked up and toward the City State of Houston. It was happening.

"What should we do?"

"Don't look at the flash," Fred said. "If there is one."

"Get down!" Cotton shouted. "Face down to the ground."

Everyone dropped as the rumbling grew louder. They could feel something akin to a pressure wave wash over them, but it was light, much lighter than they would have expected. After another moment, Cotton turned over, sat up, and looked back to the city.

"My God," he said quietly.

The rest of the group sat up and likewise turned to the former City State of Houston—engulfed by a mushroom cloud. Whoever was behind this had really done it. They had unleashed a nuclear weapon on their own people.

Everyone sat in silence as Harris drove the Winnebago down State Road Ninety-Nine, taking them around the shattered carcass of what had previously been the City State of Houston.

Cotton sat beside Sheila, turning over the data card in his hand.

"You ever get the feeling," Sheila said. "Like we just finished a warm up for the big game?"

"I don't like that feeling," Cotton said. "But I think you're right. Fred says this doesn't just have the data on the EMP on it. It's got everything. Including home base for the guy pulling the strings on all of this."

"Which is?"

"New Orleans. That's why I told Harris to head East." Cotton hesitated, then continued, "But we all need to talk about that. We're pretty banged up. When we left Oatmeal, we knew we were getting into something, but I don't think anyone knew how big. Also didn't know we'd— we'd lose the people we did."

Cotton looked across from him, where the woman, Leslie, was sitting in silence. She had not said much since they'd left the tunnel and she'd shot Gregory Wilson. She could feel Cotton's eyes on her and looked up.

"Not sure what to do about you," he said.

"I know," Leslie said. "I know that what I did could have really screwed things up." She hesitated. "But it's important to me that you know I don't take it back, and if that son-of-a-bitch was sitting here right now, I'd do it again. But I'd make sure I was looking him in the eye when I did it. I closed my eyes, because I've never killed a person before. Just those things. It's not the same."

Cotton smiled.

"Good," he said. "Most folks don't think they're cut out for the apocalypse, but I think you are. If someone is willing to take another person's life, they better be damn sure as to why they're doing it. If you tried to take it back, I probably would have booted you off this RV. That having been said, we do have to think about big picture. I get why you killed that man, but we can't let our emotions cause us to make bad decisions. Understand?"

"I understand," Leslie replied. "I don't want to be out there alone. If you let me stick with y'all, I won't let you down."

"Well," Harris said from the front seat. "This isn't good."

Everyone felt the RV slow down as Harris applied the brakes, and Cotton stood up and moved to the front seat. In the distance, he could see lines of armored vehicles, tents, and other assorted military equipment, as well as what looked like several hundred solders strewn about the landscape.

"Russians?" Harris asked.

"No," Cotton said. "Chinese. Didn't think they'd be this far north in such force."

"Try to go around?" Harris followed up.

"No way," Cotton replied.

"Are we completely screwed?" April asked.

"Not completely," Cotton said. "There might be a way out of this."

"Look, boss," Harris said as Cotton stepped out of the RV and into the road. "I don't want to sound like a doubting Thomas, but are you sure this is a good idea?"

Cotton turned back to Harris. "No," he said. "I am one hundred percent sure this is not a good idea, but it's the only play I've got."

No one said anything further as Cotton walked forward, holding the white pillowcase by his side. He had stripped away his chest rig and gun belt and even left his weapons behind. He was now wearing only his Crye combat pants and a thoroughly stained and torn black t-shirt.

In the distance, he could see two men were walking toward him, and so he held up the white pillowcase and waved it overhead in the universal sign for surrender.

Once the two Chinese men were within fifty yards, Cotton stopped and waited for them to approach him.

One man was significantly older than the other, in his late fifties by the look of him. His uniform and rank insignia indicated that he was a Senior Colonel in the People's Liberation Army Ground Force. He looked Cotton over and shook his head.

"We've got no quarrel with you," Cotton said. "We're just trying to get where we're going."

The Colonel paused for a moment before speaking. "Where is that?" he asked in heavily accented English.

"Wherever you ain't," Cotton said with a smile, hoping some humor might help defuse what was clearly a tense situation.

The Colonel laughed. "I regret to inform you," the Colonel said. "That you are now prisoners of the People's Liberation Army of China. You will be treated fairly in compliance with the Geneva accords. Please have your people exit the vehicle and surrender any weapons. There is no need for bloodshed."

Cotton pointed to his front pants pocket. "Mind if I get something?" he asked. The Colonel seemed unsure. "It's important. You'll want to see it."

The Colonel looked to the younger man beside him, who nodded his approval. The younger man wore no insignia on his uniform, and Cotton realized he was most likely an agent of the Ministry of State Security, effectively the Chinese version of the CIA.

"Fine," the Colonel said. "What is it?"

Cotton retrieved the card he had been given by Colonel Xi after the fight in the woods and handed it to the Senior Colonel.

The older man smiled and then laughed. The agent was leaning in and looking at the card as well, but his face betrayed no emotion.

The Colonel threw the card on the ground. "That means nothing," he stated. "As I said, you are a prisoner—"

The agent drew his pistol from its holster, put it to the Colonel's head, and pulled the trigger. Cotton stumbled back as the older man fell to the ground, dead.

The agent turned to Cotton, and after a moment of pause, he reholstered his pistol.

For the first time in as long as he could remember, the former SEAL was speechless, and had no idea what to do next.

"He was disloyal," the agent said slowly in perfect English. "To the spirit of the Chinese people.

To honor and debt. Men like him, who gained control during the soft times, they need to be rooted out. You are indeed owed a debt because of your past actions, and because of that, you are free to go. But back the way you came, not this way. And know that our debt to you is now satisfied."

"I know," Cotton said as he stepped backward.

"You see now, don't you?" the agent asked. "Why you can't win?"

Cotton said nothing.

The agent smiled. "I will see you soon," he said.

Cotton opened his eyes and looked around. He didn't know how long he had been asleep, but he could see from the landscape that they had gone much further into East Texas, possibly even into Louisiana.

"Sleeping beauty has awoken," Harris said with a smile from where he sat in the driver's seat.

Cotton looked around and saw that everyone else was fast asleep.

"I pass out?" he asked.

"Right after we left the barricade," Harris said. "Only been a couple hours though. I think y'all will need a lot more sleep than that to recover from the past few days."

The rest of the group was beginning to stir, and Jean was the first to sit up and look out the window.

"Where are we?" she asked.

"You ain't gonna believe this," Harris said and pointed to a clearly handmade city limits sign by the side of the road. "We're in a town called China."

"You're shitting me," Sheila said.

"Nope, I shit you not. Jefferson County." Harris paused. "We staying?"

Cotton stood up and could feel his joints screaming at him in protest. "Hate to do this," he said. "But we'll do a recon, and if it checks out as safe, we'll stay here for a day or two."

Everyone moved much more slowly getting geared back up and checking their weapons. It was clear that the beating they had taken over the past few days was more than just physical.

"Okay," Cotton said. "Keep it simple. First sign of trouble, call it in and we exfil. We're not trying to clear this place or save anyone. Roger that?"

The group nodded their approval.

"Harris, take Fred. Sheila and Jean, you're together, and April, you're on me."

There wasn't much of a town to clear, with just City Hall, a school, the post office, and some scattered shops. Cotton walked down Main Street with April, scanning the perimeter.

"There was a reason I wanted you to come with me," he said.

April stopped.

"I don't want a lecture," she said. "If that's where this is going."

"It's not," he said. "I've got a feeling. In the pit of my stomach. Something bad."

"Worse than everything that's already happened?" April asked, before she suddenly understood what he was implying. "Oh. Look, I think we're all having that feeling right now."

"This is different," Cotton said. "I think I'm getting close to my luck running out."

"Don't say that."

"I get why you did what you did. Truth to tell, If I'm being honest about it, I was pretty sure I was going to be burying you in the next day or two, as beat down as you were. You did the right thing."

"Thank you," April said. "That means a lot."

"While I'm in the business of being honest, it's just that I can feel that cloud hanging over me, and wishing ain't gonna make it go away. If that rain does come down, and I see my end of days... I need to make sure you're going to watch out for Jean."

"I think you've got that backwards," April said with a smile.

"I'm serious," Cotton said.

April's smile faded. "I'll watch over her," she said. "You have my word."

"Town's clear," Harris said as the group met back up at the RV. "Figure the few folks that lived here probably left a long time ago."

"Good a place as any to rack out," Sheila said.

Cotton looked at the group for a moment. "I'm sorry," he said. "That I got you into this."

"What are you talking about?" Fred asked.

"This thing we're doing. I think it's too much," Cotton went on. "In the beginning, we had a good amount of seasoned war fighters. Now..."

"What the hell do you think we are?" Harris asked. "You know, I always thought I wanted this. The whole special forces fantasy, kicking in doors and all that bullshit. I daydreamed about it all the time. Even kind of thought I was doing it up until a few days ago. Then things got real. Now I know.... I don't want to do this anymore. Whatever you've got and she's got," Harris indicated Cotton and Jean, "I ain't got it. I ain't in this for the thrill of the fight. I'm in it for the future.

"Crazy thing about it is, back when I was married, I never wanted kids. Always said some bullshit about how I wouldn't want to raise a kid in this messed up world. Now, it's all I want. I just want to see if we can push through to the other side, somehow make things right again. Then, maybe then, I can find myself the man I always wanted to be."

His speech was met with thoughtful silence.

"I didn't mean to get all serious," Harris said. "But I thought it needed to be said."

"You're right," Cotton nodded. "And we've lost too many good people to turn back now."

"So, we keep going then?" Jean asked. "All the way to New Orleans?"

"We'll take a day or two here first," Cotton replied. "Once we're fully recovered, with clear heads, we'll make that decision together."

. . .

"Can I talk to you?" Fred asked.

Cotton looked up from where he was sitting on one of the folding chairs they had pulled from the RV and smiled. For once, he was fairly certain this was not going to be bad news.

"Of course," he replied.

"Am I acting normal?" Fred asked. "Because I don't think I'm acting normal. I don't think any of us are."

"What do you mean?"

"Jorge died. In front of me. In front of you."

"I know," Cotton said, his voice taking on a more solemn tone. "And I'm guessing you feel like there should be... something said about it."

"I just... first Roland died. I've known him for a real long time. Over twenty years. But no one said anything. And then Jorge died. He saved me, back at Tow. If it weren't for him, I'd be dead. But... again, no one said anything."

"I get it," Cotton said. "And you're right. Even through all this shit, we have to make sure we stay human. And the human thing is to mourn those we've lost."

. . .

Harris had taken on the assignment of fashioning a wooden cross and the group walked into a nearby field where the marker was sunk into the ground. It had been decided to only erect the one marker, as too many had been killed in Houston to carry that many crosses.

"I guess I'll start," Cotton said. "I knew Roland a long time, and I'll just say it, he was a real son-of-a-bitch. He liked puttin' the hurt on folks, both in training and out on missions. He was divorced twice and he earned them both. He never had any kids and that's a good thing, because he probably would have left them on the roof of his car and driven off or some crazy bullshit like that."

"I think you're bad at this," April interjected.

"What I'm gettin' at," Cotton went on. "Is some folks aren't cut out for civilization, and it ain't their fault. It's like sayin' a screwdriver ain't cut out to be a hammer. Well, Roland was a hammer. He was the hammer this world needed to do the dirty work most folks don't even want to know gets done, but it's what has to happen so they can sleep safe in their beds at night...

"Well, those times are gone now. No one's sleeping peacefully anymore, but we can get back there. I'm starting to see that now. Because if a man like Roland can sacrifice himself like that for the greater good... maybe we all have a chance after all."

There was silence.

"Jorge told me that he thought I was a fucking joke," Harris said. "And he was right, but there was a reason he said it. He said it to make me better. He said it to make me want to be better. Not many folks have done that in my life, and maybe it's because I never let them. Jorge also taught me that life isn't fair, and death isn't either. I wasn't there when he died, but... Cotton told me how it happened. It wasn't some crazy last stand like Roland had. It was just... it was brutal and senseless. Just the wrong place at the wrong time. One false move and it was over."

"He saved me," Fred said. "He didn't have to. I keep going through these waves of feeling terrified and then knowing that I can make it through all of this if I just keep going. Then I'm scared again. Then, apparently, I pass out." Everyone laughed. "He said something to me after we met though, that keeps circling around in my head, like it's an idea I need to grab onto and not let go of. When the black-eyed cannibals first came, he told me he could kill me, if I wanted him to. Said if I just wanted to get it over with, he would do that for me. I told him that I wanted to live. He said maybe we need to say that out loud once in a while, so we don't forget." Fred looked around at the battered group. "We're about to go do something terrifying, something that none of us asked for, but we all know what has to be done. So, I'm saying it again. I want to live."

"That was good," Cotton said. "You were right. We needed to get that out."

Fred looked around to make sure no one else was within earshot, and then reached into her messenger bag and pulled out a sheet of paper and handed it to Cotton.

"What is this?" He asked.

"That's the analysis I did in the lab on the blood we pulled from those dogs."

"The dogs?" Cotton asked with a raised eyebrow.

"We knew they were vaccinated," Fred went on. "That much was obvious. Remember back in the lab when I told you there was something that shouldn't be there?"

"Am I not gonna like this?" Cotton asked.

"I don't think that quite covers it," Fred said and pointed to a line at the bottom of the page.

Cotton scanned the line and then looked back to Fred.

"Explain it like I don't have a PhD," he said.

"There was talk about using Artificial Intelligence in the vaccine. The idea was that it would allow the vaccine to learn from its mistakes, to evolve and become more efficient at killing threats. The science was sound, in fact it was brilliant, but it also had the potential to become dangerous."

"I saw 'Terminator,'" Cotton said. "I know how that story ends."

"I think it already happened," Fred said. "If you think about it, what is the most efficient way for an organism to regenerate itself? To consume the exact material it's made of. To cut out the middleman."

"Cannibalism," Cotton said, understanding what Fred was getting at. "That's why the first recipients didn't turn."

"And remember that in the beginning the vaccine didn't seem to work very well? Then it went from not working, to literally killing nearly every disease known to man. It learned. By the time it would have been obvious what was happening, civilization had collapsed, and no one was around to uncover it."

"But I thought this stuff was tested. Didn't it go through the FDA and all that?"

"There are a dozen ways they could have gotten around that, and they only needed one."

"So, what does this mean now?"

"It's like terminator, except instead of the A.I. building killer robots, it turns us into them. It will keep evolving, keep upgrading until there is some kind of apex event."

"Like what?"

At a minimum?" Fred asked. "No more humans."

Bill Rampart stared at the screen on the wall of the conference room. To be more specific, he stared at the crater that now occupied what had previously been the city center of Houston. Logically, he knew that if there were any innocents left in that city prior to the strike from Rouge One, they had been very few, but still, he couldn't get the thought out of his head that he may have just murdered women and children.

Behind him, he heard the sound of a woman clearing her throat. He turned and saw a young woman standing in his door holding a smart tablet. She was attractive in a librarian sort of way, with long red hair pulled into a loose bun on her head and the requisite '50s style librarian glasses framing her milky white eyes.

"Mister Rampart," she said matter-of-factly. "I'm Jeanine."

"Jeanine?" He asked, his confusion clear.

"I'm— well, I'm Jared's..."

"Ah," Bill said, understanding who she was and why she was here. "We won't call it a replacement."

Jeanine nodded. "Of course," she said. "I'm just here to do what I can to assist you."

Bill turned back to the screen. "Do you know what every genocidal maniac in history had in common, Jeanine?"

"I'm... not sure I do."

"They all thought that they were the hero. Every single one of them thought that they were just doing what was necessary to protect their people. At least in the beginning. For some of them, it changed later as they developed a taste for power, but at least in that nascent stage, they thought they were doing the right thing."

"That's not what's happening here," Jeanine blurted.

Bill turned sharply toward her, not accustomed to subordinates he barely knew questioning him.

"I'm sorry," Jeanine said. "I over-stepped."

"No," Bill said and made a 'give it to me' gesture with his hands. "I want to hear your thoughts."

"People have forgotten about the virus." Bill could see that her hands were shaking as she spoke, gently, but it was there, and there was a wetness in her eyes. "I have not. I buried my parents and my husband in my backyard. When it started getting bad, when the hospitals were shutting down and they were stacking bodies in the parking lots, there was nowhere to go. When they got sick, I was on the internet trying to figure out what to do— and I— I spent so much time doing that and now I know I should have been spending that time with them."

"You don't have to talk about this," Bill said.

"No! You need to know. After I buried them, a story came out about the virus contaminating the topsoil. So, I dug them back up and I burned them. Do you know why that all happened?"

Bill shook his head.

"Because they wouldn't take the fucking poke. Because they heard stories about people turning into cannibals. Were the stories true? Yes, but they're still dead. It's easy to look back and see all the mistakes we've made, but it's also easy to miss the things we did right. You and Fluid Dynamics saved this country."

"That might be a stretch," Bill said with a weak smile.

"People forget that the kill rate for the virus hit fifty percent before your company stepped in with the vaccine. Remember that it even got to seventy percent in Afghanistan?"

"Yes," Bill said. "They think it had something to do with the extreme heat."

"How do we know it wasn't going to hit a hundred?"

Rampart was silent for a moment. It was clear that he understood what his new aide was trying to communicate.

"Subjective analysis is challenging," Bill said. "Sometimes, it takes an outside observer to reveal the truth of a thing."

"I know that Jared was an exceptional man," Jeanine said. "I'm not trying to replace him. I just want to do my part to help, so that maybe someday we can get on the other side of this thing."

Bill looked down and saw that the red conference call light on his desk was lit up. He turned back to Jeanine.

"I appreciate that," he said. "But I need to take this incoming call privately. Please secure the door and hold all other calls and visitors."

. . .

The panel of screens on the wall flickered to life, but only one had an occupant. The rest were just empty desks.

"Where is everyone?" Bill asked.

Klaus Andersson looked up at his own bank of monitors and then back to Bill.

"I believe we have made a... miscalculation," Klaus said slowly. "The others are attending to their own individual outbreaks."

"I heard," Bill said. "Why did they deploy it? It was for study purposes only. I thought that was quite clear."

"Their vaccines were failing. Empires were rapidly becoming graveyards, and no one wants to rule over a kingdom of bones."

"I would have told them not to deploy it!" Bill snapped. "If I thought for a moment, they would do something so foolish!"

"You could have put some kind of warning on the package."

"We did!"

Klaus turned to his right, reached across his desk, and pulled a box toward him. He looked closely at the package.

"Oh. Might I suggest a larger type-face next time?" he asked. "And in any event, no one reads the insert. You run a pharmaceutical company, you must know that."

"What was your distribution percentage?"

"Eighty."

Bill's eyes went wide.

"You only had it for a week! How on earth did you make that much and distribute it?"

"It wasn't hard to re-tool the existing vaccine production facilities, and the distribution was already there from our last attempt. What we need now, though, is not a lecture."

"You don't know what you did," Bill said. He waited a moment and then continued. "What do you need?"

"That is the question of the hour," Klaus replied. "Current projections from a collaboration between the Ministry of Health and Military Strategic Command suggest the fall of the European countries within fourteen days. China within twenty-one. And then within thirty days... it's..."

Klaus' voice trailed off.

"Everyone else," Bill finished for him.

"But you must know something," Klaus went on.

"You developed this. What is the next step? How do we stop this?"

Bill stared blankly at Klaus, realizing for the first time that the man truly did not understand what he was up against.

"We don't," Bill said, in the same tone he might use trying to explain death to a child. "We've lost."

Klaus smiled nervously.

"No. That's not right. That's not how this ends. This isn't how it ends."

Bill Rampart reached forward to press the 'end call' button.

"I'm sorry, Klaus, but this is in fact how the world ends."

EPILOGUE

JUNE KENNEDY STOPPED and surveyed the carnage that surrounded her. They had swept through this encampment of Russian soldiers just as they had through all the others. Like the others these had tried to put up a fight, but they had been no match for her thousands of followers.

She looked down at her hands and saw that the pink glow had returned to them. She had just eaten, and her life force had re-generated. For the first time since her conversation with her reflection in the woods she contemplated her own mortality. If the figure was right, she would almost certainly be gone soon.

June turned back to her followers and thought of them. They, also would soon be gone.

Then something caught her attention. One of the black-eyed things was standing motionless while the rest swirled around him, consuming the fallen Russians. He was looking at something. June watched him intently and then saw that he knelt down and picked up a discarded AK-47 rifle. His movements were smooth and deliberate, not like the others, but he wasn't the only one.

A handful of the black-eyed cannibals were now also moving in this more deliberate fashion, investigating their surroundings, going through the pockets of the dead bodies and picking up weapons. Something was changing, there had clearly been some sort of a shift in their behavior.

She turned back to the first cannibal, the one who had picked up the rifle. He brought it to his shoulder, pointed it at a man on the ground who was still barely clinging to life and fired a round into the Russian soldier's head. He then lowered the weapon and turned to June.

"What are you?" June asked.

The cannibal said nothing.

"Do you have a name?" She asked. "What is your name?"

Thus far these creatures had just been a swirling mass, part of the hive mind, but she could send that the hive was breaking apart and they were becoming more individualized. Up until this point none of them had spoken a single word.

He paused for a moment and then answered.

"Mark," he said in a gravely voice. "My name is... Mark."

ABOUT THE AUTHOR

Jordan Vezina is a fiction writer living in Austin, Texas with his wife Emily where they run a business together. Jordan served in both the Marine Corps and Army Infantry, and worked as a bodyguard. This background provided much of the detail regarding weapons and tactics in Jordan's books.

jordanvezina.com
hello@jordanvezina.com